bad at love

BAD AT LOVE
BOOK ONE

CHRISTINE MICHELLE

Cover Design ©2023 Christine Michelle

Paperback Edition
ISBN: 979-8-89706-005-4

about the book

POSIE

I fell in love with the idea of Maxwell Carter when I was too young to understand just how that beautiful boy would break my heart one day.

I was never his best friend.

Never a girlfriend.

We were strangers turned pen pals.

Through those letters, we each grew more complicated feelings, especially since he never actually came home to see me in person.

Maxwell was bad at love and I had to let the hope of ever being with him go.

I managed that, right up until a very special person in both of our lives brought us back together in an unexpected way.

MAX

Pops used to give me what he called "woman advice".

When I was younger, I blew it all off, thinking I knew everything there was to know about the opposite sex.

Failed relationship after failed relationship proved I should have listened to the old coot before it was too late.

It wasn't until I came back to my hometown at thirty-three that I realized the most important thing he tried to convey to me. The love of a good woman – the perfect woman for me – had been in my grasp all that time, only I'd failed to see her for what she was until it was too late.

I was finally coming home, and she was free once more.
Both of us were a little worse for the wear, but Pops' lessons had finally sunk in and I wouldn't stop trying until I finally made her mine.

AUTHOR'S NOTE

I am not a fan of flashback sequences or telling a story out of sequence. Sometimes, it is necessary for a story with suspense, but that isn't the case with this book. I wanted to take the reader on a full journey from the beginning of unrequited feelings until the happily ever after is achieved. That means starting in the teen years, however briefly. The majority of this book is about navigating a bumpy adult relationship.

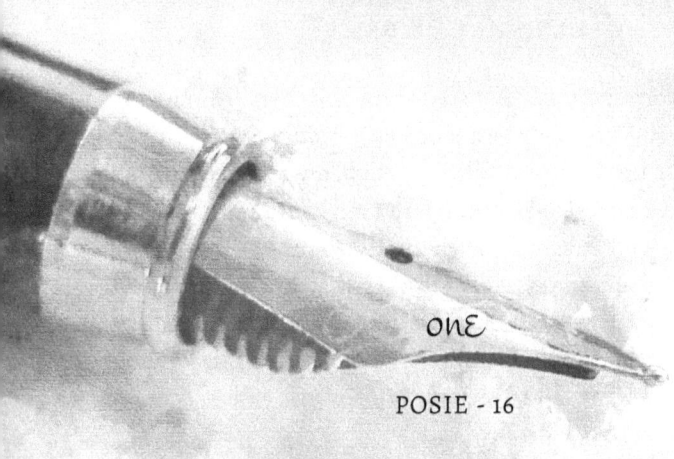

one

POSIE - 16

is lips were so close, I could almost taste them. My heart was stuck somewhere in my throat as his tongue darted out and slid across that plump lower lip that captivated me in the strangest ways.

"Kiss me." It was a demand that made my heart clench tightly in my chest, almost like it would stop and never start again.

My eyes shuttered themselves, so I wouldn't have to see. For some horrible, sick reason they wouldn't stay shut. When my eyes opened again, it was to see his hand in her shiny blond hair as their mouths came together in a sensual dance I'd been dreaming of experiencing for years. Only, those weren't my lips he was tasting. It wasn't my hair that he gripped so tightly in his fist that I could imagine exactly what it would feel like.

It was, however, my heart that cracked wide open at having to witness their kiss so closely. Knowing you're invisible to the one person who holds your heart in their hands is bad enough, but he didn't even realize I was there in the same space with them. I'd come up here to escape another one of my mother's dark rages. Everyone thought she was so sweet. The town baker, who made fabulous cookies and cakes and sold them with a smile on her face every day, couldn't possibly be a monster at home.

She didn't use to be, not until my father died. Now, my only solace was to come to Jack Carter's farm and hide away in his barn. It was slightly embarrassing that he knew about my crush on his grandson. Nothing near as painful as watching Max kissing Cheyenne. She'd never been outright mean to me or anything, but I was just as invisible to her as I was to Max. That was saying something, considering she and I shared three classes, and we were on the volleyball team together.

I rubbed my hand over the center of my chest, where everything felt far too tight as they continued kissing. Each smacking sound that came from them, every moan, and heart-wrenching sigh made it feel even tighter until the barn door opened. Jack stuck his head inside and called out my name.

"Posie, you in here?"

Max and Cheyenne quickly pulled apart, their attention going to Jack, whose eyes travelled from them to my own.

"What's going on, Pops?"

"What in the hell are you doing in my barn, boy?"

Max seemed stunned by his grandfather's angry response to seeing him there. "Don't answer. I can see for myself what you thought you were doin'. This ain't a hotel for you to bring your latest girlfriend to."

Cheyenne gasped at the implication that she hadn't been the only one. Truthfully, I didn't know if that was the case, as this was the first time I'd run into Max here.

"You two need to go," Pops insisted before his eyes ghosted back to mine briefly, the worry there tore at my heart. Unfortunately, that one look made Max turn my way. His eyes grew wide when he finally noticed me there in the corner with my sketchbook and my headphones on. His eyes quickly shifted down to Cheyenne, who was still clueless to my presence.

"Shit," Max huffed before he grabbed his girlfriend's hand. I was so jealous of that touch. If I closed my eyes and imagined it was me in her place, I could almost feel the heat of his touch against my palm. When the tear fell down my cheek, I couldn't even move to brush it away without drawing more attention to myself. Instead, I allowed it to fall unhindered without looking up to see who may have noticed.

"Pops, I didn't know," I heard Max say.

"Just go, boy." After a few minutes, I heard the engine of Max's old Chevy rev. It was odd that I hadn't heard him when he arrived, but then again, I'd had my music cranked up pretty loudly when I first came to hide out in the barn. Jack sat beside me as I thought about it, and he patted my knee.

"Bad day, Posie?"

The nod of my head was the only answer I could offer because my throat felt like it was too tight to form a response. Jack sighed and then reached over to swipe away the tears that ran down my cheeks, but it did no good. The tears refused to dry up.

"Sorry," I muttered.

"What in the hell are you apologizing for?"

I shook my head back and forth, not knowing how to answer that. "I didn't hear them come in. I came to get away and," my eyes dropped to the sketchpad in my lap, "try to forget."

"What did she do, Posie?"

I shook my head again. "I'm sorry that I didn't say anything to them when I realized they were here, but they didn't see me, and by the time I noticed them, it would have been embarrassing." We sat there quietly for a moment before Jack pulled me into his side and let me cry. "No one ever really sees me, so I just stayed invisible, Jack." The admission was so quiet, I didn't know if he really heard me or not.

"Posie," he started to say when the door of the barn slammed shut and I wasn't sure who had been there. "Sweet girl, seeing you like this breaks an old man's heart." Jack held me like that for a while before he stood and held his hand out to help me up.

"Come on, let's go get you cleaned up and I'll make you some supper before you have to go home."

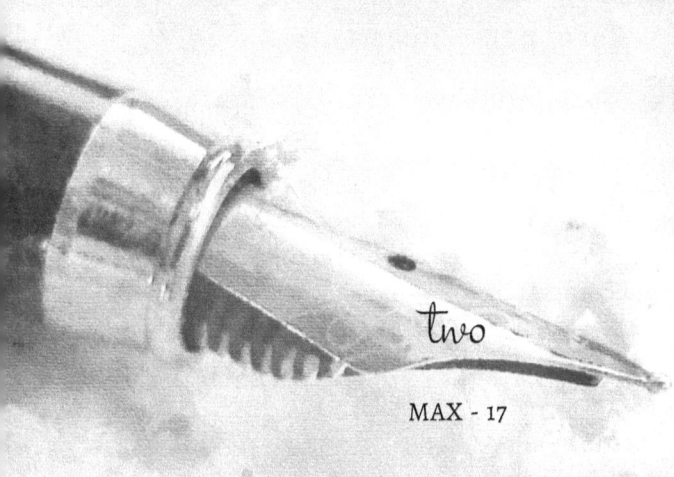

two

MAX - 17

One minute, I was making out with my girlfriend in my Pops' barn. The next, he was yelling at us to get out. Pops never yelled at anyone, least of all me, so it was a shock to my system. Then he made it sound like this might be a regular occurrence for me, and Cheyenne stiffened in my arms, her accusing eyes lifted to meet mine, as they pleaded silently for me to tell her it wasn't true.

I was about to be disrespectful to my Pops for the first time in my life when I caught his eyes looking past where we were sitting in the hay that had been piled up. My eyes followed his line of sight, and I was shocked as hell to see there was a girl sitting there with her knees pulled up damn near to her chest. The only thing stopping those two parts of her body from meeting was a notebook.

She looked somewhat familiar, though I couldn't place who she was or why she might be in my grandfather's barn. It didn't matter that she was a stranger. My heart lodged in my throat as I watched a single tear track down her face. The girl looked so fucking sad that I could feel it in my own soul. Her dark eyes shuttered closed for a moment as her head tilted down to shelter herself from being seen.

5

"You two need to go," Pops said, drawing my attention back to him.

"Shit." The word slipped free before I could pull it back. I got Cheyenne out of there before she even noticed that there was another person in the barn. There was no way to tell how she would have reacted to another girl being there, especially after what my Pops had said in anger. I jumped in my truck and started it up before I realized Cheyenne stood there staring at me like I'd grown two heads.

She huffed and then moved to the car that was parked on the other side of my truck. Fuck! That was going to go over like a ball of fucking lead. I forgot she met me here because she had to meet her parents in town later.

"Cheyenne," I called out to her as I hopped back out of my truck.

She flipped me off and left. That was going to require some groveling to fix later. Right then, curiosity got the better of me instead of worries about my girlfriend. I moved quietly back into the barn to observe whatever the fuck was going on with the stow-away in there. Pops had called the girl by name, so she wasn't just some random kid crashing in his barn.

I stuck to the shadows and creeped close enough to overhear what they were saying.

"What in the hell are you apologizing for?"

The girl removed her headphones as she shook her head, causing the light brownish-blonde locks to fall further into her face and obscure my view of her. "I didn't hear them come in. I came to get away and," her eyes dropped to the sketchpad in her lap, "try to forget."

"What did she do, Posie?"

What the hell could that mean? Cheyenne hadn't even known she was there. I was about to step in and tell Pops that before this little waif of a girl made up stories to go with her fake tears, but her head slowly did that back-and-forth motion again, almost as if she didn't even realize she was answering him that way.

"I'm sorry that I didn't say anything to them when I realized they were here, but they didn't see me, and by the time I noticed them, it would have been embarrassing."

I watched as my grandfather pulled her into a hug, as if she was one of his own kin. It was weird to see, since I still didn't even know who the hell she was.

"No one ever really sees me, so I just stayed invisible, Jack."

Damn. I might not have known the girl, but once again, my heart ached for her. What the hell had she been through to make her feel that way? And who in the hell was she to my grandfather? I couldn't interrupt them to ask Pops, so I turned and left, knowing someone who might be able to tell me something. Unfortunately, I wasn't as stealthy on my way out because I tripped and the barn door ended up slamming shut, giving away the fact that I'd been there.

The whole way back to my house, I couldn't get the look of the girl's tearstained face out of my mind. The sadness seemed to weigh her down and make her appear smaller than she probably was. Then again, being all bunched up and hidden in the corner like that didn't help much.

"Dad!" I yelled the minute I got out of the truck. I'd seen him under the hood of my mom's car. There probably wasn't anything wrong with it. He just liked to tinker on engines. Still, his head popped up immediately and his grimy face offered up a bright smile in contrast as he flashed me his pearly whites.

"What's going on Max?"

"We need to talk about Pops," I stated.

The smile slipped from his face as he closed the hood of my mom's car and started wiping his hands on the rag he had hanging from his back jeans pocket. "What about Pops?" He asked. Then, as if an epiphany hit, he chuckled. "Let me guess? He caught you taking your girl to the barn?"

"How in the hell?" Was the old man psychic or what?

Dad kept right on chuckling. "Son, your fly is down, hair's a mess, and if I'm not mistaken, that's hay you have on your shirt."

"I guess nothing gets by you," I tossed back, full of sarcasm. "Except maybe that Pops is keeping a sad little mouse of a girl in his barn."

"What did you just say?" My dad asked, obviously stunned by what I'd thrown at him.

"She didn't even make a peep to let Cheyenne and me know she was there. Just watched us making out and..."

"And?"

"And she was crying." For some reason that admission made me feel equal parts guilty and responsible for those tears, even though it was in no way my fault that she was squatting in my Pops' barn.

"You didn't by chance catch the girl's name, did you?" My father asked, and for the first time, I realized he wasn't all that surprised.

"Pops called her Posie."

Dad nodded his head and started walking toward the porch. "Let's go sit down while I explain a few things to you."

I followed along, suddenly worried about having left Pops there alone with the girl. I wasn't worried he was being inappropriate, but maybe that she might be taking advantage of him.

"Do you remember Eric Gamble?"

"The guy that was killed in the combine accident on the farm across from Pops'?"

"That's the one." Dad stared at me, as if that should be answer enough to all the questions I had. When I didn't clue in, he sighed heavily. "He left behind a wife and daughter. Max..." Another heavy sigh blanketed the pause before he looked me directly in the eyes. "What I'm about to say is not fodder for school rumors, you hear?"

"Yeah." He waited a moment, assessing me, as if he didn't

believe that I'd keep whatever he had to tell me quiet. The sincerity in my eyes must have finally swayed him because he leaned forward with his elbows on his knees, after taking a seat in one of the chairs. He promptly set his chin on his fists, and then sighed again.

"Eric and I were good friends. We grew up across the street from one another and often helped out on one another's farms when it was required. We were best friends for a long time."

I didn't know that. "What happened?" I asked because Alex Cole was my dad's best friend since my earliest memories.

A small smile split his otherwise serious face for a minute. "Your mom happened."

"Mom?" A light started to dawn on the topic. Former best friends and my mom. "I'm guessing you won the battle for her heart?"

"There was never really a battle. We saw her at the same time, but she immediately gravitated toward me. I was, uh, sort of seeing someone at the time. So, Eric thought he had a shot with Sharon."

"You cheated on someone to get with Mom?" I asked, unable to believe it because my parents always preached to us about loyalty and staying true to the one you loved. I'd never been in love, so that hadn't ever been a lesson I did more than role my eyes at.

"No. I broke it off with Sue before I ever took your mom out. Honestly, Sue was a lot to handle, and we were already hell and far gone from a healthy relationship, if you could even call it that. We dated, she would throw wild, jealous fits if anyone else talked to me, even if it was innocent. Anyway, I broke it off with her and started seeing your mom. Eric didn't take it too well because he'd had a thing for Sue before she and I got together.

"Long story short, because it was the second girl I'd started dating that Eric was interested in, he thought I was doing it on purpose."

"That's dumb."

Dad shrugged his shoulders. "He had some pretty big voices in his ear back then, telling him that was the truth. One of those voices turned out to be Sue's. Son, you need to understand, what I thought was over-the-top jealousy from her was a lot more. Sue and Eric ended up getting married after he got her pregnant. It wasn't long after their son was born that he came to me and apologized for the accusations and the damage he'd caused to our friendship.

"It was a little too late at that point. I'd written him off, especially since he was with Sue. We remained cordial and friendly after that, but never really worked at putting a true friendship back together because Sue was dead set against it." Dad took a breather, and I sat there wondering what in the world all this history had to do with Pops and the girl in his barn.

"When their boy was two, he drowned in the bathtub while Eric was out working the fields. Sue claimed that she just left the baby for a minute to go get a towel, and that she slipped and hit her head, knocked herself out. Eric came home and found her on the floor and the baby in the tub. When they realized what happened, Sue supposedly lost it and was institutionalized."

"Supposedly?" I asked.

Dad nodded his head slowly. "Most people think she killed their baby and pretended to be injured, especially since she refused medical treatment and there weren't any visible injuries to suggest her story was true. No lump, no blood." He shrugged his shoulders. "I told you she struggled a lot, even more so after they had that baby. It wasn't a farfetched idea that she might have hurt him."

"That's wild."

"When she came back to town, years later, around the time your mom was pregnant with you, I thought Eric would finally give her the divorce papers he'd had drawn up. I think he did at some point. Hell, he was dating another woman by then."

"He dated someone else while she was in the hospital?"

"It wasn't like that. No one begrudged him that. Eric was at the top of the list of people who thought Sue killed his son. He had to wait until she was of sound mind to take her to court for the divorce though. Everyone told him to wait, so it could be done properly, but no one wanted him to be stuck in limbo. Sue coming back made things hard on Eric's relationship. She did everything she could to sabotage them. Eventually, she even ended up pregnant again."

"Well, it takes two to get pregnant," I suggested.

"Yeah, it does, Max. It doesn't take two *willing* people though. Sue waited for his girlfriend to leave the morning after a party they'd been too. Eric had been drinking heavily. She, um, went inside and took advantage of the situation. Eric was heartbroken when he realized who was in his arms when he finally woke up. Hell, half the town was heartbroken for him because they all knew what happened. Eric deserved to be happy with his girl."

"Who was she?"

"Doesn't matter. The minute she found out; she dumped him because she couldn't take it anymore. It had been more than a year of putting up with Sue's antics by that point. Then, when Sue announced to the whole damn town that she was pregnant with Eric's child, his girl left town."

"Holy crap, Dad. That's insane. Why didn't anyone do anything?"

Dad's heavy exhale spoke volumes. "We tried. Hell, I think most of the town was in Eric's corner, wanting to prosecute Sue for what she did. It was rape, plain and simple. He kept her there, for the sake of the new baby on the way. When the girl was born, Eric took care of her. If he was in the fields, so was his baby girl. That child never was left alone with her mom. Eric allowed Sue to stay, to be a part of her daughter's life, because her doctor finally got her on some medications that helped with her issues, and he didn't want his daughter growing up without her mom."

"Seems like any kid would be better off without a mom than having one like that."

"You would think, but Sue was a good mom to her. It was obvious she loved her girl. The medication really did help."

"So, what does all this have to do with the girl in the barn."

My dad raised a brow at me, as if to ask if I was really that dumb that I hadn't put it together yet. I figured the girl was the one he was talking about, but that didn't explain much.

"Since Sue had so many issues before, certain contingencies were put into place, just in case anything ever happened to Eric. My father was named her guardian, and ready to step in, should Sue become incapable of caring for her daughter. Dad didn't think he needed to step in when Eric was killed because Sue had been doing so well. I'm guessing, if Posie was crying and hiding away in his barn, that all might be about to change."

"So, what? Pops will take her on as his own kid?" That seemed a little ridiculous to me, but after hearing the whole story, it was honestly all a bit much to swallow anyway.

"Yes, and if Pops isn't able to then I would step up, as I am next in line to take her if anything were to happen."

"You said you and Eric were no longer close."

"I did. When Sue was away, we were able to repair our relationship quite a bit. We were never as close as when we were kids, but our family was always someone Eric could trust and come to, no matter what. I was there when he put the legalities together and he asked that I step in for Posie if Pops was not here or unable to."

"Why Pops?"

"Eric's father left when he was in middle school. Your pops helped his mom figure out what to do with the farm until Eric could take over. He taught Eric everything he could, and he lives right across the street. The road literally splits their farms, so Pops was able to keep an eye on the place, and on Posie."

"Sounds like you dodged a bullet when Mom came into the picture."

Dad chuckled. "I tell that woman nearly every day that she saved me from crazy. Not that I was planning on sticking around with Sue, but if there was ever a woman who could scare even the craziest woman away, it's your mom."

"I'll take that as a compliment," Mom said as she joined us on the porch. The windows were open, so she'd probably been listening in the whole time. "I'm guessing things aren't going so well for Posie?" She asked my dad.

"I'll check in with Dad later," he assured her.

"If I need to get a room together, I can."

"I think the tough old coot has it covered, but I'll let him know we have a room here, in case he isn't up to it."

My parents were both amazing people, and maybe I didn't get the gene, because I silently hoped the sad girl who hadn't bothered to tell a couple she was there in the barn with them wouldn't be coming to stay with us. From what I'd seen, she might be crazy just like her mom.

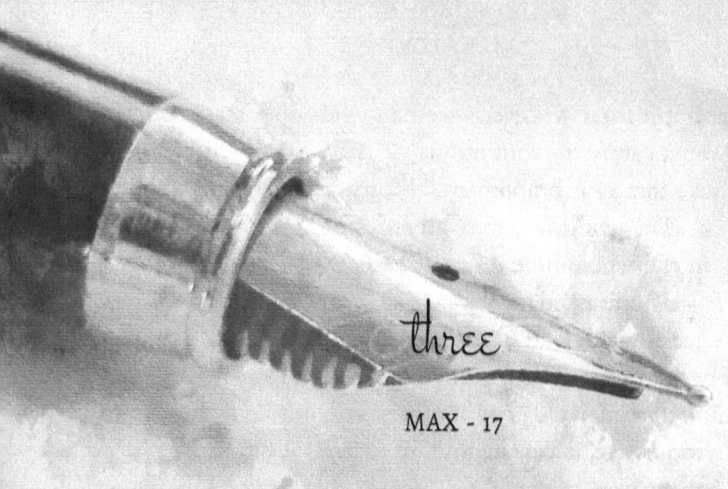

A re you sure you want to show up in that truck with it looking like that, son?"

I smirked at my grandfather, "the tough old coot", as my dad called him. My truck was a charcoal gray 1951 Chevy 3100 that I'd helped to restore. It was a classic and meant to be appreciated as such. What my pops was referring to, was the mud I hadn't been able to wash off yet after the boys insisted that my truck wasn't fit for muddin'. Proved all of them wrong.

"We live in the country, Pops. It'll wash, just not today."

"I imagine it will, Max. That don't mean that girl of yours will be impressed seeing you roll up in an oversized dirt clod to take her to prom."

"Cheyenne will be just fine."

"There's a few things you need to know about women, Max-"

"Pretty sure I already know them, Pops." I grinned widely and waggled my eyebrows at the old man to reiterate my point. I'd lost my virginity during my freshman year, to a senior girl who I was pretty sure had gone after my two older brothers as well. She was a one-time hookup, but that didn't mean the end to sex for me.

Since then, I had a string of long-term girlfriends and in-between hookups.

"Nah! None of that now, boy. You listen up! There are women who would gladly get dolled up and slip into that truck, even in the condition it's in now. That girl of yours ain't one of 'em. I keep telling you that you're pickin' wrong when it comes to your women, but you don't listen. If you don't hear anything else I'm saying to you, hear this: That girl you're seein' won't be gettin' into that truck after she gets herself all dolled up." He scoffed out a half laugh as he thought about it before adding, "Hell, don't think she'd get in it if was showroom floor ready."

He dangled a set of keys from his aged fingers, making them jingle to get my attention. "Take my Skylark, at least it's a bit fancier, and might appease that uptight girl you're courtin'."

"No offense, Pops, but I know what I'm doing. Everything will be fine." My grandfather kept looking over toward the barn where his Skylark was parked, but something made me wonder if that was what he'd been looking at when I noticed movement over there.

"Well, we tried," he said.

"Who the heck is 'we'?" The girl I'd seen there a few weeks ago might have been hiding out again. If that was the case, it just went to show that she was probably just as crazy as her momma – which I already suspected to be true.

"Never you mind. Get on outta here and go to that school dance of yours. I hope your date goes with you, but I gotta tell you, the odds don't seem to be in your favor, Max."

"Then there's always the after party," I shouted back to him as I climbed inside my truck, careful not to get any of the dried, red-clay mud on my rented tux. My momma was normally a sweet woman, but she'd kick my butt from here to the other side of the country and back if I messed up the rented tux and she had to pay outright for it.

It took me twenty minutes to get to the other side of town, where Cheyenne lived. Truthfully, I wanted to sit out in the truck and honk for her to join me, as usual. I knew that wouldn't fly this time. My girl had big ideas for how things like Prom were supposed to go. That meant I'd most likely be stuck taking pictures with her for the next thirty minutes.

I got out of my truck and walked up to the door, where her father let me in. I didn't miss the grim line his lips made as he looked over my shoulder to see my truck sitting there.

"It was a good time," I confided. The man grunted and then called for his daughter. She was halfway through her over-the-top floaty descent of the stairs when I finally looked up and noticed that she was wearing far too much dress. It would be impossible to keep that thing clean when she got in my truck, and I'd never hear the end of it.

Something nudged me in the back and brought me out of my thoughts about what an earful I would get all the way to the dance. "You look great!" I told Cheyenne excitedly.

"I look great?" She asked as confusion marred her normally flawless features.

"Yeah, that's what I said. You look..." What the fuck could I say about her dress? "There's so much..." No, that would not go over well with her. "Like you're ready for a ball or something." I settled on that little gem and glanced up to see her approving smile. It hadn't really been a compliment, but whatever got us out the door quicker.

Cheyenne was a pretty girl when we were in school. She looked glamourous for prom night. Though, maybe her type of glamour was from another era, since she looked like she just stepped off the cast of a period drama taking place in the old south. I'd had the privilege of seeing her up close and personal before she "made herself pretty" and there really wasn't a lot to be impressed with.

She was just a normal girl who knew how to put on a bunch of makeup and make herself look better. Nothing wrong with that. I still dated her, even after knowing what she looked like without all that fuss she put into her appearance. Truthfully, I think she would have been more appealing if she didn't do all that stuff to herself.

Still, if it weren't for the horrid dress she was wearing, with all those fluffy layers, she might have looked like a Hollywood starlet ready to walk a red carpet somewhere. Her light blond hair was styled to perfection, and probably meant I couldn't run my fingers through it when I kissed her, which sort of sucked. Her lips were painted a peachy color to match the dress she had on. When she smiled, it lit up the whole room and made you believe the package she presented was effortless.

Despite my grandfather's thoughts on the subject, I knew Cheyenne was high maintenance. She was being groomed by her family to be someone's trophy wife. They only put up with me dating her because my family owned nearly a thousand acres of land, some of that being prime cattle and farmland. The rest was in real estate investments and businesses my father started when he decided that farming wasn't his cup of tea.

If the Baker family wanted to keep Cheyenne in this town, one of us Carter boys was her best ticket to leading the life of splendor they all wanted for her. She hitched herself to the wrong Carter brother though. I didn't plan on sticking around after graduation. Like my father before me, I had bigger and better, albeit probably less lucrative things to do with my life.

No one but my Pops knew I was joining the Army yet. They'd find out soon enough. I turned eighteen in a week, graduated in less than a month, and then I'd be off to basic training and a new life as far from my hometown as I could get. It wasn't that I hated it here. There was just this fear in the back of my mind that if I didn't get out and explore the world while I was young, this town would be all I ever knew.

"Smile for us!" Cheyenne's mother called out. Immediately, I forced a wide grin, but that wasn't good enough. The woman giggled before coming over to arrange my date's dress for her. "This dress is a bit much, isn't it?" She commented. "It's swallowing you whole in the pictures, Max. I can't even tell you're wearing a tux and nice-"

Her voice trailed off as she got a load of my shit-kickers. She must have been about to say something about the 'nice shoes' I was supposed to be wearing with the monkey suit, but that was where I drew the line. Those kinds of shoes weren't comfortable. My boots were well-worn and a part of me. They also weren't cheap. Not that I paid for them. They'd been a gift from my pops, but they were Lucchese Boots that came with a hefty price tag because they were built to last.

Cheyenne's attention was drawn down to where her mother was looking, and both of their faces turned slightly horror-filled when realization about my footwear choice finally settled in. Her father smirked at me and gave a chin lift in acknowledgment of my little rebellion. His life was exactly what I hoped to avoid by joining the military and seeing more of the world. I didn't want to look back one day and think a kid wearing shit-kickers to his prom instead of wing-tip shoes was the height of rebellion.

"Are we ready?" I asked when the women didn't seem prepared to stop staring in judgment over my shoes.

"Yes! I can't wait to get there," Cheyenne screeched excitedly. "We're going to have so much..."

Her voice trailed off as she glanced around outside while she had huge layers of her dress bunched up in her hands so she wouldn't walk on it. How in the hell did she expect to dance in that thing if she couldn't even walk without holding it up?

"What's up?" I asked when it was clear that Cheyenne stopped moving.

"Where is the limo?"

"What limo?"

"The limo we're supposed to arrive to prom in?"

I shook my head, lost as to what she was talking about. "Did you order a limo?"

"No! You were supposed to order a limo, Max. That was your job!"

"Um, no one told me that was a requirement."

"Max!" My name sounded more like a word that would have gotten my mouth washed out with soap when I was a kid. "We've only all been talking about the limo for months now!"

"Yeah, but you said you didn't want to go in the limo with a group, that you just wanted to go with me alone." I didn't bother reminding her why she'd said that, since her parents were still standing there watching our back-and-forth like it was a damn table tennis match.

"Yes," she gritted out through clenched teeth. "I wanted our own limo, so that we didn't have to deal with your idiot friends and brother messing things up and spilling something on my dress."

She glanced around again, and I knew the minute she saw the truck. "You have got to be kidding me! Please, tell me you don't expect me to get in that heap of rolling mud with you."

I shrugged my shoulders. "It was sparkling clean yesterday, but Jake kept saying how my truck wasn't useful and that it couldn't even be taken out muddin'. Everyone else agreed with the assho-jerk," I changed the word so as not to cuss in front of Cheyenne's parents. Truthfully, I didn't care, but my momma did teach us some manners.

"My mom and dad and even Pops had a bunch of shi-stuff for me to do today, so I didn't get a chance to wash it up again."

"I am not going to prom in that truck!" Cheyenne stomped her foot and let go of the mounds of material she'd been holding up, so that she could cross her arms under her breasts. Being stubborn always made her look better because with her arms crossed like that, her cleavage was on full display, and the one thing my girl had going for her – that didn't require enhancements or extra prep time – was her impressive rack.

"Well?!" She questioned in a snotty tone.

"Well, what?"

"Are you going to call for a limo?"

I laughed, which made her expectant look slip further into a frown.

"No, I'm not calling for a limo. There probably isn't one available at this late notice anyway."

"Fine, then we'll borrow Daddy's car for the night."

I turned to look at the angry scowl that slid onto her dad's face. "I don't think he's okay with that and besides, I'm not insured to drive his car and you don't have a license, since you failed the test again."

"Oh my God! I can't believe you brought that up," she huffed. Mr. Baker's face relaxed into something akin to enjoyment as I let him off the hook and he watched his daughter begin to throw a tantrum.

"If you don't call your brother and have the group limo come here to pick us up, I will not be going to prom."

"Their limo is full, since they got someone else to take our spots when you refused to share it with the group," I reminded her. "Plus, we didn't pay our share to use it."

"Maxwell Carter!" She screeched. "I will not get into that truck with you!"

I took one slow step back from the porch and then another quicker step, putting distance between us. Her jaw looked like it came unhinged with my third step. "What are you doing?" She asked.

"I'm taking my truck to the prom."

"You're going without me?"

"I guess you have to be dropped off. I'm not leaving my truck here overnight because then I'll need a ride to pick it up." I shrugged my shoulders again. "If you won't ride with me, I guess I'll meet you there."

"You're not serious?" I couldn't tell if it was a question or a statement. In answer, I turned my back to her and walked to my truck. Before I got in, I glanced up one more time.

"Are you coming with me, or not?"

"You are unbelievable!" She shouted at me before turning and stumbling over her dress while trying to run into her house.

"At least I'm not ruining my own night by being overly dramatic," I called back. Cheyenne's mom stomped into the house behind her daughter. Her father stood there smiling on the porch steps.

"Good call. Wish I'd made the same one myself," he said before turning and following the furious women into the house.

I hopped in my muddy truck and patted the dash. "You probably just helped me dodge a bullet, buddy." I praised the thing as I cranked it up and headed to prom - solo.

My dad was on my mind, and I wondered if one of my friends would end up falling in with Cheyenne and going through what Eric Gamble did. The shiver that ran up my spine made me turn the radio on and crank it up loudly. No use thinking about stray bullets that might land somewhere else. I'd just be thankful the Cheyenne-shaped bullet missed me.

Mom would probably be pissed that she didn't get any pictures with me dressed in the monkey suit she laid down a pretty penny to rent, but she would get over it pretty quickly when she realized it meant she didn't have to deal with my girlfriend coming around anymore.

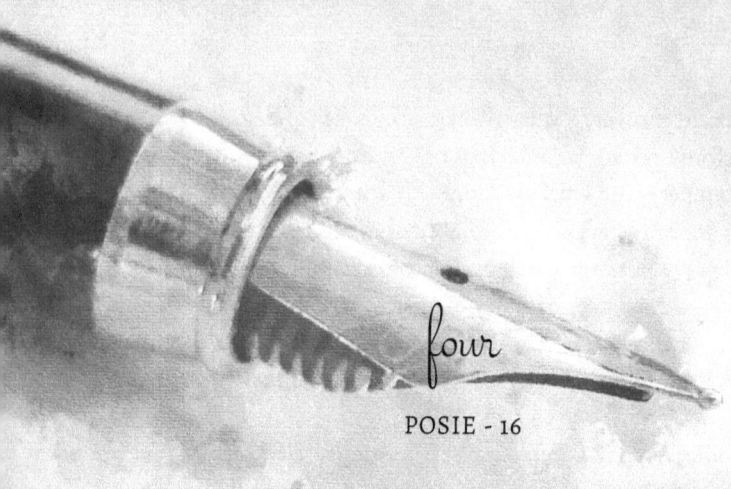

four

POSIE - 16

Y ou can come on over now. He won't be back anytime
soon, even if she tells him where to go with that muddy
truck of his." The old man that I'd come to love as if he
were my own grandfather chuckled at his own assessment of his
clueless grandson.

I made my way over to him, noting that there seemed to be a
little more silver in his hair than there was just a few months
before. His wife died when I was 12 and ever since then, my mom
started sending me across the street with baked goods at least once
a week. It quickly became our thing to have pastries together and
talk about everything and anything. I wasn't stupid. My mother
hadn't done it to be nice. She'd done it to get rid of me.

Mr. Carter, Jack as he told me to call him all the time, was a
wealth of wisdom, even if his grandson was too stupid to take a
hint. I loved sitting on his porch and listening to the stories he told
about how he met his wife, the way they loved one another so
fiercely, right until the end. Some days, he'd lament the fact that
she was gone, and we would just sit in peaceful quiet.

My father was gone as well. He was killed in a farming accident
only two short months before Jack's wife died. So, in those quiet

moments, on the darker days, we sat in silence and shared our grief before saying our farewells and going about our days.

"Do you really think he'll still go to the prom, even if she refuses to get into that truck?" I asked as I climbed up the porch steps and took the rocking chair beside Jack's. It used to be the one his wife occupied when they sat on the porch together. At first, I wouldn't go near it because I felt like it held her ghost, but eventually Jack convinced me his Shelly would have wanted me to sit there and keep him company.

"Knowin' my grandson, I'd expect no less."

I rolled my eyes in response, which made Jack laugh. "Why aren't you all dressed up with your dancing shoes on?"

"I'm only a sophomore and I wasn't invited by anyone."

"I forget there's two school years between you and Max, not the one. When you're sixteen and he's still seventeen, it feels like you should just be one grade apart."

"I only turned sixteen two months ago. Max turns eighteen soon, so there's the difference. For most of the year, we're two years apart in age."

Jack glanced over at me with a thoughtful expression on his face. "That he does." After taking a sip of the lemonade I'd made him earlier he turned his storm-gray eyes on me. "What do you have planned for the summer this year?"

It was sweet of him to ask, like I could enjoy the summer as a normal teenager. That wasn't in the cards for me. My mom started a bakery in town after my father passed. She didn't know a thing about farming, but she knew plenty about baking. So, she hired out a farm manager and some hands to take care of things, but it became obvious rather quickly that paying someone to do the jobs my father used to do took a huge bite out of the profits we used to have. Her bakery was our salvation, especially in the summertime when tourists came to spend time on the lake.

I suppose my silence spoke for itself as Jack finally asked, "Bakery again?"

"Yep. I'll be going from four in the morning to mid-afternoon most days. This year, Mom said she's going to pay me a real wage for my time, so I can put it aside for college."

"That's good to hear. I know you don't mind helping your mom out to keep things afloat, but you both need to be preparing for your future. It's coming faster than I think she realizes."

I nodded my head. "I worry about what will happen to her. You know... If I leave for college."

"I don't want to hear no 'if I leave' business, Miss Posie. You are going to leave and get a good darn education while you're out there. Your momma will be just fine, I'll see to it."

There was no doubt in my mind that Jack would keep his word. He was one of the last good men, in my eyes. My father had been a lot like him. Those men cherished family above all else, even the land they both tended came in second place. My dad never missed a meal with us, even if that meant having to go back out to the fields after supper for a little while. He was always there to tuck me into bed at night too. When I was younger, he would even take me out to the field and sit me on the tractor with him as he worked.

I still miss being able to sit with him while he worked. It always made me feel special, like I was too important for him to leave behind. I stared out across the street to the land our family owned – I owned. My father left it all to me, which was probably why Mom was so angry all the time.

She couldn't sell the place without my permission, and I wouldn't give it. Pops had reminded her a time or two that my permission couldn't be given until I was eighteen anyway. When I'd asked how he knew that, Jack told me that my dad put some things in order for me long before he passed, to make sure I was always protected and had a home. I guessed he never trusted my mother.

"I miss him, but I worry my mom is wasting away just missing him instead of finding someone else to be happy with."

Jack seemed startled by my revelation. "You want your mom to date again?"

I shrugged my shoulders. "I don't exactly look forward to having a man come in and try to take over our lives, but I've seen the way Andy looks at her when he doesn't think anyone is paying attention." Andy was the man running the show on our land already. I had a suspicion that he came around to see my mom during those times she sent me to spend time with Jack, but I couldn't be sure.

Jack chuckled before taking another swig of his lemonade. "Matchmaking is sticky business, little Petal. Don't go pushing for what your momma isn't."

I grinned at Jack's nickname for me, but that didn't stop my scheming mind from finding ways to get my mom to notice Andy, or to make her notice of him a public thing. He had done a great job managing the farm for us, and I knew in my heart, he would be good for her. At the very least, it would keep her focus off me.

"What about you?" He asked after we were quiet for a spell. I took my eyes off the stars that appeared brighter now that the sun had gone all the way down.

"What about me?"

"Is there anyone special that's taken notice of you the way you think Andy sees your mom?"

"No, I'm mostly invisible."

"I thought we talked about this before. You aren't invisible, Petal. You just don't put yourself out there. You won't ever get much back if you don't try."

I bounced my shoulders to my ears and back. "No one really notices me, Jack. The girls don't hang out with me much because I'm not into dresses, makeup, and shopping the way most of them are. Plus, even the ones on the Volleyball team with me keep their distance. I hear them mumbling sometimes about our family being crazy in the head. I guess being quiet means I'm mental to them.

Then there are the boys who don't notice me because I look more like one of them than I do a girl."

Jack choked on his lemonade. "Christ, are the boys your age blind nowadays?" He commented before his cheeks turned red with embarrassment. "Sorry, that was inappropriate, and I didn't mean it..."

I waved him off. "I'll take the compliment, even if it was from an old guy."

He laughed at me, knowing I was teasing him. Also, it was a little true. Jack made me feel like I was a pretty girl when no one else even looked at me twice.

"My grandson is an idiot," he mumbled.

"I thought we established that when he took a muddy truck to pick up his princess of a prom date?" I asked good-naturedly.

"Yeah, but here you are," he pointed down to my boots, "wearing shoes that match his own. Let me give you some man advice, sweetheart."

"Okay, shoot."

"My grandson, along with all the idiots you go to school with, they're not men yet. They think they are, but they're just fools playing a game they still don't understand. Don't you worry none about those jackasses not noticing you just yet. When they do, they'll be kicking their own butts for not snatching you up sooner. Then, it will be you who will have the pick of the litter, so to speak."

"That's sort of what my mom told me." She had been a bit blunter, telling me I was probably a late bloomer since I was still only rocking an A-cup bra and had no other curves to speak of. She said once I blossomed, boys would take notice, and I'd know exactly which ones to steer clear of because they will have already shown their true colors in how they treated other girls in school and around town.

If I went by my mother's standards, my heart wouldn't yearn for a certain cowboy-boot-wearing, muddy-truck-riding Carter boy who was not long for our town, according to his grandfather. Some days, I wished I could get over the crush that plagued my heart for Max. It was painful seeing him all dressed up and looking so handsome earlier, knowing he was going to pick up a date who wouldn't appreciate any of his quirks the way I did.

Then again, I'd been living across the street from his grandfather my whole life and he'd never even said so much as "hello" to me. If that wasn't bad enough, the first time he ever really noticed me, I was hiding out in his grandfather's barn, just a few feet away from him, as he made out with his girlfriend. So, he noticed me at the exact moment where I would come off as some sort of pervert or creeper. The weird thing was, while I'd been all but invisible to him before, each of his other brothers at least acknowledged that I was a living person from time-to-time.

I sighed deeply as those thoughts drifted here and away again as time shuffled on. Jack sighed too while his eyes remained trained on the stars in the sky.

"Posie!" Mom called from our house across the street. She stood there on our weather-beaten porch with a hand on her hip, but a smile on her face. It was a forced smile. I called it her 'public face'. When she had that on while home, it was only because she knew Jack would see her. It also didn't bode well for the kind of mood she was in. I never told Jack the real reason I wanted Andy's interest to flare for my mom and for her to reciprocate. If she had someone else to focus on, things wouldn't be so bad for me.

"Evenin', Susan," Jack called out.

"Jack," she responded. "Come on, Posie. You need to help at the bakery early tomorrow."

It was the weekend, and no one had asked me to prom, so I had to take the shifts the normal weekend high school crew held at my mom's bakery. Just another day in the life of a small-town invisible girl.

"See ya, Mr. Carter."

"Jack," he corrected.

27

"No, you're Jack, I'm Posie," I teased in our usual goodbye.

"Okay, little Petal, go get some rest."

When I went to sleep that night, I dreamed that Max had asked me to the prom and we'd worn our matching boots and he took me in his truck, mud and all. In my dreams, it was the best night of my life. Since reality sucked for my sixteen-year-old self, I'd have to cling to the dreams until I blossomed into whatever the adults thought would make me less invisible to the opposite sex.

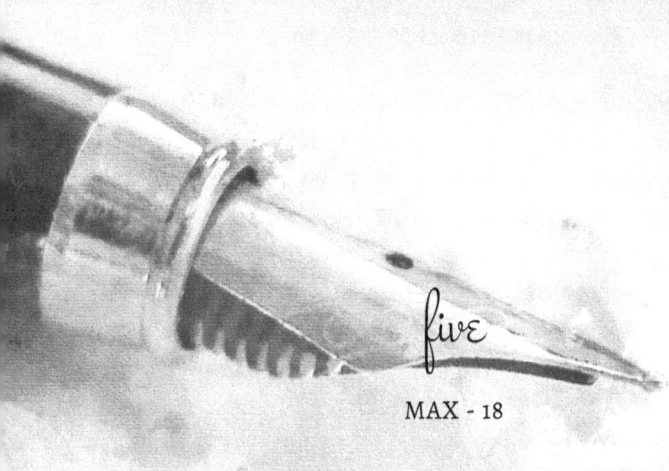

Dev and Evan both came to see me off, so we drove to our grandfather's house first before heading to the Army recruiter's office. Evan was starting his junior year of high school next year. Devon already had a degree in horticulture and was using what he'd learned to help streamline our grandfather's farm. Our other brother, Michael, was in his second year of college, and close to obtaining his business degree. He hoped to follow in my father's footsteps with real estate and investments.

As we rounded the bend and closed in on our Pop's house, I noticed he was talking to someone on his porch.

"I swear, that girl is going to steal our inheritance one day," Evan complained.

"What? Why would you say that. She's just the weird girl that lives across the street, right?" I knew the story my father had told me about her family, but he had sworn me to secrecy, so I had to play dumb even as my curiosity about the girl was piqued.

"Seriously, Max? Where have you been for the last four or five years?" My older brother asked instead of just answering my damn question.

"I'm being for real. Why is Evan worried she'll steal our inheritance?"

Evan was the one to answer. "I think her name is Petal, or Flower or something weird. Pretty sure that's what I heard Pops call her."

"Don't you guys think it's weird that she's always hanging out with Pops?"

"You really are a clueless asshole, man," Devon answered. He glared at me and then at our little brother. "You are, too, since you're in the same grade as her, Evan. Her name is Posie Gamble. That's her family's farm across the street and her mom owns the bakery in town."

"Wait, that's her mom's bakery? How did I not know this?" I asked, honestly curious how something so major could slip right by me. I tried to remember my whole conversation with my dad. Did he mention that? Maybe I was too hung up on the rest of the crazy story he told me to hear that part.

"Because you're a self-absorbed idiot who only sees girls when they wear pounds of makeup, barely any clothes, and are ready to jump on your Johnson when you tell them to. Posie is a sweet girl, so I'm not surprised she fell under your radar."

"What is she doing with Pops?"

"He really never talked to you about her?" Devon asked as we pulled into the driveway. My eyes tracked her path as she hightailed it off the porch and across the street to her house.

"No. I think he mentioned that I should get to know the girl across the street a few times. He said we'd have a lot in common, but I had no clue who he was talking about." I shrugged and hauled my butt out of the truck, not giving it any further thought.

"Pops!" I yelled as he stood there on the porch with worried eyes trained across the street. "What's got you so interested in the Gamble kid?" I asked. My Pops' angry glare sent a chill up my spine as my older brother popped me in the back of the head for good measure.

"Is everything okay?" Pops called to the girl while ignoring me. She stood there, frozen in front of the door, the only movement a subtle shaking of her shoulders.

Slowly, her head slid back and forth, and her body pivoted so that her watery eyes connected with Pops'. He was off the porch and on his way to her before any of us could even blink.

We all watched as he pulled her into his arms and rocked her back and forth. Pops took a note from her hands and read it before crumpling the thing and throwing it to the ground. I don't know when my feet started moving beneath me, but my brothers shadowed my movement as we all drew closer to the edge of the road.

"Do you have a key, little Petal?"

She shook her head. "I didn't think I'd need it, since I was just across the street."

"Okay, come back to my house, and we'll figure everything out. I'll get Johnny down here to open the house for you."

"What's going to happen if she doesn't come back?"

"Don't you worry about that. Nothing is going to happen to you."

"How do you know?"

"Your dad made sure of it a long time ago, sweetheart. I'll explain everything once we get you settled."

The whole conversation sounded like a strange puzzle to me. I guessed the girl didn't know her own family's history. Pops ignored us as he sheltered the girl from our view when he brought her back across the street to his house. "Devon, I need you for a minute."

Devon complied and followed immediately after our grandfather, but I had clues to gather instead. I walked in the opposite direction and went to collect the crumpled piece of paper that Pops had thrown on the porch.

"What's it say?" Evan asked.

I uncrumpled the letter and started to read it out loud for Evan's benefit.

Posie,

The bakery is in default with the bank. I know how to bake, not run a business. I sold it off to Mrs. Fisher rather than have the bank take it back. There wasn't much left after the bank was paid, but the rest is in an account for you.

I can't do this anymore. Your father was my everything, even if I wasn't his. It hurts too much to breathe without him. I promised if anything ever happened, I would wait until you were older. Waiting just became too much. Go to Jack, he'll know what to do.

Mom

"What did you just read, Max?" My startled brother couldn't hide the panic in his voice as I side-stepped him and moved to look into the window. Thank Christ the girl hadn't done the same. Her mother was hanging from the rafter not ten feet from the front door. That's the image she wanted her daughter to have after reading her note. What a sadistic piece of work. I wanted to bring her back to life and throttle her until she was dead again. Posie might have been a stranger to me, but no one deserved to come home to this kind of a shit show.

Devon came jogging over to us. "Pops said he called a locksmith to come out and open the house, so she can get some of her things."

"You can't let her in there. We need to call the police."

"What? Why?"

I pulled my older brother to the window and told him to look. Judging by the surprised intake of breath, he hadn't been prepared for what he saw, which meant my grandfather might have misunderstood the note. "She never left," Devon whispered.

"She left, but in a permanent way."

"Go, quietly tell Pops." Devon told our younger brother, then he kicked the front door in and charged inside to try to save a woman who I could already tell was long past saving.

"She didn't even tell the poor girl she loved her," I mentioned as my brother spun away from the window and toward me. I handed him the note and he read it, despite his shaking hands.

"Damn. Poor girl."

"Do I need to call my recruiter and tell him I can't leave right now?"

"Nah, no need. You didn't even know her. I'm going to let Pops know that I have to get you there before they count you as absent without leave or some shit."

"I don't think you can be AWOL when you haven't even gone to basic training yet," I countered, although, I'd signed a contract, so that might not be entirely accurate. I had a lot to learn about the military, considering I was the first in my family to join.

Devon ran inside and I stayed out by his truck. When he came out he indicated with a nod for me to get in. "What's going on?" I asked.

"Mom's coming to help Pops with whatever needs to be handled for Posie. I'm going to take you to the recruiter so he can get you off to the bus or whatever they're putting you on to ship you to Fort Benning."

"So, that girl is suddenly an orphan, and I'm supposed to just leave?"

"Not quite," Devon hummed his answer.

"What's that mean?"

"I think Pops is going to take her in. He's been acting as a surrogate grandparent to her for years, anyway. I guess there was something legal in place in case anything ever happened to her parents he would get custody of her. And you said yourself that you don't know her, so why they hell would you stay behind? There's nothing you can do for her." For some reason that didn't sit well with me. All the times Pops had tried to talk me into meeting the neighbor girl came back to mind.

"Why in the hell didn't this girl factor into our lives more, if they're so close?"

"For me, it was because I was older. I remember her being at Pops' house a lot after Grams passed away, just before I headed off to college. Not sure why you never noticed her."

"This feels like the wrong time to leave," I admitted again.

"It's now or never, Max. There's always going to be something that makes it feel like the wrong time. Go, do your thing. Figure out what you want out of life. I'm proud of you, man. The Army is no small thing, but I think you're going to make the most of it. Stay safe and come back home to us when you've had your fill of adventure."

I watched my grandfather's farm grow further and further away in the rearview as we drove in the opposite direction of where I wanted to be in that moment. My brother was right, though. No matter when I left, there would always be something here that tried to hold me back. This town had a way of latching onto you and holding tight.

"Make sure Pops isn't taken advantage of," I instructed my brother.

"Don't worry, I'm pretty sure Pops has been handling his own shit long enough to be able to protect himself. That girl means something to him."

I nodded and we both stayed silent for the rest of the drive. Once we got there, I hugged my brother and sent him back on his way from the parking lot.

"Where's your family?" Sgt. Hayes asked as he looked past me when I opened the door.

"There was an emergency," I admitted.

"Well, we can push your leave date if need be."

"Nah, it's all good. My grandfather's neighbor kid lost her mom today. Suicide. He's taking her in. I don't even know her, so there's no need to push anything."

"That's tough." I nodded in agreement with Sgt. Hayes' assessment. "If you're sure?"

"Positive."

"Let's get you downrange then."

"Downrange?" I asked.

Sgt. Hayes chuckled at me. "It's weird having a recruit in these parts that isn't from a military family. Don't worry, you'll pick up on our language quickly."

He never did explain what he meant, just grabbed the things he needed and put me in his car as we drove away from my hometown and toward my future.

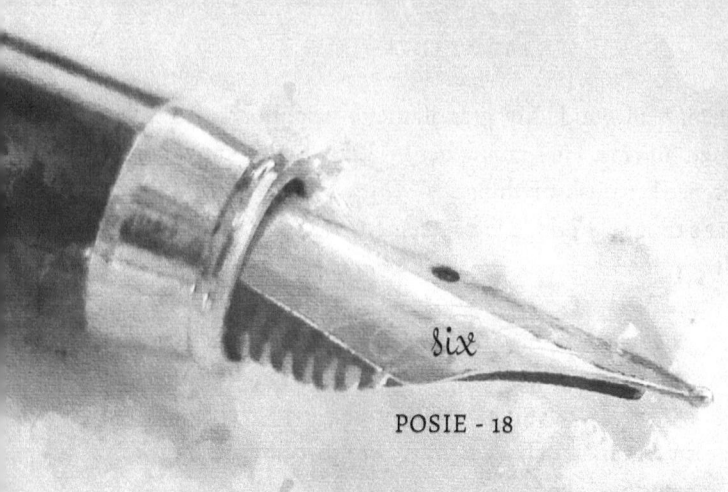

Six

POSIE - 18

S ix years ago, I lost my father in a farming accident. Two years ago, I lost my mother to suicide."

Come to find out, I'd lost a brother years before, as well. There were secrets in this town, and they only started coming to light after my mom took her life. That wasn't something I addressed in my speech though. Instead, I continued with what I knew back then.

"Their deaths left me with no blood relations. I had been an orphan for all of two minutes, until the man from across the street, who lost his wife the same year I lost my dad, came to my rescue. He had become my surrogate grandfather from the time I was 12 until two years ago. Then, I became his ward, and he my surrogate father. I am standing here today because the strength of that one man, who held me up all these years.

"Thanks to our shared experience, I can also tell you that life will throw you curveballs. Sometimes, it feels like too much to bear, but there are people out there who are willing to catch you and pick you up when you fall. Our successes don't belong to us alone. They belong to everyone who helped prop us up on our journey toward our goals. This celebration is as much for them as it is for us, and I wanted to acknowledge that.

"I learned far too early and often in life that tomorrow isn't promised. It's great to have goals and achieve them, but not at the expense of living. When you leave here today, do so with joy in your hearts for the accomplishment you achieved, and go celebrate before moving on to the next goal. These milestones mean nothing if we're constantly chugging forward to the next one and the next without stopping to appreciate what we've already done. My parting gift to my fellow graduates is to impart a little bit of wisdom my Pops, Jack Carter, has instilled in me. "Live for the moment while you learn for tomorrow."

"I'm so proud of you, my little Petal."

Jack pulled me in for a hug to go with his praise the minute we got back to his house after graduation. I held onto him as if my life depended on that hug, and for a while there, he had been my very literal lifeline.

"I sent the video to Max to guilt him into coming home and spending more time with family when he has leave."

"You sent what video to Max?" I asked.

"The one I took of your Valedictorian speech."

I ran a hand down my face to hide the embarrassment that stained my cheeks red. "Why on Earth would you do that?"

"Are you kidding? Max has always fought for the "favorite" spot amongst my grandkids. If he thinks there's stiff competition, he'll haul ass back here and show his face."

"You're a bit of a nutter, Jack."

"A nutter who loves you to pieces, Petal."

"Thank you-" I started to say more but was interrupted when a cheer broke out in the house that had been steadily filling with the Carter family.

"There's our other graduate!" Jack called to his youngest grandson. "Get over here, boy." He flung his arms wide open to welcome Evan and give him the same congratulatory hug he'd offered me moments ago.

"Hey, Evan. Congratulations."

When Evan was done hugging Jack he turned and wrapped his arms around me. "What in the hell are you congratulating me for? That speech brought tears to my eyes. This old coot needed you just as much as you needed him. Never doubt that." The last bit was whispered into my ear conspiratorially.

Since the day my mother took her own life, I'd been coddled by the Carter family, most of them anyway. Michael had been away at Boston University, but whenever he came home, he was always standoffish and avoided me where possible. Devon and Evan, the oldest and youngest of the Carter boys, had become like brothers to me. I wasn't sure where I'd be without them. Jack kept me afloat, but they managed to make me smile again, even if it did take a while.

Then there was Max. I'd like to say I knew where Max stood, but the truth was, he hadn't come home since the day he left for the Army. Part of that was simply bad timing, since he went to basic training, advanced individual training, and then was shipped off for a year to South Korea so fast that the whole family had whiplash trying to keep up with his fast-paced schedule.

I read up about some things, though, and knew that he probably had an option to take leave before heading out of the country. Max opted not to take it for some reason, and I worried that it might have had to do with me. Not that my head was so big that I thought the world revolved around me. It just had to be somewhat surreal for him to leave in the middle of his Pop's involvement in my family tragedy.

"What are you two doing hiding over in the corner?" Greg Carter, Jack's son and father to the four Carter boys, asked.

"Well, after that stunning speech she gave earlier, I was asking Posie for some life advice. She should be one of those wackadoodle types who people pay good money to, just to dole out common sense to everyone in our generation who doesn't have it."

Greg rolled his eyes at his youngest son. "And you should have studied harder, then maybe you could have made it another family business."

"I was never going to make Salutatorian, let alone Valedictorian with Mitchell Graves and Posie Gamble as my competition, Dad. Let's be realistic." Evan wasn't wrong about that. Mitchell and I had been competing for those honors for our whole high school careers. My dear, pseudo-brother was more worried about football and girls, though I'd admit he was smarter than most people gave him credit for.

Greg turned his attention back to me. "Sharon has a gift for you."

"You guys didn't have to get me anything," I protested. The Carter family had already done far too much for me.

"Petal, when are you going to understand that you're family?" Jack asked as he joined our little huddle.

I leaned into his side and smiled up at the man who had become a second father to me. Times like these, I couldn't stop the tears from building in my eyes, though I did my best to keep them from falling because the Carter men did not do tears.

"Peace! I'm out. I see crocodile tears on the way. You know that's not my scene." Evan kissed me on the top of my head, squeezed my arm affectionately, and then he raced off toward the front door.

"I guess he didn't want his present," his dad teased. Maybe we should give it to you, since you're the one who always sticks around when the Carter boys are hot footing it out of here like their shorts are on fire."

"Their shorts might just be on fire. Your boys do tend to get around," I joked back.

Greg and Jack both scrunched up their noses at me and tried to shake off my comment. "Nope. You can't say things like that."

"What? Evan says things like that all the time."

"Yeah, but you're our sweet Petal," Jack announced. "We'd like to at least have the illusion that you will always remain sweet, innocent, and untainted by the world."

Sadness swept through the center of my being and bowed my shoulders with its weight. "That ship sailed years ago, Jack." It was my turn to walk away from the Carter men.

"Maybe we should have let her have a tiny, dirty joke at our boys' expense," Greg mumbled to his father.

"She'll be okay. That one has strong bones and a solid soul." I had no clue what that meant, but every time I doubted myself or things went wrong, it was something Jack used to tell me. I had strong bones and a solid soul.

I was a tiny, petite thing who never really did get that growth spurt everyone kept promising me. So, I was fairly certain I didn't have strong or sturdy bones. As for the soul, mine had been pierced by the darkness of what my mother did when I unknowingly stood feet away from her body as I read her goodbye to me.

My own mother took the time to say goodbye, but not once did she mention that she ever loved me. I had already told Jack, that very day, that I still felt invisible to everyone, but having my mom fail to acknowledge her love, or the loss I would face when she was gone, made it that much harder to overcome that feeling.

I moved in with Jack after what happened to my mother. The property across the street sat, waiting for me to become an adult and figure out what I wanted to do with it. Technically, I became an adult three months ago. It was still hard for me to even allow my gaze to fall on the house. That property had both of my parents' deaths staining it.

I made my way to the bedroom that had become mine two

years earlier and found a box, two cards, and a giant teddy bear sitting there with a graduation cap parked on its head.

On closer inspection, I noticed that the package was post-marked from South Korea and my heart ticked up a few beats. Was it possible, after all this time, that Max Carter acknowledged I was a real living and breathing being?

Ignoring everything else, I dove into the package and found a treasure trove of things inside. There were Couque D'Assi White Torte Cookies, a box of Pepero sticks, and Korean Sweet Cakes. I pulled each of the sweet treats out of the box and set them aside.

There was another box to open. Inside that was a black lacquered music box with a gorgeous mother of pearl inlaid scene consisting of a moon in the top left corner, trees in the lower right that bled into water and two cranes taking flight near one another, as if one was chasing the other. It was stunning. Once I took it out, and got the jewelry box open, there was a letter waiting for me inside.

> Posie,
> It feels weird writing this because technically, we don't really know one another. I'm sorry that it wasn't possible for me to stick around after what happened my last day in town. I've thought of you, that day, and what must have transpired for you many times during training.
> Oddly enough, you're the reason I had the strength to keep going, even on the days when I felt like I bit off more than I could chew and wanted nothing more than to come home.
> Is that weird?
> Everyone gave me updates on how you were doing,

and I always thought, if she can handle that, then this is nothing.

In a way, you gave me strength to keep pushing forward. I've wanted to thank you for that, but honestly it never seemed appropriate. I thought it might be now, considering you're graduating at the top of your class. Your strength amazes me. Congratulations on everything you managed to accomplish and welcome to the family – though according to everyone else, I'm far more than just two years late on giving that welcome.

I tried closing this letter out like ten different ways in my head. Not knowing what you are to me is weird. Did Pops adopt you? No one ever said. So, I guess you could be like my aunt – wow, that's too weird. You can see what I went with instead.

Before I sign off, you have my new address (at the bottom of this letter). It won't be good for another two weeks (by the time you get this, I might already be there, now that I think of it), but that's my next duty station. I expect at least one awkward letter back before you head off to college and the rest of your life.

Your friend,
Max

I HAD ABSOLUTELY NO IDEA WHAT TO DO WITH HIS letter. This was the boy I'd always had a crush on, and he acknowledged that we don't really know one another. It was somewhat heartbreaking that he acknowledged he didn't even really know I existed prior to the day my mother died. Unless you counted the barn incident, which he obviously did not. That was a crushing blow to my ego, not that I had much of one to begin with.

To know I was a source of strength for him when just being me was a struggle... That part was nice, I supposed. At least my pain was inspirational to other people, I guess. And then he ended the letter with a roundhouse kick to my heart by wondering if I was his aunt now.

I growled out loud as I flung the letter down beside me.

"Everything okay?" Greg and Jack stood there in my doorway with mirrored amused looks on their faces.

"Max sent me a package," I explained.

"Did he send something foul?" Greg asked, and the menacing look he gave, said if his son sent anything inappropriate he'd be on the next fight to South Korea to put a boot up Max's ass.

"No." I started to show them my haul and they both seemed puzzled by my reaction, so I flung the letter out toward them.

Greg held onto it, but Jack proceeded to read over his son's shoulder. They both got a little teary-eyed when they no doubt read the part about my strength inspiring Max. Then they started chuckling and I assumed that was over the part at the bottom about me being his aunt now.

"Which part did you have a problem with Petal?" Jack asked as he came to sit down next to me.

"Honestly?"

"Always."

"First, he said he never knew who I was. That's weird because I was at your house a lot when he was around."

"True, but you always hid whenever he showed up."

"Oh." I had forgotten that part and my cheeks flamed in response and worsened as Jack chuckled, clearly amused by my humiliation.

"Why did you hide from my son?" Greg asked, genuinely curious.

"Um, no reason."

"She had a crush on the boy," Jack ratted me out.

"Jack!"

Greg stayed silent, thankfully.

"So, in the wake of that resounding revelation, I'm assuming the growl was more than likely as a result of the 'aunt' thing," Jack surmised with a grin on his face after scanning the letter.

"Ah, I see where that could be upsetting," Greg concurred.

"Please, don't placate me. It was a stupid girl crush. Honestly, I think I just envied his boots. No offense, Greg, but your son was a bit of a moron when it came to girls."

"Obviously, if he failed to ever notice you," he offered and winked as he turned to leave the room. "I'll leave you two to this discussion. There's a reason I never had girls."

"That's biology, not because you didn't want them," I called out to his retreating back. I heard his laughter echo down the hall.

"Don't let my son fool you. He'd trade places with me in a hot second. He always wanted a daughter to dote on."

"You have both been very kind to me over the years. He's a lot like you."

"The real estate mogul is like the farm boy, huh?"

"Are you kidding? The only thing not alike about you two is your jobs. You passed on the very best things about yourself to your son. He's a good man."

"Aw, Petal, you're really itchin' to make an old man cry today."

"Maybe the estrogen is catching," I teased.

He poked me in the ribs and we both laughed before he lifted a sealed envelope up. "What's the rest of this?"

"I don't know. Call me greedy, but I opened the package first."

"I doubt greed had anything to do with that. I'm betting the return address on a flat envelope would have made you open it if that package had a different postmark on it."

He had me there. One of the cards was from Devon, and surprisingly the other had been from Michael. It didn't say much, just congratulations on graduating, and he included a hundred-dollar gift card with it. The giant bear, along with the card and gift card that was hidden underneath the graduation cap, was from Sharon and Greg.

I sat down and wrote them each a thank you note that night. Then I wound the music box and fell asleep listening to the sweet little tune it played as I thought about Max. If he saw me now, would he think of me as his newly minted aunt or a woman worthy of a second glance? There was no way of knowing and it didn't seem likely to happen anytime soon.

He was still in another country, and I was off to college in a couple of months. Our paths back home would probably narrowly miss one another. So, I sat down and wrote my first letter to Max.

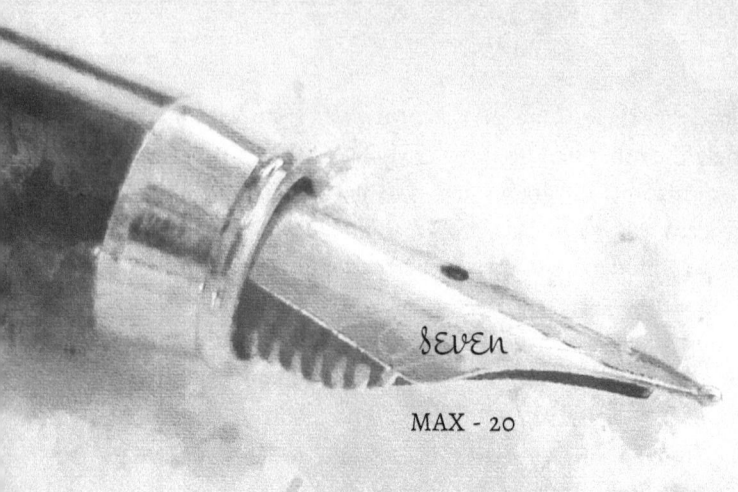

W hen I got in from pulling duty, the first thing I did was check my mailbox. It was the same thing every day since I got back to the US. Checking my mailbox had become a ritual, and usually one that disappointed. That wasn't the case as I opened it this time. There was a thing envelope inside, and it was from her.

After grabbing the letter, I hauled ass to my room and locked the door behind me, so that none of the assholes on my floor would be able to barge in and bug me. I couldn't explain the way I felt at seeing her name in a sort of scrolling, fancy script across the plain face of the envelope. My heart beat faster in my chest while I hesitated in opening it.

I sent the package to her as a way to placate Pops. As I chose the things that would go in it, I had to admit that I also did it because Posie deserved something special. She made Valedictorian, and according to my little brother, that was a hard-won accomplishment. When I told her in the letter that I expected her to write back, it was just something to say. There really wasn't an expectation, and yet, after seeing the video of her speech, it was all I thought about.

The girl who stood up and gave that speech about living in the moment, and how my pops had taught her that, was beautiful and confident in a way she never had been when I'd seen her before. I was curious how those two years and a tragedy led her to become so much more than she was before. There was no way she could hide out in the shadows any longer. It simply wasn't possible to miss her.

I sat on my bed, took a deep breath, and then ripped open the envelop and pulled out the one-page letter. It was short and sweet, a lot like the woman who penned the words.

Dear Max,

First, thank you for the incredible gifts you sent me for graduation. The music box is stunning, and I treasure it. The white chocolate cookies — I'm ashamed to say, I devoured them far too fast and now can't remember what they tasted like except to say they were divine. They were gone too quickly, which makes me sad. Jack told me he would see if there was anywhere stateside to get some. Don't laugh. It's all your fault. You're like a drug dealer, but with cookies instead of meth or coke or something. Ha!

I start college in a few months. I'm going to stay local because I have a full-ride scholarship here and it doesn't make sense to spend money to go somewhere else to learn the same things. Evan will be there with me, so I'll at least know someone else starting out.

I can't even imagine what it's like to see another city in our country, let alone to experience one in a *foreign land. I bet you have some amazing stories. If you're ever bored, I'd love to hear some of them.*

Thanks again for everything!

Definitely your friend — not your aunt,

Posie

I RE-READ THAT LETTER FIVE TIMES IN A ROW. EVERY time she talked about me being a cookie dealer, it brought a smile to my face. Thinking of her starting college and meeting new people, or hanging out with my brother, made me feel a bit jealous. I would never have that experience. I did enough college to earn a bachelor's degree in criminal justice while I was on active duty, but it wasn't the same. My degree was completed through distance learning and my peers were a bunch of military assholes just like me. From what I had been told, it was a completely different experience to kids who go off to college. The weapons and uniforms were just a small part of that difference.

We had our own culture – a military culture – that some people would never understand. As I thought that, I pulled a pen and paper out and got busy writing Posie back. She might not have realized it yet, but she'd just become my letter writing friend. I sat there and put to words what it was like to be in the military and how my peers behaved.

I made her promise to tell me all about how college was different. Then I promised to find her more cookies – even if they weren't the same ones. She could try new ones each time and then maybe her next favorites wouldn't be so inaccessible. Writing that letter to her and rereading the one she had written me put a smile on my face that I couldn't describe. It felt good to be able to talk to someone, and not have to hold back anything. It was the first interaction, in a good long while, where I felt like I was being true to myself first.

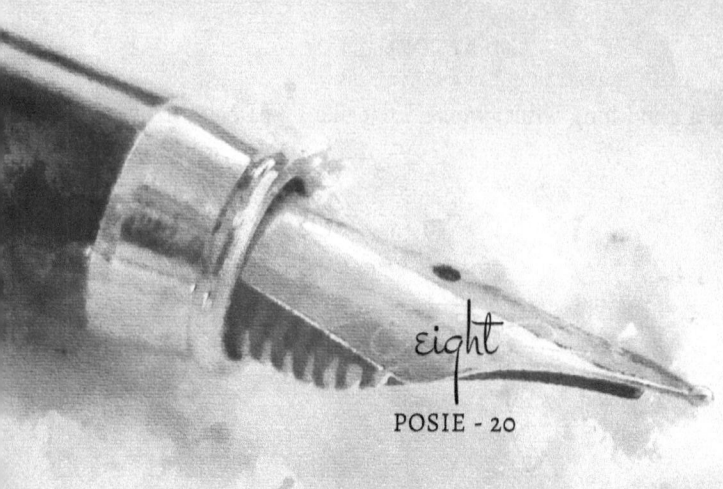

eight

"They're here!" I yelled excitedly as Evan plopped down on my bed. We both decided to stay close to home and attend the local university. I did so because I earned a full scholarship and was able to pocket some cash in the deal since there was no need to pay for a dorm room or meal card. Plus, I wasn't ready to leave Jack behind just yet.

"Well, let me see," Evan demanded with his greedy, grabby hands aimed at the package.

That was my cue to rip open the box. We both stared, awestruck at our collective work for a few minutes before Evan leaned in and picked one up.

"Holy shit, Posie! These look... Wow. I know I saw your concept drawings, but this is beyond even my wildest imagination."

The grin on my face was so wide, it was surprising that my head didn't split in two and fall right off. "I can't believe they look so good," I admitted.

"Seriously, who cares about my story because your artwork is what will draw everyone in and keep them there." He thumbed through the pages so gently, as if afraid he'd damage the images. It warmed my heart and filled me with so much pride.

"What are you two doing?" Jack asked from the door. I quickly turned and put my body in front of the box to hide it.

"N-nothing," I stammered like a guilty fool.

Evan laughed hysterically. "Jesus, Captain Obvious, if he wasn't curious before, he will be now."

My panicked eyes found his as I turned my attention back to Evan. There wasn't an explanation for why I didn't' want Jack, or anyone else in the family, knowing what Ev and I had been up to. The fear of being judged was probably the only thing stopping me from handing the box to him and telling the man who had become my father just how happy I was with our accomplishment.

"Petal?" He questioned and my shoulders slumped, knowing I'd have to show him.

"I thought you were proud of our work?" Evan asked, and his hurt tone made me feel even worse.

"I am, Ev. You wrote such a wonderful story. I'm just afraid of what everyone will think of my work." I shrugged. "All I did was draw the pictures."

"Are you kidding me? I knew what was coming and you still blew me away with this. He held up our graphic novel, and before I could even process what he was doing, it was placed into Jack's hands.

"I wrote the story, but all of that artwork is Posie's. She brought my words to life. She did it so well, people may never actually read the words." The pride in Evan's voice made me blush as Jack took in the cover and then lifted his eyes back to meet mine.

"You did this?" He asked.

"I did."

"I knew you drew a lot, but..." He hesitated a minute as he flipped through the pages. "What in the hell are you doing studying agriculture at school when you have all this talent?"

"I wanted to be able to help you with the farm and," I glanced out the window, but couldn't bring myself to remind everyone in the room – me included – that I owned a whole lot of farm acreage as well.

"No, sweet girl. We're going to sit down and talk about getting you a proper staff to run your place. Your focus needs to be on this." Jack walked over and sat down in my desk chair, kicked one ankle up to rest on his other knee, and placed our graphic novel in his lap. Then, he started to read it. Evan came over to me and sat down, clearly just as nervous as me now. My artwork was in your face – the first thing you noticed when looking at the cover. Now, Jack was reading his words and checking out the artwork that went with it.

We waited until he was halfway through before Jack finally raised his head and looked at both of us as if he hadn't ever seen us before. "This is something else. I didn't even realize you were working together so closely."

"We mainly worked on it during our breaks on campus," I admitted.

"This is my first time seeing the finished product on Posie's art," Evan explained. "I only ever saw the initial concept sketches as I developed the story."

"You two are going to keep working together, right?"

We grinned at one another. "That's the plan, Jack."

"Good, because this is truly something else." His eyes drifted back down to the graphic novel in his hands. "Can I have this one?"

"Of course," I said at the same time Evan answered, "It's yours."

"You both need to find a spot to sign it for me."

We looked at one another and grinned again. It would be the first signed copy of our very first graphic novel. As Evan and I signed the back of the book for Jack, his eyes flitted between Evan and me.

"Maybe I kept telling the wrong grandson to get to know you better." He winked at me as Evan smirked.

"We work well together. That's all," I insisted.

"That sounds like a good foundation to me."

It was a bit embarrassing, especially since neither of us felt that way about one another. Evan had his eyes on someone else while my attention had already been diverted to another Carter brother. Maybe, if Jack had pushed earlier, that would have been different, but I doubted it.

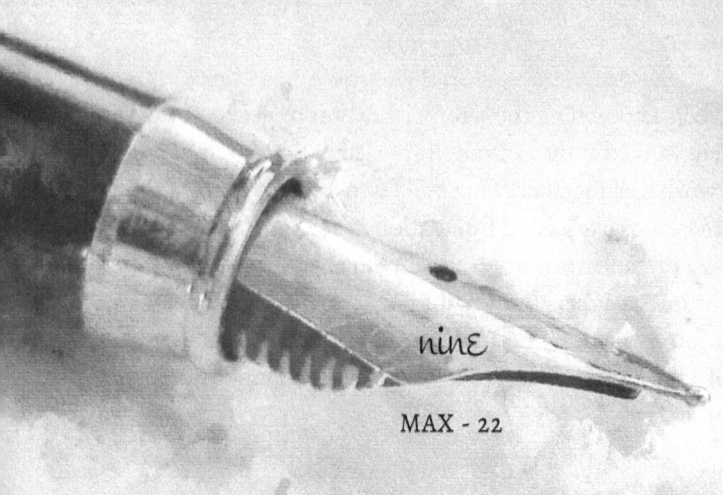

ninE

MAX - 22

It was a strange thing to be disappointed when staring into your mailbox. There was plenty of mail waiting on me after working my shift, but nothing from the one person I wanted to hear from. Posie hadn't even responded to a single one of my letters over the past month and I wasn't sure what to make of that.

My phone ringing pulled me out of my thoughts of the girl who had been taking up residence in my brain far too often over the past couple years. Her letters, those simple words written on paper, were the main thing I looked forward to. When I finally saw Posie again, I had a feeling things would be a lot different between us.

"Did you get it?"

"What are you talking about, Pops?"

His excitement turned into a grumble, which made me chuckle at his expense. "You haven't received a package from Posie, or maybe Evan?"

That got my attention. Posie had written letters to me weekly ever since I sent her a graduation gift two years ago. We had gotten to know one another pretty well, but she never mentioned my little brother in them. Evan never mentioned her either when we spoke on the phone. Pops and Devon were the only ones who ever spoke about her, besides my parents.

"What would I have received that involves both Posie and Evan?"

"Oh, I guess she kept it a secret from you, too." The old man sighed. "There was a time, I hoped that she would open up and trust you with everything. I suppose proximity is why she chose to grow closer to Evan instead."

I wasn't stupid. Pops kept pushing for me to come home and every time he did, Posie's name was on the tip of his tongue. Truthfully, it made me not want to come back. It was weird, but I liked having someone to talk to while knowing that we'd probably never see one another. Writing to Posie was like writing in a diary, only I'd get responses to the things I said, and she would get them back from me. Seeing each other in person might ruin the dynamic we had. It wasn't something I'd admit out loud, but I was afraid to lose that. Then again, I was also afraid not meeting up with her in person would end just as badly.

"What's going on, Pops?"

"Posie and your brother wrote a book together."

"A book?" Not once in the two years we'd been communicating had she ever even hinted at writing more than our letters.

"It's more of a comic book. What did they call it? A comic novel? No..."

"A graphic novel?"

"Yes, that's it. Your brother wrote the story and Posie did all the artwork."

"And its published?"

"Yeah, they even signed a copy for me."

Why did my chest feel tight when I thought about the fact that she didn't want to share this with me? Thinking about it made me realize that there hadn't been any letters from Posie in a few weeks. That wasn't like her. I wondered if maybe the novelty of having what amounted to a pen-pal friendship with me had grown stale.

"Hey, babe! Please, tell me you're naked and waiting!" I turned to watch as my girlfriend walked down the hall, leaving a trail of her clothes behind as she got closer to the bedroom we now shared.

"Who is that?" Pops asked.

"Rebecca," I answered honestly, even though I didn't give away who she was to me.

"And who is Rebecca?" Pops asked at the same time my live-in girlfriend spoke as she finally made it to the bedroom door.

"Why aren't you naked?"

"I'm talking to my Pops," I explained to her.

"Oh! Are you finally going to tell your family we're living together?" She asked, and I didn't miss the fact that her voice grew louder as she did so.

"Shit!" I heard Pops hiss into the phone. "Gotta go," he called out quickly before hanging up.

I frowned down at my phone, not liking the way that sounded. When I attempted to call back, the phone rang out as if no one was there to answer it.

Rebecca crawled up to straddle me where I'd been sitting against the headboard. "Aren't you going to play with me?" She pouted.

"Stop. My Pops just got off the phone in a hurry and now no one is answering."

"He's probably just mad because you hadn't told him anything about me yet." Her lips turned down as she reminded me once again that it was weird how my family didn't even know I was dating anyone, let alone living with a woman. It was a fight we'd been having for the past month, when I told her that we wouldn't be going home for Fourth of July, despite the invite she overheard from my brother, Devon.

"Are you ashamed of me?" She asked.

"No, I'm not. Can we table this until I find out if something is wrong with my family?"

"Something's wrong, all right. The fact that you won't tell them about me."

"Jesus, Rebecca. Stop for a minute."

She scrambled off me and over the to the closet. "You know what? I'm done being your dirty little secret you keep from your family."

"You're not a damn secret. Can you give me a minute to make sure my pops is okay before you throw your fit?"

She huffed even louder as I continued to watch her throw clothes into her bag. Then, she reached up to the shelf in the top of the closet in an attempt to reach a box of keepsakes or whatever. I got up to go help her while I tried to get Evan on the phone.

She smacked at me when I touched the box and in doing so, made it fall. The contents scattered all over the floor of the closet, but a vivid splash of color caught my eye along with two names. Evan Carter and Posie Gamble.

It was a graphic novel. How in the hell? I glance up to see a guilt-stricken look on Rebecca's face before I looked back down and saw letters. There were letters from Posie, but also the letters I'd stuck in the mailbox to send to her were there. All of them had been opened.

"What the fuck is going on?" I asked through clenched teeth.

"I can explain," Rebecca tried to say as she took a step back.

"There's no fucking explanation good enough for what I'm seeing. What the hell did you do?"

"You wouldn't tell your family about me, and the way your grandfather kept talking about that girl, I got jealous and needed to know if she was the reason. So, I looked at her letter that came in before you could. When I went to put it in the mailbox again the next day, I saw yours there that you were sending to her, and I had to know what you talked about with her. It obviously hasn't been me – your girlfriend. One thing led to another and suddenly, I couldn't put them back because the next letter was asking why you hadn't written to her."

"Are you fucking kidding me?"

"She's in love with you!" Rebecca hissed.

"She's not in love with me. All we have are the letters. We only ever met twice in our lives before I left for the Army."

"That doesn't mean she isn't in love with you."

"You had no fucking right! No matter what you thought was going on. Posie is family. You had no right to hinder our communication."

"She's not family!" Rebecca shouted. "She's a girl who is in love with you and taking advantage of your too-kind family."

"Kind of like how you took advantage of my too-kind heart when I let you move in here after your roommate moved out without notice?"

She cringed back. "We were on track to move in together anyway," she insisted.

"No, we really fucking weren't." I glared at her. "Pack YOUR shit and get out. Only your shit. As a matter of fact, I'm going to watch to make sure everything you pack belongs to you."

"Are you kidding? Now, you think I'd steal from you?"

"You *did* steal from me! You probably stole my fucking friendship with Posie while you were at it because she's going to hate me for not writing her back, especially about the book she and my brother worked on together. Fucking hell! My brother is going to hate me for not saying anything to either of them about it."

"Her reaction is more important to you, though."

"Fuck you! Who cares? You don't get a say in how I communicate with anyone, who I write or speak to, or how I feel about them. You were nothing more than a regular fuck who conned her way into living with me."

Rebecca sucked in a huge breath and then began sobbing. "That's not true. I thought we had something. I thought our relationship was going somewhere."

"I'm twenty-fucking-one years old. The assholes in my unit might be eager to settle down with local girls looking for a military man to hitch their ride to, but I'm not. I never told you otherwise, not even after you moved in here."

Becca kept floundering back-and-forth between trying to change my mind and excusing her behavior of hindering my communication with Posie. Tuning her out was the only way to maintain my temper while she packed her shit up. As soon as she was done, I walked her to the door.

"Key," I demanded with my palm outstretched to receive it.

"I don't know where it is," she argued.

"That's fine, I'll have the locks changed today."

"I don't understand how you could do this to me over some stupid letters. Especially if she really doesn't mean anything to you. You said yourself that you're basically strangers. You don't even know that girl, but you're going to throw me out for her?"

"You're damn right," I told her as I slammed my front door in her face.

I picked up my phone and dialed my buddy, Travers.

"What's up, Carter?"

"Need new locks on my doors,"

His initial reaction was to laugh. "I'll grab some new locks and head your way. Just the two doors, right?"

"Yeah man. Thanks."

"We'll talk about what went down when I get there. I'll bring some beer with me."

"Might want to grab some whiskey while you're at it."

"Oh shit, that bad, huh? I know you're not heartbroken over Rebecca, so something else must have gone down. She's not claiming to be knocked up, is she?"

"Nah. I'll fill you in when you get here."

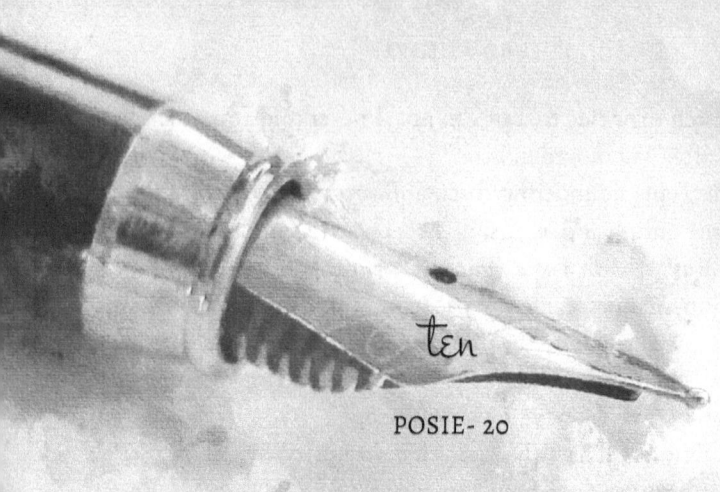

ten

POSIE- 20

"I guess we know why he never said anything to either of us about the book and why he stopped writing me. He has a girlfriend living with him now."

"Petal, I'm sure that's not the whole story. Max can be an idiot sometimes, but I don't think he'd purposely ignore you, or his brother, because he was seeing someone. You can't think this is the first time he's been with a girl since you two started writing letters."

"I bet it's the first time he's lived with one. That changes things." I was pretty sure it changed things. If I was dating a guy who was always writing and receiving letters from another girl, I'd at least be curious about who she was and what they said to one another.

Jack looked away, contemplating what I had to say before glancing back down at his phone. "He's calling again. Maybe I should just give him your number."

"We've been writing letters to one another for two years, if he wanted my number, he would have asked for it."

"Did you ever ask for his number?"

I shook my head. "No, but I did ask for his email address

because I thought it would be easier and quicker to write one another that way. He wouldn't give it to me."

"Did he say why?"

"He said it felt more personal writing actual letters where we had to decipher one another's handwriting." I thought it was a bullshit excuse to keep me from being able to write him more often.

"Well, sounds like you got your answer then."

I shrugged my shoulders. "Either way, he stopped writing me back like a month ago, so I think we're done with even doing it that way."

Jack sighed and moved close enough to pull me in for a side hug. "Sometimes, people grow apart as they grow up."

"We never grew together," I reminded him.

Jack laughed softly as he held me. "Sweetheart, I know those letters meant a lot to you. Wish you had told me he stopped writing them. I don't want you to let this get you down. There are too many things in your life to celebrate right now. That book of yours is selling well according to Evan."

I rolled my eyes. "He won't stop bragging about it."

"And he shouldn't. You two did something truly amazing, Petal."

"Lots of people can write and draw, Jack."

"True, but not all of them have the confidence to chase down their dreams and make them happen. What you and Evan did took courage, passion, and commitment. Don't ever sell yourself short."

"Thanks Jack."

"When are you going to call me Pops?"

"Never," I tossed back callously. A little sinkhole formed in my stomach when I saw the hurt on his face. "It's not what you think," I quickly explained. "I never want to call you Pops because you're not a grandfather to me like you are to the boys. You have taken over where my father left off. You're my second-chance dad,

Jack. I never called you that because I was worried you wouldn't like it."

"Petal," he choked on my nickname as emotion made it hard to get the word out. He made up for it by nearly smothering me in the biggest hug I'd ever received. "I'd be proud to be called your dad. Not taking anything from Eric either. He was, and always will be, your true father but I don't think he'd mind one bit if you had someone else step in to fill those shoes, since he can't be here to do it himself."

I nodded and swiped away the tears that fell freely down my face. For some reason, I didn't think my dad would mind Jack taking his place either, since he couldn't be here with me.

"One day, when I get married, I want you to walk me down the aisle," I admitted.

"It would be an honor, sweetheart."

I grinned up at him as his phone started ringing again. "Should I answer it this time?" He held it up to show that Max was calling. I nodded my head, and he held me close, so that I could hear what his grandson had to say.

"Pops! Is something wrong? You hung up so quickly, I've been worried."

"No, Max. Everything is okay here. So, you have a girl living with you?"

"Not anymore."

"Why not? Sounded like you two were about to get cozy when I spoke to you earlier." I bristled at that, but Jack patted my back reassuringly as Max answered him.

"No, we weren't. We got into a fight because I haven't told the family about her."

"Why didn't you?"

"Because I didn't think she was serious," he explained.

"Then why in the hell was she living with you?"

"It's complicated, but basically she couldn't afford her place when her roommate up and left with no notice and I told her she could stay here until she could find something more affordable."

"I see, and then she made herself comfortable instead of looking for somewhere else to live?"

"Pretty much. Made herself comfortable with my mail, too."

"How's that?"

"Is Posie there? I really need to apologize to her. I only just got her letters and the graphic novel today. I got the letters I thought I'd been sending to her today, too."

"You might need to explain that to me, Max. Hang on, Posie is here, so I'm putting you on the loudspeaker."

I giggled and I heard Max do the same.

"It's speakerphone, Pops."

"Whatever. It makes you louder, so she can hear." Jack winked at me. He knew damn well what it was called. He was just trying to cast some light on the situation.

"Okay, now explain what happened. Don't leave us in the dark, boy."

"Becca was curious about Posie's letters. When she intercepted one from the mail before I could get to it, she opened it and read it. Then, when she went to put it back in the mail, she saw that I had put an outgoing letter to Posie there, and she took that too. After that, she realized she had to keep intercepting them because otherwise I'd know Posie hadn't received her letters. At least, that's what she told me when I found them after I got off the phone with you."

"So, this girl was not only hiding your incoming but outgoing mail concerning Posie?" Jack asked him.

"Yeah, I haven't even had a chance to look at them yet, but Posie?"

"Yeah?"

"I wanted you to know that the cover of that book is on fucking fire. I knew you sketched stuff all the time, but I never realized you were that good."

"Thanks," I offered as my cheeks blazed with heat.

"Considering what happened, I think you were right about the email thing. We should do that."

For some reason, it felt like a consolation prize to have him finally agree to emailing rather than sending handwritten letters. It was because of another woman that he was finally willing to allow me that level of access. There was a part of me that wanted to shoot his offer down, but with Jack standing there watching me so carefully, I didn't dare.

He'd always wanted Max and me to have a relationship for some reason. It wasn't harming me, so I figured there was no reason not to try.

"Okay."

I heard his laughter through the line. "I'm going to need your email address," he reminded me.

"I gave it to you in my letter. Did you throw it out?"

"No, I still have all of them. I figured it would be easier to get it from you now than to go hunting it down."

I gave him my email and he hung up shortly after.

"At least now you know he wasn't ignoring you on purpose," Jack mentioned.

"I suppose not," was my only answer as I contemplated what it must have been like for that woman to live with Max, knowing he was writing letters to another female, and she was writing him back. Would I have done the same thing in her position? I'd like to think that I'd just ask him about it.

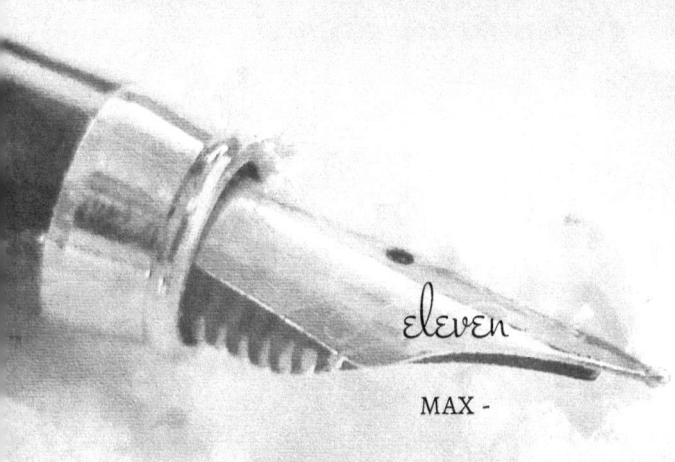

Eleven

MAX -

"You're officially done with the Army, so explain to me again why you can't come home. Your mother is worried sick."

"Dad, I told you that the police department here recruited me before the ink was even dry on my discharge. Thanks to my background in the military, I've been given the opportunity to take the exam and become a detective."

"Son." Dad sighed that one word like my decision was the end of the world. "We have a police department here," he finally mentioned as an alternative.

"I understand that, but they're not going to offer me the same deal. They'll want me to start from scratch as a beat cop. I've already done that and put in the work to move up. Taking a step backward isn't what I want. Maybe, after I get some time in here, I can move closer to home and not have to worry about backsliding in my career."

"Are you at least ever going to come home to visit?" He asked, sounding worn down by our conversation already, even though we'd only been on the phone for five minutes.

"I'm starting a new job right away. That means building up

time off before I can come home. It'll be a while, but I promise to get back as soon as I can."

My father sighed. The fact that I hadn't been back since leaving for the Army was a point of contention for my family. I missed them, and I know they missed me. The problem was that going home didn't feel like an option. Maybe it was fear holding me back, or the fact that I'd simply outgrown the small town, but it felt as though I'd be trapped there forever the minute I set foot in town again. I didn't want anything to keep me bound there, and my family would try their best to do just that.

There was also the issue of the other person who might make me want to stay. It was one thing to communicate with her through our letters and e-mails, but I didn't think I'd be able to walk away if I saw Posie in person. She would never agree to come back here with me, considering she worked so closely with my brother.

That was yet another reason I couldn't get home. I didn't know if I could handle seeing them so close and chummy. Pops swore up and down that there was nothing between them, but I knew firsthand what happened to people who were attracted to one another and worked closely together. My brother looked enough like me that I knew he was physically desirable to women. And Posie, well, even back when I first noticed her in that barn, there had been something about her.

She'd been waifish, in that she was a tiny thing, but there was a beauty to her features too. I often imagined how she looked now. I purposely avoided pictures of her because I didn't need that kind of temptation.

Pops and Dad were both two very big trees who cast wide shadows. It was hard to step out from under them and make a mark on the world that was my own. I didn't feel like I could do that while living so close to them and Posie was just type who would make it okay to never feel the sun firsthand again.

"Max, I wish you'd talk to me about whatever is keeping you

from coming home. Your mom is beginning to worry that we did something to upset you."

"I swear, you guys are fine. I'm just trying to establish a career. She didn't want me in the service any longer, and I listened."

Dad chuckled. "You went from the boiling pot to the frying pan full of scalding oil, son. Being a cop isn't any easier on her nerves, and she thought it meant you'd at least be home to watch her chewing her fingernails off."

It was my turn to chuckle. "I promise, as soon as I have time in my position, I'll start looking for an opening over your way and come closer to home."

"Famous last words, Son. Don't put it off too long," Dad warned. "You never know what you'll be missing out on by hiding out away from home."

"What's that supposed to mean?"

"Guess if you want to know, you'll have to make an appearance and find out," he teased.

"Guilt doesn't work, so you think you're going to bait me back home with intrigue?" I asked.

"Did it work?"

"Almost."

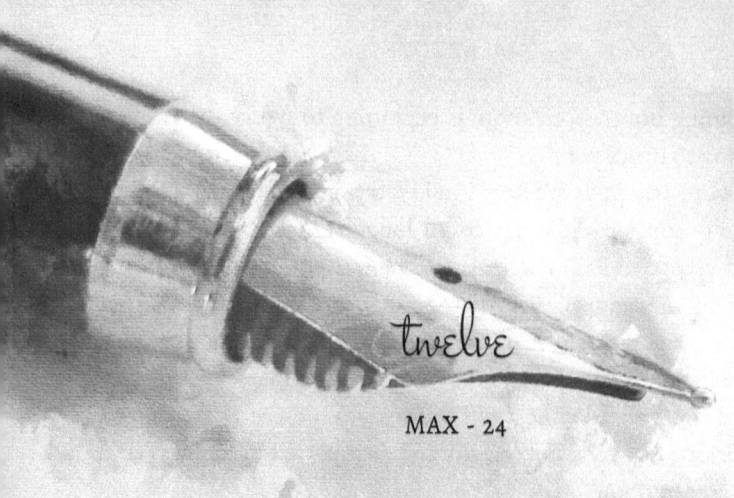

twelve

The best part of my day was always when I was able to go home, take a breather, and have a letter from Posie. Sometimes, it would be an old, snail mail version. Other times they were e-mails. I never told anyone, but I refused to read them on the computer or from my phone. The printer on my desk that only had one use was testament to that. Every time she sent an e-mail, they got printed before they were read. I don't know why the act of touching the paper made it feel more real, more connected to her, since it was no longer in her handwriting, but it did.

I printed out the latest letter and sat in my chair to get comfortable and read it. That familiar prickle in my chest exploded when I saw that Evan was the immediate topic of conversation. Posie and I didn't really talk much about our dating life and my brother refused to talk about Posie with me, so the question was always there in the back of my mind. Were they a couple now or still just collaborators on their graphic novels? An uncomfortable tightness in my chest always accompanied that thought, but Posie wasn't mine. She could never be mine since we had two different goals in life.

. . .

Dear Max,

Your brother thinks I'm ridiculous for opening my emails to you that way. He says it's antiquated and proves that I'm an old lady trapped in a hot chick's body.

I LAUGHED AT THAT, WONDERING WHAT SHE'D THINK IF she knew that I was just as much of an old man for wanting to read the physical letters.

We have another graphic novel in the works. Evan swears this one is going to be bigger and better than the last one, which is selling really well. Better than expected! Can you believe people want to read our stuff?

Evan says they love my art, but I still can't bring myself to look at the reviews it gets. Maybe I'm a coward, but I don't want to read about people tearing my work apart and nitpicking every little detail. My heart and soul went into those drawings. I guess, there is a part of me that still feels a bit like a fraud, like it was all a fluke and the next one we put out will be the proof of that.

. . .

I WANTED TO TAKE POSIE IN MY ARMS, WRAP HER UP, and reassure her that she was amazing. I had been blown away by her sheer talent, and the one thing my brother would say about our mutual friend was that she did every bit of so effortlessly, that it made his job as a storyteller easy because he could picture everything down to the finest detail and the words just melted from his hands onto the paper as a result. That had been simply from her concept sketches. He'd shown me a side-by-side comparison of one concept sketch versus the final, published image.

I'd have to make sure Posie knew to stop underestimating herself and her talent. She was amazing. Unfortunately, because of my life choices, it would have to be my brother who pulled Posie into a hug and reassured her in person. I shook off that thought when my chest pulled tight again and dove back into her letter instead.

Enough about that stuff, though, as I'm sure you find it boring, Mr. Bigshot Detective. How goes everything in the world of real life crimefighting? Have you caught many bad guys yet? What about your house? Have you moved into the new place yet? It's weird, I know we have email now and it goes faster than snail mail, but the little day-to-day pieces of life seem to be lost in the mix. I want to know what you're having for dinner — it better not be takeout again! You need a proper meal, Max!

MY DEEP CHUCKLE RUMBLED THROUGH MY CHEST AS her words lifted a smile from my tired, grumpy face. Posie wasn't wrong. I needed a good home-cooked meal. While that thought usually conjured up images of my mom's cooking and sitting around the table with my family, all I could picture was sitting at a far more intimate setting with a girl who I couldn't quite picture.

It made me want to ask for a recent photo of her, so that I could fully form that oddly domestic little fantasy scenario in my mind, but I knew better. It wasn't time yet. I hadn't lied to my father when I spoke to him a few weeks ago. My intention was to try to move closer to home eventually. I had to pay my dues and get enough time under my belt as a detective first, and then I needed for a position to open up. It felt a whole lot like waiting for the stars to align. The prize seemed less about being close to family and more about finally getting to be near Posie in person. The girl had wormed her way under my skin over the years we'd been corresponding.

She had burrowed herself so deep, I felt myself comparing everyone who came into my orbit to her. Women rarely matched the bar Posie had been unknowingly setting for them over the years. She was sweet, thoughtful, funny, caring, and sometimes seemed far too innocent for this world. Other times, she seemed far too jaded. There was a delicate balance where she'd been touched by too much tragedy so there was an edge to her sweet innocence that made her not seem totally out of reach for a guy like me.

I shook that thought off as quickly as it appeared. Posie would eventually end up with my brother – if he ever got his head out of his ass and realized what he had in front of him. If not Evan, though, it would be someone like him. It would never be me – the man who refused to go home to be seen as living under the blanket of his family's wild successes. I turned my attention back to her letter.

I made chicken and dumplings for Jack and me tonight. He loved it.

Okay, he told me he loved it as he choked it down. It was my first time making the dish and I may have accidentally added too much salt. How was I supposed to know a little goes a long way? Don't worry, I didn't let him finish his after I tried mine. That Pops of yours certainly did try to stick it out so he didn't hurt my feelings. We laughed so hard! Then we drank a ton of water and went to get takeout. Don't judge! At least I tried to make a hearty, homecooked meal.

Your mom promised to give me lessons on how to use spices and stuff. She said everything else looked good, except the heart attack inducing level of sodium. Maybe, if you ever come to visit, I'll be able to cook you a meal that won't kill you.

I have to run. We're all going out tonight to see that new action movie with the actor everyone loves. Can I be honest with you? I wish it was an at-home viewing so I could pause it and study the way explosions look at different points, so I can get them right in my drawings. It's going to annoy the hell out of me that I can't do that. I'll just plaster a fake smile on my face while I inwardly fume about my lack of a pause button in a movie theater.

My ride's here. Gotta go.

Always,
Posie

. . .

I LOVED HER QUIRKINESS, BUT DAMN IF I DIDN'T WANT to know who the hell her ride was and who all was going to a movie together. None of it was my business. None of it should have mattered. The tightness in my chest seemed to disagree with logic though.

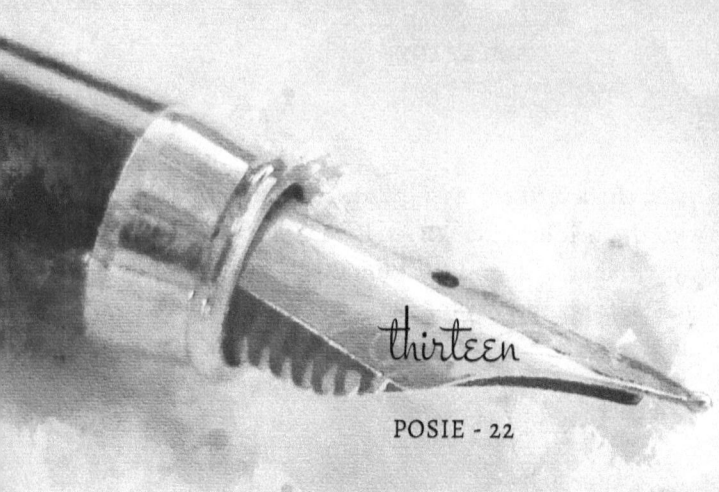

thirteen

POSIE - 22

I cherished the days when Max sent a handwritten letter instead of an email. I stared down at the letter and traced the scroll of his letters. The man had better penmanship than most women. Thankfully, no one was there to see me pick that same letter up to my nose and sniff it. His scent lingered on the pages along, mixed with the ink. There was a lingering cedar wood fragrance with a hint of citrus. It smelled wonderful, but I knew it wouldn't last.

Part of me wanted to ask Max what kind of cologne he wore. Was it creeperish to want to buy a small bottle to spray on the letters he sent when it eventually wore away over time? Probably. Did that stop me from wishing I could do it? Nope. I loved that each of his handwritten letters came with that extra little bit of him.

Dear Posie,

Fuck my brother! He doesn't get it. It's not old fashioned to start a letter that way and I don't want you to ever change your style for anyone. Whether it's handwritten or email, I love knowing that you're consistent in some things. It's comforting in a weird way. Kind of like coming home and settling into your favorite chair after work and the stress of the day immediately starts to drain away. When I sit down and see 'Dear Max' written to me, I'm automatically taken to a better place.

Wow! Did he really just say that? I wasn't sure if it should be a compliment to be compared to someone's comfortable "favorite chair", but I understood the sentiment all the same. Giddy little butterflies danced around in my belly as I thought about the fact that my letters took Max to a better place in his life. I hated that he needed that escape, but considering he was a police detective, it made sense. That was why I always tried to keep my letters to him upbeat.

You never said who you were going to the movies with. I wondered if you've suddenly made a bunch of famous friends in the industry, but I can't see famous people heading to our hometown to hang out at The Seven Screens. I'm still not sure how a town as small as ours can support a theater with that many screens, but then again, I seem to remember helping to keep them in business in high school.

Did you ever go back then? I don't think I ever saw you there.

. . .

THE BUTTERFLIES IN MY BELLY STOPPED FLUTTERING about and took a steep nosedive into the bottom of my gut. Of course he wouldn't have seen me there, even if I'd been able to have the free time to go. If I wasn't working in the bakery, I escaped to Jack's barn. Mom couldn't complain and come drag me back home from Jack's place because my guardian angel would never allow that, and Mom knew it. The barn had been my safe space. Going to the theater had been a dream. Going with friends seemed impossible, since I didn't really have any.

Max hadn't even noticed me in the barn the one time he showed up and made out with his girlfriend just feet away from where I'd been sitting. There was no doubt in my mind that he wouldn't have noticed me had I been allowed to go to the theater.

I shook off the morose thoughts and tried to remind myself that I was no longer that little girl hiding in the shadows. There were people who I could consider friends in my life now. Evan being the biggest one. Max, I suppose, was a friend even if only paper. Then there were Evan's friends who I considered more acquaintances because they tolerated my presence for him more so than welcomed me into the fold.

Since I couldn't answer Max out loud, I would probably leave that last bit out of my response to him. He already knew I was an invisible loser before he left town, he didn't need to hear from me that not much had changed.

Some days, I wish we could pack up and go things like that together. Is that weird? We never hung out when I lived there, but whenever I go things like try a new restaurant or run into a street artist as I walk through the city, I wonder what you would think. What would you order in the new Mexican joint I tried last week? Would you like the artist who makes funny caricatures more or the guy who does spray painted images of the solar system?

Maybe all that goes beyond our letter-writing friendship for you, but those are things I think about. I hope you had fun at the movies. I'm kind of jealous that I wasn't there to enjoy it with you. I want to know if you laugh out loud at the good parts, ask questions through the whole movie that annoy people, or if you're too afraid to get concessions because chewing seems like too much noise.

My guess is the latter. You were always so quiet and assuming, I can't imagine you being the person in the theater everyone hates.

Anyway, I just caught a new case and have to run. I hope you had fun and that you've come out of your shell enough to at least enjoy the popcorn. Fuck everyone else. Some days, you need to live for your own enjoyment.

Catch you later,

Max

MY HEART FLUTTERED SO FAST, I WORRIED THAT IT might explode. Max thought about me outside of our letters. Sure, it seemed stupid to think that he didn't, but he really wanted to know what it would be like to go places with me and what I would think of things. If only he knew that I often wondered those same things about him. I bet if he was sitting next to me in the theater, he would insist that I eat the popcorn and make squeaky noises with my straw.

I took the time to gather my thoughts together before I pulled out my pen and paper and started to write down my own thoughts. All the while, my stupid heart concocted all sorts of fantasies about me going to Max's city to surprise him with a visit. I wondered how he would take it. Would he be happy I showed up and take me to a movie or would he send me packing back home where I could remain out of sight and out of mind until he was ready to write a few more words that would unknowingly give me hope that he never intended?

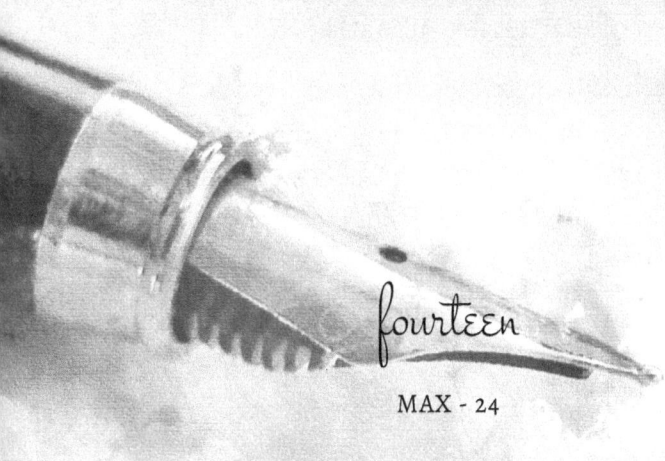

fourteen

MAX - 24

A normal letter came about a week after I last dropped one in the mail for Posie. It sucked that she didn't send an email. As much as I loved the handwritten letters over the emails, the wait to read her response was almost unbearable. I'd given away a bit too much in the last letter I sent.

I promised myself that I wouldn't give her a bunch of platitudes and false hope. It would probably be a couple years before I was able to move closer to home and it wouldn't be fair to her to string her along. Even though it killed me to think that some man might swoop in and make her his, I had to hold out hope that Posie would still be there when I was ready to come home. The biggest danger to that was my brother, and if I heard even the faintest hint that they were together, then coming home would be out of the question.

I pulled my blazer off, hung it in the little closet just inside my front door. Then I pulled off my shoulder holster and hung it from the hook inside the door before stowing my HK45 in my gun safe. Afterward, I tossed Posie's letter on the side table next to my chair and went to wash the day off me.

Once I finally got settled into my chair, and tore into the mint green envelope, my hands started to shake. What if she told me I'd gone too far in my last letter? What if she told me that she didn't think about me at all? Fuck, even when I was in my teens and still new to dating, I don't think I ever even worried about what a girl thought about me the way I did with Posie.

> *Dear Max,*
>
> *I won't take it personally that you basically compared me to your favorite piece of furniture. No, I never did go to the theater when you were still around in high school. Evan took me to my first theater movie about six months after you left town. I never went before because I was either working in my mom's bakery, busy with volleyball, or hiding out from life in Jack's barn — the one place my mother couldn't drag me away from.*

SHIT. IT FELT LIKE SOMEONE PUNCHED ME IN THE fucking stomach. I knew that Posie didn't have the easiest time. More importantly, after what my dad told me about how crazy her mother was, coupled with her suicide, I should have put two-and-two together a lot sooner. Posie wasn't just shy. She didn't try to stay hidden. No one ever noticed her because she was never around for anything. Except volleyball.

That was where the gut punch came from. I'd been to plenty of the volleyball games when I dated Cheyenne, and I can't remember a single one where I noticed Posie. It made me a feel like a dick all over again. I hadn't noticed her at Pops' place. I hadn't noticed her in school and certainly not during those games because

I'd been too busy watching my girlfriend's tits jiggling when she jumped up to spike a fucking ball. My eyes scanned back down the letter until I found where I left off.

I went with Evan and his friends this last time. It was a good time. While I wished I could pause the movie to figure out how to draw those explosions, you are absolutely right, there is no way that would get voiced out loud. I have this irrational fear that someone will come kick me out of the theater if I don't remain absolutely still and quiet for the duration. Besides, I hate missing the fun little nuances that 'those people' seem to miss because they're too busy being annoying.

Of course, there are times when I wonder what it would be like to go somewhere with you. I never really picture you here for those things, though. For some reason, it feels like you'll never come back here. So, when I picture those moments, it's usually as you describe some new place you tried, or a fun new spot you got to hang out. I've even pictured what it would be like to see you in action.

You want to hear something funny? Sometimes I watch an episode of Law and Order or Criminal Minds and I wonder who would play you if someone made a show about one of your cases. Whose character would be most like you when you're at work. I remember the Max who used to roll around town in his dirt-caked pickup truck like he owned the world. I know the man who writes these letters to me, too. What I don't know is what kind of man are you when you're at work. That's the question that always keeps me wondering.

I'm kind of a boring person to take to a Mexican restaurant. I panic and never know what to order, so I'll just automatically ask for a Quesadilla or Chimichanga. Sometimes, if I don't have to drive, I'll spice it up by ordering a Margarita.

I HAD TO LAUGH AT THAT UNTIL I WONDERED WHO WAS driving her around when she was drinking. Maybe it was my brother. I tried not to be jealous, especially of my brother's time spent with Posie. Mom mentioned that he was dating someone, and while I couldn't remember her name, it wasn't Posie. That would have been a big deal in the family. There's no way anyone would have kept that from me, least of all Pops. The old coot would have called me personally to tell me how I missed out on the best woman in the world.

That's what he thought of her, and I was hard pressed to disagree with his assessment lately. I turned my attention back to the letter in my hands. She thought about me, my work, what it would be like to be here with me. That was something I wanted to see her expand on. Hopefully, she did.

I have a confession to make. This is going to make

me sound like a complete loser, please don't hold it against me.

I've never really been on a date before. Evan convinced me to go on a double date with one him and his new girlfriend. I'm not a big fan of hers, so I'm guessing it's going to be uncomfortable. The thing is — I think Evan needs me to do this so that she'll stop giving me the side-eye like I'm about to steal her man. Evan and I have to work together. I don't see him like that at all. He's come to mean so much to me — like a brother, really. I could never see him in a romantic light, but there's no convincing this girl of that.

So, I guess I'm going on my first official date with some guy that they're setting me up with. Truthfully, I don't want to go. I kind of hope the guys stands me up and lets me off the hook. It's still two weeks away because of everyone's conflicting schedules, so there's time for a catastrophe to happen first, right? I'm sure it's just first-time nerves getting to me.

I've been thinking about getting away for the weekend coming up. Wish me luck on my trip!

Always,
Posie

A DATE?

Posie was going on a date. Her first date. She was 22. I thought about that for a minute. It wouldn't be too much longer, and she'd be 23 years old. How in the hell could she be that old and never been on a date? What the absolute fuck? Part of me wanted to haul ass back to my hometown and pick her up before she had a chance to go anywhere this weekend. I could be the first man to take her on a date.

Then I thought about it. Nothing had changed for either of us. Posie needed to be in our hometown because her business partner lived there. I had to be here for the time being because I was still logging my hours on the job as a detective and building a reputation.

I sighed as I folded her letter and stuffed it back into the mint-green envelope she'd sent it in. I sat there and held that envelope in my hands until I realized it was getting crinkled up thanks to the frustrated death-grip I had on it. It didn't take long for me to get to the closet in my bedroom, open my safe, and tuck the letter in with all the rest she had sent over the years.

My phone buzzed in my pocket as I closed the safe and made sure it latched securely. When I pulled it out, I was surprised to see my brother's name and picture pop up.

"Evan?" I turned his name into a question.

"That's me," came his smartass reply.

"What's up?"

He made a noise, like he was a bit uncomfortable with something. "What are you up to this weekend?"

"Why? You planning to come up here?" I lived six hours away by car. It wasn't a terrible drive, but it was enough of a barrier to act as a deterrent most of the time for me coming home and my family coming to see me. It wasn't that I didn't want to see them. I did. I missed my family so much it made me sick when I thought about it. I'd even had a hard time justifying how long I'd been away lately. Still, it wasn't like Evan to want to just come hang out, especially since he had apparently had a new girlfriend with a jealous streak.

"I'm not sure. It's my weekend off. Honestly, it's been a crazy two weeks on the job, and chilling at the house sounds like an amazing time."

"Damn, man. You sound like you belong Pops' porch with him and Posie. You old fuckers wouldn't know how to have a good time if it smacked you in the ass and told you to bend over."

I chuckled at that. "You have someone telling you to bend over for a good time, baby brother?"

"Shut the fuck up, you know what I meant."

"You planning a trip to see me this weekend?"

"Well, not really. I have a new girl and…" His nervous laugh made me wonder what the fuck was going on."

"Mom and Dad aren't planning to surprise me, are they?"

"Would they walk on in to find you balls deep in some cop chasing woman who wants you to use your cuffs on her?"

"Fuck's sake, Evan. What is wrong with you? No, they wouldn't walk in on that shit. I don't even bring women to my place after the last one that made herself cozy in my apartment and decided to hide my mail from me."

"Yeah, that's probably a good call. Also, don't date crazy."

"Sometimes, you don't know they're crazy up front, Ev."

"Ain't that a bitch. I'm worried my new girl might be a bit crazy. She gets twitchy around Posie."

"Any reason why she should?"

"Nah, you should know better than that. Don't you two talk all the time? Posie isn't into me. She's into someone else pretty hardcore."

"I just read a letter that said she's dreading going on some setup date with you and the new girl and some mystery guy. If she's so into someone else, why would she agree to that?"

"She's dreading it?" Evan asked. "Dammit, I knew I shouldn't push her into it."

"Ev, answer my question."

"What question?"

"Why would she agree to date some random setup if she has her eyes on someone else?"

Evan chuckled in my ear. "Dude, she would never look at another person if the guys she liked ever noticed her."

"He doesn't know she exists?" I remembered what it was like the first time I saw Posie. It was shocking to hear her tell my Pops that she was invisible to everyone, but after conversing with her over the years, I understood it was a common occurrence for people to just overlook her for some reason.

"Nope, the dipshit knows she exists. He's just too fucking dumb to understand she's the best he'd ever get. My Posie is the best anyone would ever get. If we didn't work together and she didn't treat me like a brother from another mother, I'd..."

"You'd what?" I asked cutting him off before he could even finish his own sentence.

"I'd date the hell out of her. Who knows, maybe even wife her up," he stated. I could hear him trying to hold in his laughter. The fucker knew he was getting under my skin and I didn't like it. I liked it even less that Posie had been fawning all over some guy and if he ever pulled his head out of his ass and realized what a catch she was, I would lose any chance that ever existed of making her mine.

"Hey, Ev, unless we need to make plans for the weekend, I'm gonna get off the call and go grab some food before I crash and wake up hungrier than a post-hibernation bear."

"You know bears don't really hibernate, right?"

"Ev, is someone planning a trip here this weekend that I need to be aware of?"

"Nah." He didn't seem too sure of his answer, but didn't change it either.

"All right then, I need to go."

"Yeah, have a good night, bro." I got ready to click off the call when my brother spoke up again. "I hope you have an amazing weekend, no matter what ends up happening."

"Yeah, man, you too, Ev. Later."

"Later," he said and that time I did hang up.

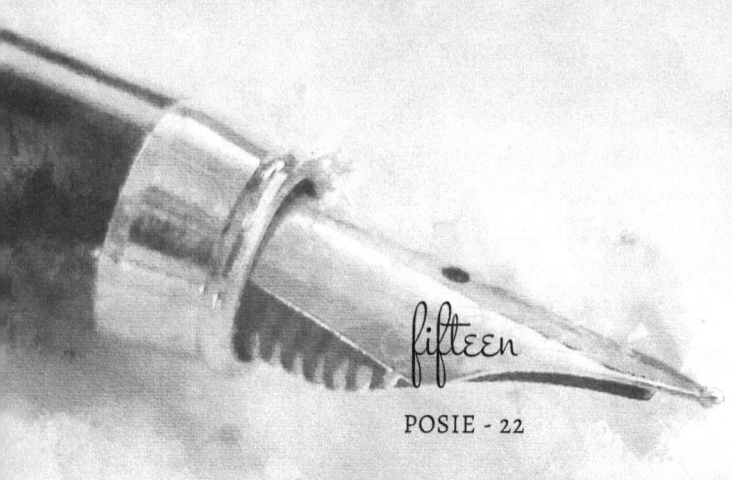

"Are you sure about this?"

I stopped stuffing my shirt in my bag and turned to look at Evan. It wasn't his question that pulled me up short so much as the tone in his voice. He was worried.

"Of course, I'm sure. It will be an adventure. I've never really had the time to get away from our town, and now that we're making pretty good money, I don't have to feel guilty about spending money on myself for once."

"It's not that. I mean, are you sure you want to waste your first trip away on my brother?"

"I..." My mouth moved like the words were going to come out any minute, but Evan left me speechless. "What is that supposed to mean?"

"Come on, Posie. We all know you've had a crush on him since high school. I love you. You're my best friend, my sister for all intents and purposes, but he's my brother."

"And?" My one-word question came out sounding a bit indignant, I'd admit, but it felt a little like Evan was choosing and it wasn't mine.

"And I know Max. If he was interested in you like that, he

would have been here, in person, to come hang out with you. My brother doesn't just sit and wait on something or someone he wants. He dives in headfirst, more often than not without thinking of the consequences. He hasn't even come home once. Not for us and," he grew quieter, as if to soften the blow, "not for you."

I yanked out the letter that I planned to take with me to justify my actions and then thrust it at my best friend. "Read it."

I watched as Evan read through the letter and saw when his expression turned a bit stunned. "Okay, I wasn't expecting that, but this doesn't mean..."

"I know it doesn't mean he's suddenly fallen in love with me or something, Evan. I'm not an idiot. I also don't want to be a coward my whole life. You literally just told me all about how Max would behave if he liked me 'like that', but I'd hate to hear what your opinion of me is. If he's the type that acts first, dives in headfirst, takes chances, goes after what he wants... Then what does that make me? A fucking coward for sitting back for years. It's been seven years since I first watched him kissing Cheyenne in that barn."

I pointed toward the barn that had been turned into our studio, thanks to Pops. I'd probably live in it instead of keeping a room in Pops' house if it wasn't for the fact that it was shared workspace between Evan and me.

"I watched him kiss that girl, who never deserved him, and I hated it then. When that bitch who was stealing his mail lived with him, it physically hurt me to find that out and still, I did nothing but give your brother my email address. I wanted the cute boy to notice me in high school. That was the end of my expectations back then. I just wanted him to see me, to know I was a person worth noticing." I swiped at an angry tear that slid down my face.

"Over the years, we've established a friendship. He knows who I am in here now," I said as I tapped my chest over my heart. "He knows the inside me. He wonders what it would be like to do things with the outside me, too. He admitting to having the same daydreams I do. Even if nothing more comes from this than realizing we're just friends on paper, it's something I have to do, Evan. I can't spend the rest of my life living in limbo and regretting the fact that I was too scared to take a chance."

"Can I at least go with you? It's a long drive and he doesn't know to expect you. Anything could happen."

"No, but I'll keep you updated every single time I stop and when I get there. I promise."

"Fine. Please, be careful, and if I don't hear from you at least every two hours of the trip, I will call him and tell him you're on the way."

"Please, don't do that. I really want to surprise him. It's important to me."

"Fine. For the record, I don't think surprising him is the way to go."

"Why? Is there something I should know? If he has a girlfriend, he would have told me, right? You would tell me before I go make a fool of myself."

"He doesn't," Evan admitted and that was all I needed to hear. It was time. Truthfully, it was years past time for me to finally get the nerve to do this. Max's last letter had bolstered my confidence. If he pictured me there, hanging out with him, then it was a sign that I meant enough to him that he should at least be happy his friend showed up out of the blue. I wasn't naïve enough to think it might mean that he wanted me as anything more, but I had to know for sure.

IT TOOK A LITTLE OVER SIX HOURS OF DRIVING, HAVING to stop to pee – more often than should have been necessary because of nerves – and grabbing a bite to eat. Not that I had been able to choke down much of my lunch, but I needed the sustenance to keep me going. It was later than I anticipated when I finally arrived. Max's truck was in his driveway, so I parked along the street just before his drive. My nerves screamed at me to turn around and leave before he noticed my stalker ass sitting out here, but I pushed through the self-doubt, got out of my car, and walked my overly excited butt up to his door and knocked.

I waited.

I knocked again, a little louder that time.

Nothing.

Nervously, my eyes shifted back to his truck that was in the driveway and then to the door again before I hung my head and decided to go call Evan from my car. I got inside, pulled my phone out, and was stopped by the rumbling of a loud pickup truck coming down the road. It slowed as it passed me and stopped on the opposite side of the driveway just in front of Max's mailbox. Max hopped out of the passenger side and said something to the driver just as the passenger side back door slid open.

A beautiful brunette woman hopped out and giggled as she nearly lost her footing. Max quickly moved over to steady the woman on her feet.

"My hero," she cooed at him. My eyes couldn't have rolled harder in my head if I'd tried. "I had so much fun tonight, Max. You were the best date."

Date? My gut bubbled with anxiety at the thought I was sitting there like a creeper, only feet away, watching as once again Max had another perfect, perky, confident woman in his arms. How the hell was it possible to live out my teenage heartbreak all over again? It was like the universe had to remind me of my place at every step of the way. I was still just as invisible as ever.

The woman wrapped her arms around his neck and pulled herself up onto her tiptoes so she could attack his mouth with her lips. In Max's defense, he seemed completely caught off guard by her aggressive kiss. Then again, that might have just been my jealousy clouding my perspective. Still, I'd seen Max kiss a girl who he wanted before, and he certainly put forth more of an effort back then.

Maybe he was losing his touch in his old age. I chuckled to myself over how he would react to me saying that. Then, I reminded myself that those conversations only took place via letters and emails, so I would never get his true reaction anyway.

Max gently moved the girl away from him using the hands he still had wrapped around her hips. Even though it wasn't healthy for me to do so, I wondered what it would be like to have them on me like that. I bet it would feel wonderful, like he was taking ownership of my body for the time being and I would have let him. The woman he was with would have too. The disappointed pout on her face as Max stepped back and bumped into his mailbox was testament enough that she did not like the fact that he was no longer touching her.

"I thought we had a good time tonight?" The woman questioned.

"We all had a great time hanging out."

"We all?" She asked with an elevated pitch to her voice that spoke of her annoyance to be lumped in as a group.

"Yeah." Max circled his fingers to indicate them and the other people still in the truck who had to be watching this take place. "All of us who went out together."

Max took a step to the side, which put him directly in the circle of light being cast by the light post. His jaw was darkened in with a heavy five o'clock shadow and his hair, while still short was starting to curl a bit at the ends near his collar. It seemed a bit messy on top, as if he, or someone else, had been running their fingers through it.

His hair was only the first thing that struck me. The rest followed quickly behind as I got my first look at him since the last time I'd seen him seven years ago. Max was no longer the boy I remembered. He was a solid man with broad shoulders that tapered down to a trim waist and strong legs that strained the thighs of his denim pants just enough to be enticing, but not enough that it looked uncomfortable for him.

His feet were tucked into cowboy boots that made me smile as I remembered that he wore a similar pair to the prom all those years ago. He might have grown into a man's body, but there were still parts of the boy I'd once crushed on there too. I watched as he took a bigger step to the left, presumably to move away from the mailbox that had been digging into his backside. The woman's pout grew more dramatic.

"Come on, Tasha, we need to drop you off too." Another woman, one with red hair and a very short skirt had jumped out of the truck and made her way around to the passenger seat that Max had vacated. "Jake and I have plans for the rest of the night, sweetie. Unless Max is going to take you into his house and ravish you like you deserve, we have to go."

Well, that woman wasn't pulling any punches as she attempted to be a very blunt wing-woman for her friend.

"Sorry, ladies. Having company over tonight was not on the agenda."

"I don't mind if your house a little messy."

"What I meant to say was that I didn't realize this was supposed to be some kind of..." he flapped a hand between them and took another step back. "I had fun, but it's been a hell of a couple weeks at work and I just want to catch some sleep."

"Well, that's no fun. I can work the stress out of you, so you sleep better." Tasha refused to give up.

"Maybe another time," Max muttered before he turned and started to walk to his house.

"Get in the truck, Tash. He's not interested and you're embarrassing yourself at this point." I noticed Max's shoulders go up when he heard the friend berating the girl. I wondered what about that bothered him. Was I the way the woman's friend called her out, the loss of a potential 'other time', or did he wish he could sink into the ground and pretend the day hadn't happened?

Personally, I wished I could sink into my upholstery because his buddy, Jake, had taken notice of me a couple times from his rearview mirror. I wanted them to leave and Max to go inside, so I could take off and pretend I never drove here.

Unfortunately for me, I had the worst luck in the world because my cell phone rang with another worried call from Evan. Since my windows were cracked and my volume was turned to deafening levels, so I'd be able to hear it over my radio on the ride, everyone else heard too. Several heads turned my way, including Max's.

The minute he took a step in my direction, I put my car in drive and took off. Luckily, the woman who had been throwing herself at Max still hadn't gotten in her truck, so Max's friend couldn't follow me. When I got far enough away, I snatched my phone up with shaky hands.

"Call Evan."

After two rings, he answered. "I tried calling you."

"I know, and then I had to get the hell out of there because I looked like a creepy fucking stalker. Thanks a lot, you jackass."

"What the fuck, Posie?"

"Oh my God! I'm so mortified, Ev."

"Okay, calm down and tell me exactly what happened."

By the time I was done explaining, in great detail, everything that had just transpired, I couldn't get a word in edgewise about how I felt because Evan's hysterical laughter drowned out anything I could have said.

"Dammit, Evan!" I yelled into the phone.

"Sorry, Posie, but that's some funny shit." He wheezed as he pulled himself together again. "You have to go back and explain."

"What? No, I don't. I'm not doing that."

"What happened to not wanting to be a coward?"

"One – he's obviously dating people, so he isn't thinking about me like that. No matter how much I deluded myself into believing otherwise."

"Posie," Evan tried to placate me.

"No!" I shouted into the phone. "And two, I literally just sat there at the end of his driveway watching a woman kiss on him and throw herself at him for a good fifteen minutes without announcing my presence, Ev. I wasn't trying to be creepy. I just wanted to wait them out until they went away. Then, I was going to let Max know I was there – even though my whole reason for showing was kind of thwarted already. But then you called and drew attention to me. EVERYONE'S ATTENTION! Now, I just look like a psycho stalker."

I groaned loudly into my car and then pulled into a gas station to park for a minute because my hands were still shaking, and my heart was racing like there was a prize if it could beat so hard that I passed out.

"Posie, I'm sure Max will understand once you explain."

"Please, don't tell him I ever came here. Please, Evan. I'm begging you to keep this one secret for me because I can't take the humiliation."

"Seriously, he'll understand."

"You don't understand. The first time your brother ever noticed me was when I was sitting in a corner watching him make out with another girl."

"Yikes. Deja vu, huh?"

"Exactly. He's going to think I make it a habit, especially since he knows exactly how nutso my mom was."

Evan sighed deeply. "Posie, I really think you should just tell him. Remember that whole speech you gave me about not wanting to be a coward?"

"Yeah, I do. I'd rather be a coward than a weird kiss-watching stalker!"

"I knew it was a bad idea for you to go." He huffed and then relented. "Fine. I'll keep your secret for you. Are you going to find a place for the night? You shouldn't drive straight back, that's too much driving in one day."

"Yeah, I already had a hotel room reserved."

"Damn, you went there with no expectations for my brother, huh?"

"What do you mean?"

"You didn't think he'd invite you to stay with him if you showed up?"

"Considering how everything just played out, I think it was a wise choice. Besides, I would never expect someone to put me up for the night after showing up out of the blue."

"One of these days, you're going to learn that people love you and want you to be around."

"Well, I kind of know that about you and Jack and even your parents. Max is a wild card though."

"I don't think he's as much of a wild card as you seem to think he is."

"Did you not listen to everything that went down tonight?"

"I did. Sounds like he went out with a group and came home with a clinger trying to make it into something it wasn't and you were unfortunately there to witness it."

It was my turn to sigh. Somewhere, deep down inside, I knew his assessment was probably correct. That didn't stop me from being absolutely mortified that I was almost caught skulking around outside of Max's house, waiting for him to come back home, and then watching him kiss another woman.

Maybe it was the trauma of learning what my mother had done to my big brother, how she'd run off the woman my father had been in love with, or how she left me by killing herself. Our whole town knew my mother was batshit crazy, and I couldn't help but think that was the reason everyone treated me like I was the invisible child for so long that it became habit. It felt like they were all waiting for my crazy bomb to go off too. No one bothered to think that I might favor the men in my life instead. My father who kept me tucked to his side until the day he died, so that Mom couldn't harm me and Jack who took me in and made sure I was loved. They were the examples I wanted to emulate. For some reason, when it came to Max, I always came off looking more like my mom, though.

Thankfully, Max never asked me about that day. Maybe he thought it was someone else watching him. Part of me felt bad about it because I didn't want him to think he had a stalker watching him or something. Considering the job he did, there were probably no good scenarios where someone would be parked up outside of his house watching him carry on with someone. Still, I couldn't bring myself to ever confess that it had been me and he never posed it as a question to me, so I didn't think he ever knew.

One thing I was certain of was that I needed to stop living solely for the hope that something would ever happen between Maxwell Carter and me. It was pretty fair to say that he just wasn't that interested in me and I refused to come off as crazy as my mom.

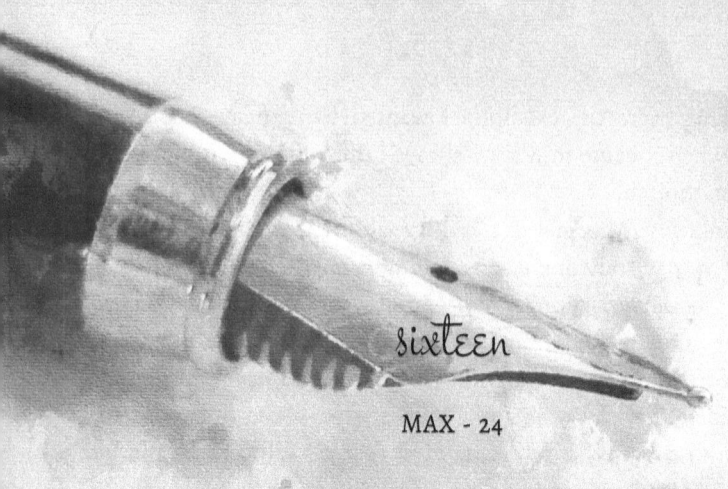

After Jake took his date and her clingy friend home, I walked over to my neighbor's house. There was something not quite right about having a woman sitting in a car outside of my house when I got home. It put me even more on edge that she took off the minute we all noticed her there.

"Hey, did someone happen to set off your ring camera earlier while I was out?" I asked after Mr. Stevens greeted me.

"Yeah, pretty girl showed up. I thought she stuck around to wait for you. The wife and were taking bets on whether you were about to be notified you're going to be a dad."

"Nothing like that, I can assure you. She didn't stick around, so I was wondering if I could see the footage, and have it forwarded to me?"

Mr. Stevens took on a less amused stance then. "This about the job?"

"I'm not sure yet but want to be able to set eyes on whoever it was, just in case."

"All right, Son, give me just a minute and I'll have it all put on a flash drive for you. I'll make sure you get the footage from when

98

she showed up until you came to the door. It'll be better if you go through all that, since I don't know what you're looking for."

Twenty minutes later, Jake was back. He wasn't an idiot. I'd been busy trying to fend of the handsy brat he'd stuck me with all night, but he had noticed the woman sitting in the car before her cell phone went off.

"My neighbor just got me his ring camera footage, so let's take a look."

As soon as the footage started, we saw a woman walk up to the front door. Thankfully, because my front door was to the left of the house and Mr. Steven's front door was to the right, his camera caught a great view of my front stoop. As the blonde woman approached, it was obvious that she was nervous. She was wringing her hands and glancing back and forth between my truck and the front door as she approached.

She knocked, stepped back into the camera's view again to wait, continued to ring her hands and look back and forth between the truck and the door. Then, she moved forward and knocked again. When no one answered, she finally turned to walk away. We watched as her shoulders visibly slumped, but the camera caught the perfect image of her face. I backed it up and paused the frame. Something about her seemed so familiar. Her eyes were round and expressive, the little button nose looked like a cute addition to the perfection that was her elfin features. The tips of her ears even seemed the slightest bit pointy rather than fully rounded.

She was also wearing a pair of shit-kickers that made me want to know who the hell she was. It was the button pinned to her oversized bag that caught my attention the most though. It had a logo that was a bit too blurry to make out, but the words were clear. "Ask me how graphic I get."

I snapped a picture of the TV screen and sent it to my brother along with a question.

Max: Is this who I think it is?

I didn't get an answer back from him. Instead, my phone rang. I put it on speaker so Jake could hear him too.

"Where did you get that picture?" Evan asked. His non-answer was answer enough. She had come to see me. My beautiful little Posie had driven all the way here to come talk to me and then she just left before...

"Fuck!" I hissed. Jake stared at me as Evan cussed down the other side of the line.

"She's already 'so mortified,' her words, not mine. You can't tell her you know."

"Why the hell not?" I asked.

"Listen, Max, I promised I wouldn't tell you she was there, but she was humiliated. If she knew that you were aware she was there, I promise you would never get another letter from her again."

"Wait," Jake chimed in. "That gorgeous girl is your little pen pal? You have some explaining to do, man."

"Why is she humiliated, Ev? I don't understand. I wouldn't have been mad that she came here. Shit, I want to see her." My heart was about to hammer its way out of my chest. Did I want to see her? With all my heart. The timing wasn't right just yet, though. That's the only reason I hadn't made it happen yet.

"Do you remember the first time you ever met Posie?" My brother asked me. His question had Jake leaning in to hear the answer.

"Of course, I do. Her freaking mom had just offed herself."

"Nah, man. Before that."

"Well, we didn't exactly meet the first time I noticed her," I informed my brother.

"Yeah, well, do you remember the situation she ended up sitting through?"

"Yeah?" I questioned as Jake asked, "What situation?"

"I took my girlfriend to my Pops' barn and climbed up to the loft to make out in peace." I chuckled at the memory because it wasn't so peaceful once Pops busted us.

"Dumbass failed to even take notice that there was a sad girl sitting in the corner listening to music with earbuds in and drawing to try to drown out her crappy life."

"Letter girl?" Jake asked. I nodded as Evan confirmed it in words. "Okay, I get where you're going with this."

"Well, I'm glad you do, Jake, but I don't see what that has to do with shit."

"The girl in that car tonight was already there waiting for you to show up," Jake informed me. I'd already figured that much out. When I didn't say anything he continued. "So, she sat there and watched Tasha climb all over you and try to shove her tongue down your throat. It probably felt a whole lot like being transported back in time to when you didn't notice she was there, and you were making out with your girlfriend."

"Bingo," My brother added.

"Fucking hell. I didn't even want Tasha's attention. I had no control over that shit. She had to have seen that I pushed Tasha away and told her I didn't want her coming to my house."

"Yeah, she did. Posie told me all about it and didn't leave anything out. The thing is, she has a lot of baggage that her mom left her with. She got it in her head that everyone in town treated her like she was invisible because she was her mother's daughter. Honestly, I don't think she's that far off the mark. So, as she got older, no one bothered to notice her. Do you know that in our freshmen year Posie was moved to the varsity volleyball team? When you were dating Cheyenne, Posie was the leading scorer for the volleyball team three years in a row and they still made Cheyenne the team captain.

"Wait, you're telling me that everyone purposely overlooked that beautiful woman who was banging on Max's door earlier?"

"That's exactly what I'm telling you. She thinks it's because everyone knows how crazy her mom was. So, imagine how she felt when it looked like she was stalking you while you made out with another woman in front of her without noticing that she was there."

"I saw the car there, but I didn't look too hard."

"I saw there was a woman in the car, but I didn't know she was there for Max," Jake added.

"Tell me she didn't drive straight home after coming all this way, Ev."

"She didn't, but I'm also not going to tell you where she's staying."

"Why the fuck not? I can put her worries to rest. She was more than welcome to be here. I wasn't out on a fucking date. That bitch literally ruined my night in every way." I glared at Jake then because I fully blamed him for putting me in the position to be mauled by the stage-five clinger all night while he tried to charm her friend.

"I already told you, she feels horrible and I made her a promise."

"That's not good enough, Ev. I need to go make things right. She didn't do anything wrong. I appreciate the surprise, but if anyone had told me she was coming, I would have been here to greet her."

"I asked if you had anything going on and you said you'd be home all weekend trying to catch some rest and relaxation time."

"That's why you asked what I was up to this weekend?"

"Yup," my brother answered.

"Fucking Christ, a head's up would have been nice."

"Max, I didn't want to give you a head's up. I wanted her to get there and see you hooking up with someone, which is what I thought 'rest and relaxation' at home meant to you, even if you didn't want to spell it out."

"Why the fuck would you want that?"

"She's a Goddamn 22-year-old virgin, for Christ's sake. She needs to get over her crush on you and start dating people who are available to her."

"That Goddess is a freaking virgin who has never been on a date?" Jake's eyes bugged out as his head swiveled back to her image that was still paused on my TV screen. "Are all the men in your town blind?"

"It will make her feel better about the trip if she knows I don't think she's crazy, man," I argued with my brother while ignoring Jake.

"Max, you like her, right?"

"Of course, I like her."

"I mean, if you guys lived in the same town, you'd want to date her."

"Yeah, that's what I've been holding out for."

"Holding out for?" Evan scoffed.

"Yeah, I don't want to start anything long distance. I have at least another year here before I can transfer, if I can find a department with an opening closer to home. She works with you, so she needs to be back there. The timing isn't right yet. I hoped she'd still be single by the time I got back to town, but damn man... Up until I got one of her last letters, I didn't know she hadn't been dating at all. That can't be because of me."

Evan scoffed again. "I mean her stupid crush on you doesn't help, but I already told you how the people in town feel about her. They think she's as crazy as her mom, even though they've never seen her do one outlandish thing. You would think after her Valedictorian speech when we graduated, they would have realized she's a pretty cool chick, but they're all morons."

"Valedictorian?" Jake questioned. "So, she's beautiful, smart, sweet, thoughtful, and has never been touched by another man? I'm about to move to your town and take a job as a fucking paperboy if I have to. What the fuck, Max?"

"It's not time yet," I stated again. My best fucking friend in the world would end up getting punched in the nose if he didn't watch himself.

"And that right there is why I'm not going to tell you where she's staying, and you're not going to use your police shit to find her either. You're going to let her come back home, date people, and try to get over you."

"I'm not going to stop writing to her." I yelled at my brother.

"Didn't ask you to." He sighed so loudly I heard it plain as day through the phone line. "Max, I am going to encourage her to date. She's seen you with two other women now and heard about the horror story you had living with you before too. It ain't right to string her along until you're ready while you do whatever you want. I'm sure there were more women warming your bed along the way, man."

My brother wasn't wrong, but I didn't want to think about some other man in Posie's bed. He was right though. I wasn't ready for her just yet. We both had to be in a place where we wouldn't end up resenting the other for having to give something up. I wasn't ready to go home and move backward in my career and she couldn't work here when my brother and her were used to collaborating from the same room. It wasn't fair.

"Fine. I won't say anything. As far as she will know, she got away with coming here and me never knowing."

"Good," Evan said. There was a long pause and then he spoke again. "Max, if you really want to see if there's something more than letters between you, you might want to make it home sooner than later. Some other guy is going to realize what a great woman she is."

"Do I need to worry about you?" I asked, and honestly, the more I talked to my little brother about Posie, the more I thought it might be a concern.

"Nah. She's my business partner and as much as she thinks this town doesn't see her... Posie has blinders on when it comes to the Carter men. The only one she sees as anything other than family is you."

He sounded a little sad about that, but I couldn't find it in my heart to feel bad about it.

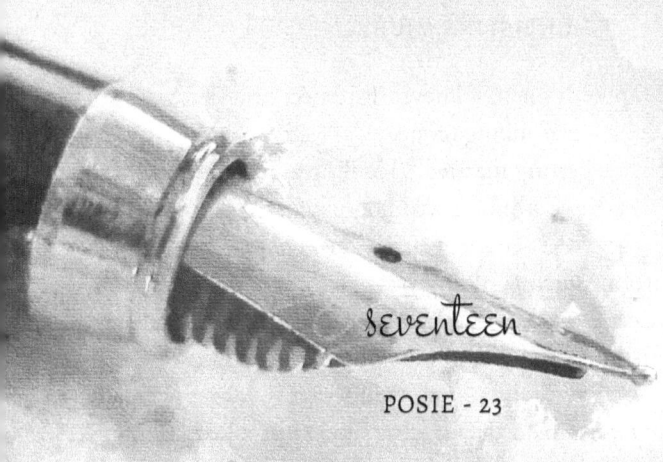

SEVENTEEN

POSIE - 23

"I can't believe he's getting married." Evan said as he stared down at the cell phone in his hands.

"Who is getting married?"

His eyes rolled up to meet mine and then he cocked his head to the side questioningly. "Figured you would know before me." I shrugged my shoulders and raised my eyebrows to question him right back. "What the hell do you and your little pen pal talk about in those letters you're always writing to one another?"

"Max?" I asked.

"Do you have another pen pal I don't know about?"

"Evan, I clearly have no clue what you're talking about. Would you just spit it out? I'm going to be late if I keep screwing around here with you."

Jack gifted me the infamous barn I'd always hidden out in and helped me turn it into an office space for Evan and me to work out of. The loft area was turned into a studio apartment for me as well. I didn't mind staying in Jack's house, but he thought that privacy might be something I needed as a young woman. It was his way of telling me that he didn't want to see if I brought someone back home to hook up with them. I'd never disrespect him that way, but it was cute that he was thinking of me.

"My brother is getting married." He flipped his phone toward me and there was a picture of a wedding invitation taking up the whole screen. Maxwell Grant Carter was to marry Elizabeth Brighton Murphy. Their wedding was set for two months from today. He hadn't even told me he was dating anyone, that he'd proposed, or that marriage was imminent.

I turned away from the phone wondering if Max ever really shared anything with me or if our letters were just a joke to him. I poured my heart out into those letters, told him about my first kiss, the fact that I was no longer a virgin and how I felt about it. He also had to hear about the inevitable breakup that followed losing my virginity. I'd given him all those important pieces of myself, and he'd given me nothing of substance. I got anecdotes from work and funny fishing trip stories.

I wished Evan would disappear because the sting in my eyes and the constriction in my chest told me that there was going to be no way to control or hide my reaction to any of this news or how it made me feel.

He hadn't even told me he was seeing anyone. In fact, more and more over the past couple months, he'd alluded to the fact that he wished I lived closer to him, so that we could go out on a date. The pencil in my hand dropped to the drawing table and I clutched at my chest, as if it would help hold the pain in that I was feeling.

"Posie?" Evan's concerned voice only made things worse. I wanted him to leave and wrap his arms around me to hold me together all at once. It was humiliating to know that he was about to witness my heartbreak over his brother. The same brother who apparently still didn't see me as a person worth his time. When would my heart get the memo? He never saw me, didn't want me, and was only stringing me along out of some sort of weird obligation to his family.

The first sob broke free as I doubled over into Evan's arms. "Holy shit, Posie. What's going on?"

"I tell him everything." Those four words were a struggle to get out. My heart ached in ways I hadn't felt in years. "Everything, Evan. And for what? I thought we were friends, he said if I lived closer he'd like to take me out on a date. He... He's never given me anything back but silly fishing stories and half-truths, and I'm only just now seeing that."

"What... Who are we talking about, Posie?" His question was a whisper on lips. His mouth entirely too close to my own. His blurry face came into view as I slowly looked up to meet his gaze.

"No! Tell me this isn't about Max. He's the one that always put that one smile on your face, the look of longing when I catch you staring off out the window? My stupid fucking brother who couldn't claim you when he should have because he was too concerned about his job. I thought you were over him. He's the same one you're still saving your heart for?"

What could I say? If I denied any of that, I'd be a liar and I wouldn't stoop to Max's level.

Evan growled and released his hold on me. "I've been fighting an uphill battle all this time against my own fucking brother," he mumbled.

"You never saw me like that," I reminded him.

"There was a time, when we worked on that first book that I did, Posie. I just wasn't willing to climb the mountain someone else put between us. When you started dating people, I thought maybe you were finally ready to move on from whatever fantasy you'd built around my brother. He was never planning on coming back home. Not for me, our family, and definitely not for you."

That callous admission brought about more violent sobbing. "Shit. I'm sorry, Posie. That wasn't fair to you."

"No, it was..." Pulling myself together was no easy feat. "It was true though. He never even told me he was dating anyone, let alone getting married. Invitations were printed and mailed out, that means this isn't something new. It's been in the works. He wrote me just yesterday and never mentioned..."

I would ignore everything Evan just confessed to. Knowing he someone held a torch for me while I pined away for his brother was just a bit too much. I'd never seen Evan as anything more than just a friend and workmate and I didn't want to lose that.

Whether Evan realized it or not, if he truly had strong romantic feelings for me, he never would have been able to stand back and watch me date someone else without imploding our lives. The Carter boys were a bit too passionate when it mattered for him to have been able to sit back and watch me love his brother from a distance and then date someone else.

"Posie, why Max?"

I shrugged my shoulders, feeling like that girl who was huddled into the corner of this very barn watching the boy she had a crush on as he made out with someone else. "I've had a crush on Max since before he knew who I was," I admitted to my best friend even though he obviously already knew. "I was crushing on him and the first time he ever even noticed me was when I was sitting right over there," I pointed to the corner of the loft where I'd been hiding and while sketching my day away.

I shook off the memory because it was entirely too painful for far too many reasons. "You would think that seeing him with someone else like that might have killed my crush, but it didn't. I just kept thinking that one day... One day, he would see me. Really see me. Then, I'd be the girl he was kissing." Evan's eyes were full of pity for me. That made everything I was feeling so much worse.

"I tried, Ev. I dated. Kissed other boys. I'm not exactly a virgin anymore, you know? I tried to forget about him, but then there were our letters. The things he said in them felt so sincere, like we were building this relationship with our words. I shared my life with him and thought he was doing the same. Sure, sometimes, that meant that we were sharing things like our experiences with other people, but it always came back to just the two of us."

I turned to stare out that stupid window again. It was the one I always checked. It was like I had been waiting for the day when I'd see him out there, knowing he would come for me when it finally dawned on him that I was the person he'd been waiting for too. That had just been a little girl's dream that carried over to an adult woman's fantasies. It was never bound to happen. If nothing else could have stripped me of that dream, that fantasy... Seeing that wedding invitation did. Not only did he never tell me about dating someone seriously, but I wasn't invited to his wedding either.

"I know we were supposed to get some work done today, but I'd appreciate it if you just left for the day."

"Posie." Evan's voice was quiet and reverent as he spoke my name and placed his hands on my upper arms. He pulled on me gently, so that my back connected with his chest. Then he wrapped his arms around me and hugged me fiercely. "I'm sorry my brother is a blind fool. It's not you. Before I found Jennifer, I would have stepped up to the challenge of making you forget Max even exists."

"Thanks."

"Do me and yourself a favor."

"What's that?"

"Maybe you need to put away childish things now. That includes your childhood crush. Stop writing to him. Stop reading any letters he sends. Let him go. Not for him and his relationship, but for you. I thought, when you started dated, that you'd already done that, but you obviously never really moved on from the idea that you two might have ended up together. It wasn't right of him to keep you dangling on the end of his line while he was busy living his best life and falling in love with someone else. You should never be someone else's second choice or backup plan, Posie. You're too amazing to be that for anyone."

Evan leaned down and placed a sweet kiss on the top of my head before hugging me one more time. Then, he let go and gave me the space I needed to mourn the loss of his brother and the future I'd been dreaming of having with him.

Once I had the place to myself again, I sat down on the over-stuffed couch with my sketchpad and started drawing. The image that came to mind was from that day so many years ago when a 16-year-old girl wondered what it would be like to feel his lips on hers like they were on the girl he'd chosen.

I closed my eyes and remembered the way my stomach had pulled tight, how my chest made it hard to breathe. Her candy-sweet perfume and his citrus and spice cologne had mixed, mingled, and wafted to me in the corner where I'd hidden myself away long before they decided to use my refuge as their make out spot.

My pencil flew across the paper as the memories assailed me. Her profile came into being, lips pursed, eyes glued adoringly to his face, and his fingers tangled in that silky, flaxen hair. Then his face started taking shape. Swollen lips as he smiled down at her face with that cocky little smirk of his tipping up just the one edge of those lips that I'd always wanted to brush my own against.

I could close my eyes and be transported back to that moment. The first time I ever felt a crack through my heart that wasn't from the death of someone I loved. I was too young then to understand it was a death of sorts. It was the death of a potential future, of my dream. I should have left it there in the shadows of that old barn instead of allowing myself to carry that same flame for him all these years later.

My phone dinged and I glanced down before thinking better of it to see a notification that I had an email from Max. Evan was right. I needed to cut him from my life before he ruined me completely. It was obvious that we weren't meant to be anything more than two strangers who wrote letters to one another out of boredom. It was time to end that.

I deleted the notification. I'd delete the unread email later when I had the strength to do it. Until then, it could sit there. After setting my phone back down beside me, I turned my attention back to the sketch in my hands. His eyes were the last thing I drew, only instead of having him look down at her, I shifted them to look back toward the corner where I'd been hiding that day. The juxtaposition of him looking back at little mousy me while loving up bold beautiful Cheyenne made it seem as if he was taunting me with that look.

It felt a lot like the blow I'd received today. I put the sketchpad on my drawing desk and took the stairs up to my bedroom in the loft. I would allow myself one day to wallow in self-pity, cry, and sleep the hurt away. Then, I had to carry on as if I'd never even known Max Carter.

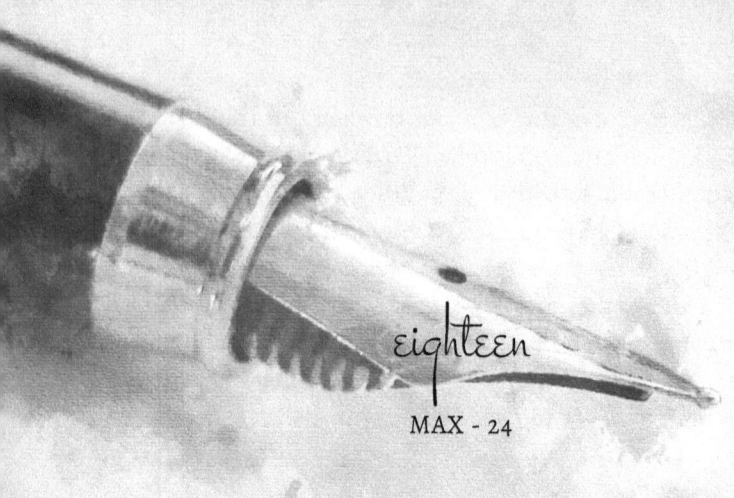

eighteen

MAX - 24

I stared at the text again. My little brother was angrier than I'd ever heard him. It was a good thing he sent that message in a text instead of yelling everything at me, especially since Beth was busy moving her things into my place.

One stupid fucking mistake in a fit of jealousy had ruined my life.

> Evan: I can't believe you never told Posie you were seeing someone, that you proposed, or that you were getting married. She's so fucking heartbroken. I wasn't going to say anything to you, but then I went back to check on her and saw what she drew. It seems like you just can't help yourself. You've been hurting this girl for years with your bullshit. Leave her alone, Max. She's had enough heartache to last a fucking lifetime, she doesn't need more of it from you.

He snapped a picture of the sketch Posie had done, so that I could see it. I recognized the event, even if she'd changed things a little. It was me and Cheyenne in the barn the first day I ever realized who she was. The sketch showed me glanced over at a ghostly, barely-there trace of the shape of a girl huddled in the corner. In reality, I had never looked at Posie like that while I was holding onto my old high school girlfriend. I'd only seen her just before we left after Pops caught us in there. It felt like she purposely shifted where my eyes were looking for the sketch though, as if I was taunting her with my relationship somehow.

I wish I could tell her that the thing with Beth and me wasn't what she thought. We'd never dated. Fuck, Beth had only ever been a one-time hookup on a night when I wanted nothing more than to get in my truck and drive home to be with Posie.

Beth had her sights on me for a while. She took full advantage when I was at a low moment. I never wanted to go there because she was my Lieutenant's daughter. I wasn't dumb enough to mix business and pleasure, especially considering men before me had done just that and found themselves walking a beat patrol again after breaking her spoiled little heart.

So, when she came to my house nearly two months later, with a pregnancy test in hand, I was crushed. There was no doubting the condom had broken, but she said she took a morning after pill to keep from getting pregnant. It was obvious that had been a lie. There was no way fate fucked me over hard enough to account for a broken condom and failed morning after pill.

My hands were tied. I could kiss my career goodbye or marry the girl.

"What are you looking at?"

"Nothing," I told her as I closed my phone down.

"I won't tolerate you cheating on me," she said.

I turned slowly until Beth stood in front of me and then leaned back. "Let me explain something to you, Beth. You manufactured this bullshit based on a romp that took place when I was so fucking drunk I barely remember seeing you that night, let alone falling into bed with you. You might have me by the balls only because my career is in harm's way, but don't fool yourself into thinking we're creating a love match here. We're not.

"I will never love you because I have zero respect for you and the bullshit you pulled. What you did that night could get your ass locked up. My parents are aware of what went down, even if the rest of my family is still in the dark."

The wind blew out of her sails completely as I spoke my truth. "You caused me to irrevocably hurt the one person on this earth that should never feel another ounce of pain. If you think, for a single minute, that you are ever going to be anything more than the mother of my child, you are deluding yourself."

Her crocodile tears didn't bother me in the least. "Why are we even doing this, if that's how you feel?"

"Because I wasn't about to become Joe Warden, Travis Blackmore, or whoever the hell else had their career tanked because they were unfortunate enough to stick their dick in you. I worked hard for my position. You're not going to take it from me."

What she didn't know was that I had feelers out for a detective position in other cities. Once I had a bite, I'd jump there, divorce her ass, and only have to see her when we had to swap the kid on custody change-over days.

"If I had known you were going to be such an insufferable prick, I'd never have slept with you."

I laughed at that. "Really? It wasn't obvious that I was an insufferable prick every time I turned you down when I was stone-cold sober? You can lie to everyone else, but not me and not yourself. There's only one reason my dick was ever even remotely close to you, Beth. That's because I was drunk off my face over another woman. That woman owns my heart and always will. You – I don't even remember being acquainted with your body and won't ever know the way that feels either because you had your one shot with me."

"We're going to be married," she insisted.

"That doesn't mean I have to fuck you. This marriage is against my will." It was also being investigated because I'd talked to the DA, who I'd become friends with since my time at the department. He didn't like the position I'd been put in any more than I did. There was no reason to let Beth in on the fact that we were trying to get the Lieutenant booted from the department for his improprieties and abuses of his position for his daughter's sake. They were both corrupt beyond belief. I hoped that everything would be wrapped up before the farce of a wedding had to take place.

It was the one reason why I hadn't sent an invitation to all of my family. It was only supposed to go to my parents. How in the hell Evan got a hold of it and managed to show it to Posie before I could tell her what was going on was beyond me. After reading my brother's message to me and looking at the sketch repeatedly since he'd sent it, I wished things could be different for the hundredth time.

I hadn't told her as much, but I'd fallen for Posie over the course of our years-long correspondence. I understood why Pops tried to push me to get to know her when we were younger. He was right. There's something special between us and now she feels as though I betrayed her and wasn't sharing anything going on in my life with her. How else would she react to a sudden wedding announcement? It would most likely seem as though I'd hidden an entire relationship from her.

I could feel the bile rise in my throat. Hopefully, when all was said and done, Posie would understand what happened and allow me to be a part of her life. I tried to reach out with an email, to let her know what happened, but she hadn't replied yet. Even if she could forgive me for the forced, hopefully never-to-happen wedding, I wasn't so sure she'd willingly sign up to help me raise a kid I had with a duplicitous woman who ruined men's careers and lives for kicks. What kind of target would that put on Posie's back?

And how large would that target get after I help the DA take down Beth's father?

It still made me sick to think that I could have knocked that woman up. There was no question she was pregnant, but we had to wait on DNA to confirm if it really was my baby she was carrying.

My mind wandered to the day Posie wrote to tell me that she'd met someone, then when she wrote about kissing him and what that had been like for her. As if she couldn't help herself, she then told me about losing her virginity to the undeserving bastard. Reading all about it in an email made me feel sick to my stomach.

It was the first time I realized that just how badly I'd fucked up by not chasing Posie down that time she came to visit me. Instead, I'd listened to my brother and let him talk me into letting her go explore dating other people. Logically, I understood that she deserved to live that part of life I had already enjoyed over the years. I didn't want her to have regrets when I finally came for her. Then again, I was at war with myself because I also wanted all her firsts.

That was why I dove headfirst into the bottom of a bottle after I read that some other man had taken all of her firsts. First boyfriend, kiss, and her virginity. Then, the motherfucker left her like it was all some sort of joke to him.

Part of me wanted to go kill him for putting his hands on her when he wasn't willing to cherish the woman the way she deserved. The other part wanted vindication for the betrayal she felt. Then, there was the dark part of my soul that grinned at the fact that the asshole had taken himself out of the running just when I was worried that I'd lost something I hadn't realized I should have been protecting.

Unfortunately, I'd already had my drunken night of trying to forget the words I'd read. I'd woken up in bed with Beth and feeling like shit for going there. I thought that would be the end of my encounter with the bitch, and we'd never speak about our drunken one-night stand, especially since I couldn't even remember most of it.

There were twisted, fractured memories that came back to me now and then. Enough to know that we'd really had sex and that I'd been smart enough in my drunken stupor to wear a condom. Then again, I was in this predicament because that condom hadn't saved me.

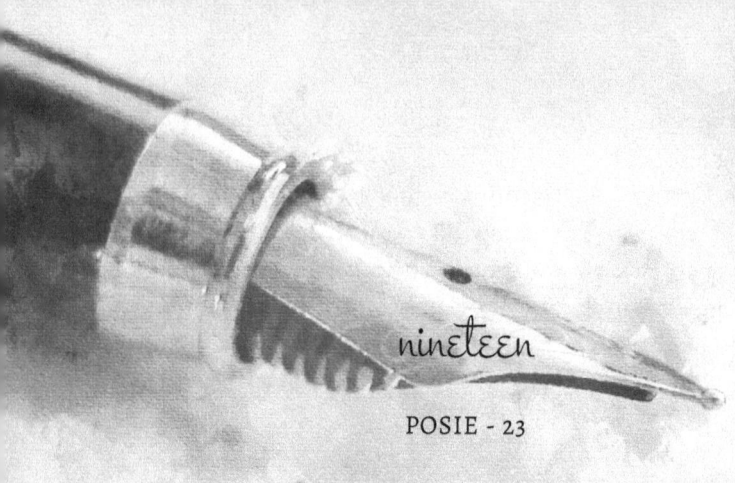

nineteen

POSIE - 23

"Max asked me to get this to you. I can't make you read it, but before you throw it out, I'm going to ask a favor of you."

"You've never asked me for anything," I told Jack.

"I know it, Petal. Wouldn't ask this of you either if I didn't think it was important." I nodded my head for him to go on. He smacked the letter against his hand before holding it out for me to take. Against my better judgement, I took the thing.

"Need you to read it, sweetheart. Things aren't what they seem, and Max wasn't able to explain them sooner, but he wanted you to know just the same."

It did nothing to make me feel better. Jack seemed so far away, lost almost. His eyes held so much sorrow that it added to the misery I felt deep inside. My eyes drifted from him to the folded-up papers I held in my hand. It took a few minutes, after Jack left me alone, to get my hands to stop shaking so that I could open the damn thing. My chest tightened at the sight of *his* handwriting. It had been so long since we'd exchanged physical letters that it was a bittersweet moment to get another one from him just when it felt like I'd finally lost him for good.

My sweet, sweet Posie,

People are always lecturing about taking things for granted and how life doesn't offer guarantees. I guess I learned that lesson the hard way, and unfortunately, I think it was at your expense too.

I didn't realize how deeply embedded in my heart you were until you told me about that jackass who stole all your firsts and didn't appreciate them.

I was determined, after reading about the asshole, that I'd never allow you to slip through my fingers again. Unfortunately, I came to that epiphany after a drunken night of feeling sorry for myself, thinking how I could have lost any chance with you.

I did something stupid.

So, fucking stupid.

Being drunk should never be an excuse, but I honestly still don't even have a full recollection of how I ended up with Beth that night.

My heart thudded heavily in my chest as I pushed the pages of his letter down into my lap. If I continued to read this letter, after the mention of her, I'd come away with a bigger fracture to my heart. There was no question about that. Hell, I already had a broken heart, but there was no denying hearing what he had to say about meeting up with his soon-to-be wife was going to crush my soul. I didn't know if I was ready for that.

I peered out my window to see Jack sitting on the porch, his hand resting on the empty rocking chair beside him. His lips were moving, which meant he was talking to his wife out there. It was something he rarely did these days. Usually, if he was talking to her, it was because the old man was having a hard damn day. I could relate. Seeing Jack talk to his lost love, as if she was still sitting there beside him, made me pull the letter back out of my lap and straighten the pages.

If Jack had the courage to keep breathing on this earth when the love his life no longer did, then I could finish reading Max's letter to me. It was that simple and that hard. My eyes scanned the first page until I found where I'd left off.

I'd gone out to drown my sorrows and ended up waking in her bed. I'm not telling you this to hurt you. Fuck, I wish I never had to tell you this part, but it led to everything else that snowballed afterward.

I was determined to come home. To come there for you. I swear to you, Posie, all I wanted then was to make you fall as in love with me as I've fallen for you. Plans were in place, and I didn't want to tell you about it until I was sure that everything would work out with the job situation and the timeframe for when I'd be back there.

Two months later, when I was still waiting to hear back from the police department there, I was called into my boss's office.

Beth is his daughter.

She wanted to tell her father and me the news at the same time. She was pregnant and claimed that I was the father.

"You have to understand, Posie. Beth had already tanked a couple other police officer's careers before the one night we spent together. Immediately, her father told me I was going to do the right thing or find myself on the losing end of a career going nowhere.

I'm not one to scare easily. I went to the District Attorney, who happens to be a friend of mine. We worked out a way to use my situation to bust my lieutenant for abuse of power. The whole wedding thing was supposed to be a farce. Honestly, I thought I'd been careful and that the baby wasn't even mine. I told her I wouldn't marry her until a test was done to confirm.

I never thought it would come to that. I truly thought there was no way.

Fuck, Posie. Fuck!

It's my baby.

I can't believe I had to write that. That you will eventually read those words. Over the past couple years, when I've pictured having a family, for some reason, it's always you and the farm, and that stupid fucking barn. That's the picture I still had in my head when the test results came back.

I can't leave now.

I can't come home because she won't go. I can't leave my kid behind with someone like her as their mother. Being a conniving bitch isn't enough to prove she wouldn't be a good mom to the courts, so I have to wait.

I'm not marrying her, Posie. There's one first of mine that I want to save for the only woman who deserves it, but I'll understand if she's not there when I'm finally ready. If she needs to move on, then it will kill me, but I'll understand.

This was my fault.

My doing.

My stupidest fucking mistake.

I'm having a kid with the wrong fucking woman, and it feels like I'm drowning, but I can't let my kid ever feel that. You know? No matter who their mother is, they're only ever going to feel loved and wanted by me. I'm so sorry that I screwed it all up. I'm so damn sorry. One day, maybe you can forgive me. You were supposed to be my forever, and I threw it away just like that idiot you dated. If you can't forgive me, then I'll understand that, too.

Yours Always,
Max

I crumpled the pages to my chest and doubled over with the ache of what his letter revealed. The man I'd been in love with since we were teenagers would never be able to come back home for me.

He was having a baby with another woman.

The first tear fell as the shock wore off and the realization settled in.

A baby.

A baby with another woman.

My heart ached worse than when Evan showed me that wedding invitation. Marriages came and went sometimes. That was hard to take but wasn't the end of the world. A baby – that was forever. That meant whatever I'd hoped for us – it was really over. There would never be anything between Max and me. He would always be stuck there with them, even if he didn't marry her. The decisions she made would always keep him chained closer to her.

The worst part was that I understood. Hadn't my father been sucked into a similar situation, after all? What would my life have been like if he hadn't taken such good care of me until he couldn't anymore? I don't think I'd still be alive.

I sat up, carefully folded the letter, and pulled the box out from under my bed that I'd used to keep all of our other correspondences in. I even printed out the emails, so that they could be kept in the box too. I laughed at my reasoning as I laid the letter inside and closed the lid. I'd been keeping them, so that one day I could show our daughters or sons how our love story started. I wanted them to know that they should never settle for less than the person who could pour their heart out to them and listen as they did the same.

What a joke.

We were never going to have those children together now because he was having one with another woman. That meant he'd never come back home, and I couldn't go there and put myself in the middle of things. If he had a chance to work things out with his child's mother, then he needed to do that. I couldn't put myself in the way and potentially keep that child from growing up with both parents around to love them together.

My parents' secrets had come to light for me over the years and I knew the sacrifice my father made for me. My father lost his son because he married the wrong woman. He chose the wrong mother for his children. He lost the love of his life when my mom came back into the picture and made life miserable for him until I came along. I was the trick that he had to pay for. I never knew, never would have known by the way my father treated me.

In that, I respected Max's decision immensely. He was repeating the mistakes of my father's past. The mistakes that kept him tied to a woman he loathed, all to make sure that his daughter didn't suffer the same fate as his son.

My father was my hero for everything he sacrificed for me, but especially for never allowing me to see what a sacrifice it was. Max would be that hero for his own child one day.

At some point, Evan found his way to me. Jack probably sent for him because his grandson was my best friend. I wished, for just a fraction of a moment, that Evan had been the one I'd crushed on all those years ago. He would have been here and wouldn't have taken forever to see me the way his brother had. Our relationship would have gone somewhere from the beginning or ended swiftly. There never would have been this long, dragged-out affair by mail that led to my heart being completely crushed in the end.

"I wonder if this is my karma."

"What karma?"

"I stole away the love of my father's life. That means I stole my father from the woman who loved him, too. They both lost that love because of me. So, this is my karma, right? The world is setting my wrongness right. I'm that woman now. Everything has come full-circle and now I truly know what it must have been like for them when my mom came around and ruined everything, because I'm living it."

"Jesus fucking Christ, Posie." Evan sat down beside me and pulled me into the tight embrace of his arms. "I'm so sorry, sweetheart. You've never done anything to earn the shit you're going through. Your mom is the one who should have paid for what she put your dad through. You're the innocent one in the scenario. I don't believe for one second that the universe is somehow punishing you for her sins."

"It feels like it, though." There was no holding back the tears at that point or way the pain rattled my body with each violent sob.

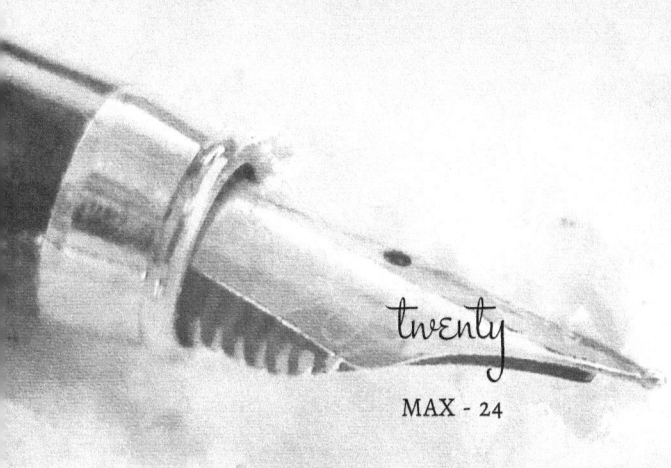

twenty

MAX - 24

My Sweet Posie,

It's a boy. I forgot those results came in too. When she had all that testing done, and they did the DNA stuff, the results came back for the gender. I guess I was too caught up in the results proving I was a going to be a father to really think about the rest of it.

Beth has been planning.

She still wants to get married.

I can't do it.

She threatened to keep the baby from me if I don't marry her. Unfortunately for her, my best friend is a lawyer, so that won't work out too well for her. Her father was thrown off the force. He was offered a chance to take his retirement, but his ego kept him from accepting that generous offer. He's lost everything now because other men came forward to say his daughter ruined them, too. I think they're lucky now. It was only their careers she ruined. I'm the one stuck having a kid with her. She ruined my life and I'm so fucking angry.

Travis, my friend who is the DA here, says that we can use everything from her father's trial to establish her pattern of destructive behavior. I'm not sure what that will do with the family courts when the time comes, but we're hopeful that it will mean that majority of custody will go to me, at the very least.

She doesn't know about my plans, obviously. She still thinks she can threaten me and convince me that marriage is our only option.

I'm still hopeful, Posie.

Maybe, one day soon, I can come home.

Always Yours,

Max

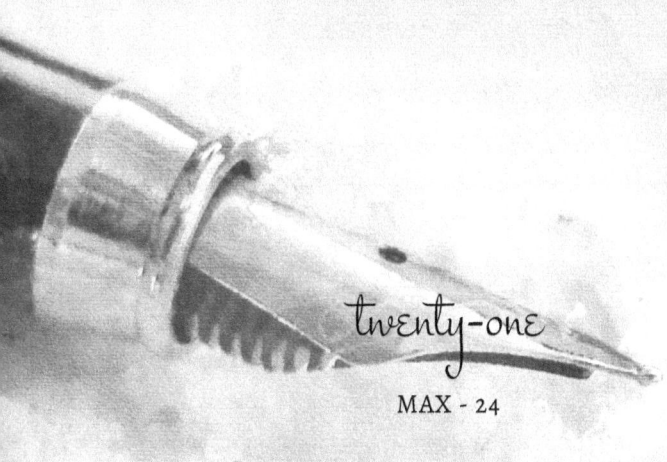

twenty-one

MAX - 24

My Sweet Posie,

I know you probably hate me, but I miss hearing from you. I wish you'd write to me again. Even as I sit here knowing it isn't fair to ask it of you.

I told you before that there were things I realized, too late, that I took for granted. Your letters, having that small piece of you to look forward to, was one of those things. It wasn't until you stopped writing that I realized just how much of a presence you were in my life. Every day, I would wait to check my mail, and then my email, until I could settle in at home to read whatever you'd written.

Those letters were my selfish time. The time where I got to spend a few minutes basking in the light that is you. I miss them, Posie. I miss you. I miss your light. It's fucking dark here right now and all I can think is that I will always be missing your light from my life because I screwed everything up. It's not fair to ask it of you, but I wish I could hear from you again. I wish my heartache hadn't caused this rift in what we used to share.

I'm not trying to guilt you. I'm sure I'd be just as quiet as you if you had been the one to tell me that you were having someone else's baby. Look what I did when you told me about giving your firsts away to some other man. I annihilated our chances of ever having anything more than these letters.

I still can't believe it's real. I can't believe I'm only weeks away from being a father now. I'm scared to death to meet him. Worried I'll fail my son. If you want my honesty, though... The worst thing out of all this is your silence. It feels like you died. I know you haven't because the family still mentions you, but to me, it feels like you died and I'm Pops sitting in a rocking chair talking to the love of my life who is no longer here.

Yours Always,

Max

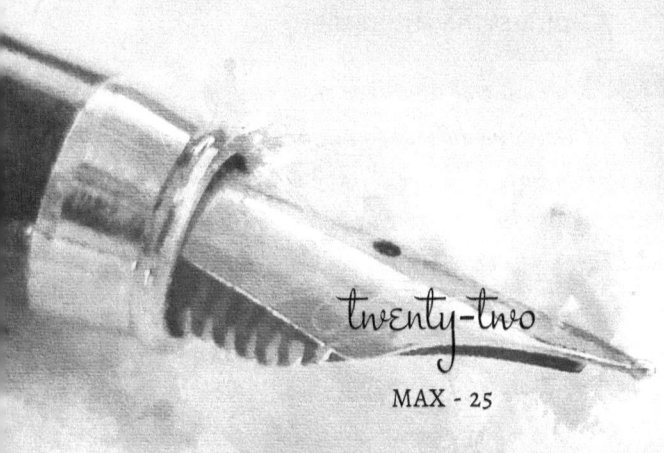

twenty-two

MAX - 25

My Sweet Posie,

Yesterday was my birthday. I almost forgot it because Beth went into labor.

My son is here.

He wasn't born on my birthday. The little guy came kicking and screaming his way into the world two hours too late for that, but he's here now.

I'm so excited that I finally got to meet him, but it feels like this cloud is sitting over my head because I couldn't share it with you — not in the way I wanted. There's only these letters that you never answer anymore. I don't even know if you read them. Maybe I should stop sending them. Maybe it isn't fair of me to keep trying. I messed everything up and took away your hope. I know that. Evan has told me as much.

Still, I feel like these letters are the last bit of hope I have that one day it will all work out. That you'll forgive me for a moment of weakness that took our future away. It would be different now, but there's still a chance we could have a future. That's what keeps me going. That's what keeps me writing to you because I don't know how to give you up even though it feels like you're already gone.

I can't believe I have a son. I wish you could be here to meet him. Even though I know how selfish that sounds. There's no doubt in my mind you'd fall just as in love with him as I did, despite the circumstances of how he got here. That's because you have that huge, beautiful heart of gold. I miss it. I miss you.

Yours Always,

Max

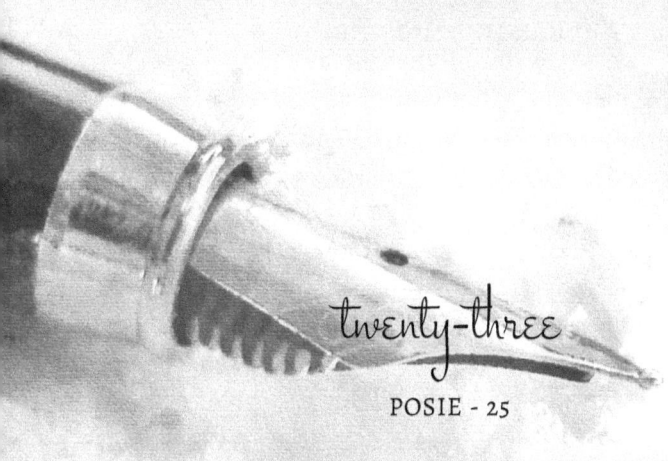

twenty-three

POSIE - 25

I t was my birthday. For some reason turning twenty-five made me feel sick to my stomach. Maybe it was because the last letter I received from Max was just after his twenty-fifth birthday, and that had been nine months ago.

"Come on, Posie, drink up!" Evan's girlfriend was getting on my last nerve. She'd been pushing me to date every man she came across. The crazy woman set up blind date after blind date for me, even when I continued to turn them down or simply not show up. I wasn't ready for that, and she refused to take 'No' for an answer.

"I've had enough," I told her.

"No, you can never have enough of your birthday!" Jennifer's gleeful voice grated on my last freaking nerve. I stood, about to leave when she grabbed my arm forcefully and dug her nails in.

"You can't go yet." Her instance made me glance around the bar. I could smell a setup a mile away now that she'd attempted this trick far too many times. Evan said he'd have a talk with her, and make her chill out, but Evan didn't understand what I did. I'd lost the Carter brother that held my heart. I worked very closely, nearly every day, with Evan. She was worried that I'd transfer my affections to him and that he'd jump at the chance.

She worried for nothing, but I was absolutely fed up with her antics. She should have been worried about pissing me off. I reached down and wrenched her wrist back and threw her hands off me.

"Whoa! Calm down, Posie, she was just trying to do you a solid."

I pulled the sleeve of my shirt up and showed my best friend the indents from her fingertips and the red marks from her fingers. "No, she wasn't. She's being pushy and doing something I asked her not to do ever again. I'm not fucking ready to date anyone right now and I'm getting sick to fucking death of your pushy-ass girlfriend trying to force these meet cutes on me. And I'm really not going to tolerate someone putting their hands on me and marking my skin. I had enough of that when my mother was alive."

"What the fuck, Jen?"

"I'm sorry, I didn't realize," she tried to say.

"Oh, you did. You realized. You know exactly what you're doing. Remember? I've been the one on the receiving end of the conversations you've had with me that you don't want Evan to know about. I'm fucking sick of it. I don't like him that way. I'm not a threat to your relationship. The only threat there is the crazy, possessive way you've been acting. Evan is a brother to me. I didn't feel that way about Max or Michael because they weren't around. Devon and Evan became my brothers years ago and it would be gross to even think of having an inappropriate relationship with either of them. So, stop your bullshit or I will get a damn restraining order against you. I mean it. I don't even want to see your face anytime soon. Thanks for ruining my birthday, but I'm done now."

"Ev, get your bitch in check because this is not okay," I turned to see Michael – who had spoken – and Devon standing there. Devon's wife scowled down at Jen too.

"No, it's not," Lisa reaffirmed before swatting her husband. "Don't call women bitches, even if they're behaving like one."

"Are you going to let them speak to me that way?" Jen had the nerve to ask Evan. He stared at her as if it was the first time he was seeing the woman for who she truly was. I hated that I was at the heart of the issue, but then again, if it wasn't me she might have pulled this crazy shit on someone else. Better that I was the target because I already had experience with how to handle people like her. *Thanks, Mom.*

"Look at her arm," he demanded. "You just did that to my best friend – a woman I consider to be my sister – my business partner. She's the person responsible for paying half my bills. Without her art, my stories wouldn't sell. Apparently, this isn't even the first time you've made her uncomfortable." Evan's eyes moved to meet mine.

"I'm sorry. You've said something before about her pushing you to date and trying to trick you, but I thought it was a joke. I didn't think it was bothering you this much or I would have put a stop to it."

He seemed to think for a minute and then frustration flared in his eyes. "Actually, I'm angry that you didn't make it a point to tell me exactly what has been going on and for how long."

"I didn't want to be a problem between the two of you, but she has made it impossible. I tried, Evan. I really tried to ignore it and brush it all off, but this can't go on. She's driving me insane."

"I know. I'm sorry." He stood and held his hand out for Jen.

"What?" She asked.

"We're leaving," he told her and waited impatiently for his girl to take his hand.

"I'm sorry, Ev."

"I'm not the one you should be apologizing to."

Jen turned to me then, and I could see it in her eyes. The fear of losing him, the anger that I'd called her out on her own bullshit, and even the regret that she pulled any of it to begin with.

"I was never a threat to your relationship until you made me one by behaving the way you did." I shook my head at her. "Even now, I'd never demand he break things off with you. I hope you can work it out because outside of whatever problem you have with me, you make my brother happy, and I don't want him to lose that."

Jen started crying as Evan led her away.

"You're too nice," Lisa told me as she took Jen's seat and pushed her drink away.

"Who is too nice?" A familiar voice asked. Chills ran up my spine before I turned to see the man I'd been pining for since I was a teenager. He was there. In the flesh, for the first time since I was 16 years old.

"Hey," he said to me. The grin on his face was something else. "Hope you don't mind that we're crashing your party. Jen called and said that she set up a party for you and that your..."

I don't know what he was about to say because a tap on my shoulder had me turning to see a man standing there who looked somewhat familiar, but I couldn't place him.

"Sorry, Jen was supposed to be here to introduce us. I'm Mark," When I appeared as clueless as I obviously was he added, "Wellington. We were supposed to have a date tonight."

It was then that I lost my damn mind and started laughing at the whole messed up birthday. *Thank you, Jen. What a bitch.* In my head, I took back everything I said about not wanting Evan to dump her ass. She deserved every bad thing that was coming to her.

"What's so funny?" A woman asked. I turned to see that a tall brunette was clutching onto Max as if he might run away at any moment. She wore a shiny diamond ring on an all too important finger. The taste of bile was sharp on my tongue, as I fought the urge to puke up everything I'd managed to get down at dinner, including the couple of cocktails I drank before Jen started to get pushy.

The tips of Max's ears turned red. "Jen said your boyfriend was going to be here with you when she invited me."

"Us, when she invited us," the woman at his side corrected.

"I don't have a boyfriend. I don't know that guy." My gaze slid pointedly toward the woman. "Don't know you either. I'm not sure why Jen invited a bunch of strangers to my birthday, why she lied to everyone, or why she hurt me earlier to keep me from leaving. I don't know anything anymore except that I'm going home because this is the worst birthday I've ever had, and if you knew half the things I never told anyone about my mom, you'd know that's a tall order. Y'all have a good night without me."

I turned to leave, but Max reached out and caught hold of my arm. "What do you mean she hurt you?"

"Look at her wrist, man," Devon told him. "If Evan doesn't drop that bitch after this shit, then I'm going to kick his ass. We've been telling him for months to rein her ass in because Posie was sick of her shit."

"Aw, isn't that sweet. All the Carter boys and their brotherly concern for you," the brunette taunted me. I knew who she was. It was a shock to see her so cozy with Max, but then again, I supposed it wasn't. They'd had months of being together with a new baby to solidify their relationship.

"Someone want to explain to me what is going on?" Max asked again. Obviously, he was left in the dark about Evan's girlfriend and her antics.

I pulled my arm free and walked away. It wasn't until I got out of the bar that I remembered Evan and Jen had been my ride there.

"Fuck!" I hissed under my breath.

A deep chuckle made me look back. I rolled my eyes at the man who was meant to me the blind date I didn't even know about.

"Listen, I'm sorry that you weren't aware why I was invited tonight. Trust me, Jen and my sister will get an earful from me because I'm not cool with a surprise setup either. I was told you agreed to this when I asked if either of them knew if you were single."

I sighed. "I realize it's not your fault, but you are number twenty-four in a long line of surprise setups over the past year. I reached my breaking point."

"You're better than me. I think my breaking point would have been about five or so."

That made me laugh. "Yeah? Why five?"

"Well, any more than that and I'd have probably said my peace a few too many times already. Any less than that and it might be pawned off as coincidence or attempted do-gooding. Five is the limit before I lose my patience, though."

"I'll keep that in mind. Sounds more logical than breaking at twenty-four."

"I'm guessing Jen and Evan were your ride?"

"You got it in one."

"Do you need a ride home?" He threw his hands up in the air and grinned at me. "I swear, no funny business, just a ride. Seems like you could use one person in your life who doesn't have an agenda tonight."

"You picked up on that, huh?"

"Not sure what was going on with Max back there, but it was obvious the chick he brought did not have good intentions toward you either. After what Jen did, I'm guessing you're done for the night."

I could see Max just inside the door, and Devon and Michael blocking his path to get to me. "Please, get me out of here," I begged.

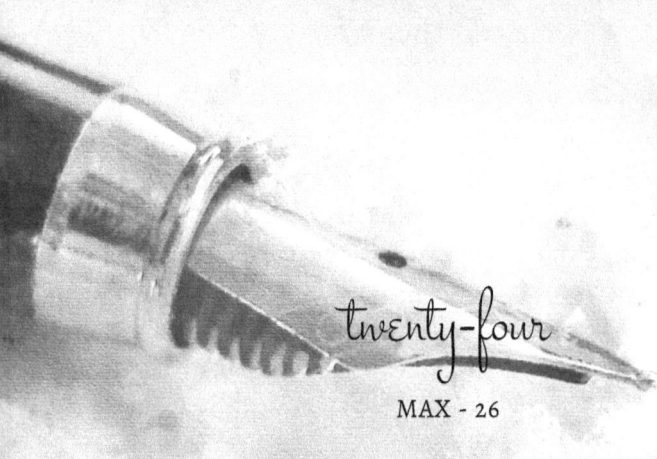

twenty-four

MAX - 26

"You need to get out of my way, so I can make sure she's okay. I don't know what the hell is going on, but something isn't right here."

"Yeah, showing up with your fiancé to Posie's birthday wasn't right, and you know it. She may have had time to deal with things, but that doesn't mean she's handling it well or that it wouldn't fucking hurt her."

"I don't have a fiancé."

"You sure about that? That bitch in there, that was hanging off of you like a fucking accessory, sure did have a nice rock on her finger."

I rolled my eyes. "She bought that herself when that shit went down, and I agreed to marry her while we got evidence against her father. I've never given her a ring."

"Posie doesn't know that."

"Fuck!"

"Why in the hell would you even bring her?"

"I didn't. She followed me here because Jen invited her to come. I got the whole *'She invited me because I'm family, too,'* speech on the way into the bar. She literally met me outside, like she'd been lying in wait the whole time."

"Swear to God, if Evan doesn't kick Jen's ass to the curb, I'm going to find a nice little hole to bury her in. She used to be a cool chick, but ever since you announced the impending birth of your son, she's gone absolute bat-shit crazy about Posie being single and involved in Evan's life."

"Why? There's nothing going on between them, right?"

"Never," Michael was the one to announce that. "They're thick as thieves of the sibling variety."

"So, what's the problem?"

"Everyone knew about Posie's crush on you. I guess she figured since you were no longer an option that maybe Posie would turn her sights to the Carter brother she's closest to. Jen's a fucking idiot," Devon informed me.

I turned my attention from my brothers back to Posie only to find that she was gone. I pushed them aside and ran out but there was no sign of her anywhere.

"She won't read my emails anymore. You guys have to tell her what happened here tonight."

"Dude, your baby momma had her hands all over you in a possessive move that told Posie everything that ring on her finger didn't."

"It was all bullshit," I argued.

"You didn't push her away, Max. Not once did you correct her for touching you like that."

I hung my head. "Jen told me that Posie has been seeing someone and that he'd be here tonight. Fuck. I didn't push Beth away because she was fucking armor."

"Well, looks like you screwed the pooch there." My oldest brother shook his head. "After breaking that girl's heart, the least you could have done was leave the armor behind and manned up for her. After all the hurt she's suffered because of you, the least you could have done, even if she had a boyfriend here, was suck it up and take it the way she had to."

I hung my head as my shoulders drooped. He was right. My chest felt tight as my other brother dropped the other bomb on me.

"Looks like that guy, Wellington, took her home. She said she made it back safe and sound," Michael announced.

"Does she even know him?"

"He was an easy escape route. She checked in." Michael shrugged. "If something comes of it, then I'll thank the man for looking out for her. This was a shitty birthday for a girl who deserves so much more."

"Evan better make this shit right," Devon stated before heading back into the bar where he left his wife.

"Sorry you got pulled into the Jen drama," Michael offered as he clapped a hand down on my shoulder. "Wish things were different, man. I really do." He shook his head and seemed equal parts angry and resigned. "First time you actually make it home in forever and this is what it amounts to. I could kill Jen. Might just do it later."

"I'll bring the shovel," I murmured. I wasn't sure he heard since he just kept walking and the door shut behind him.

"Hey! There you are!" Beth called to me when I finally made it back inside with my brothers.

"Stop," I ordered. "I don't know why you're here, and from now on, if someone gives you an invitation to a family event, you will decline it because this isn't your fucking family. We might have a kid together, but you are nothing to me beyond being his mom. Pull some shit like that again, and I'll see what I can do to keep you from him altogether."

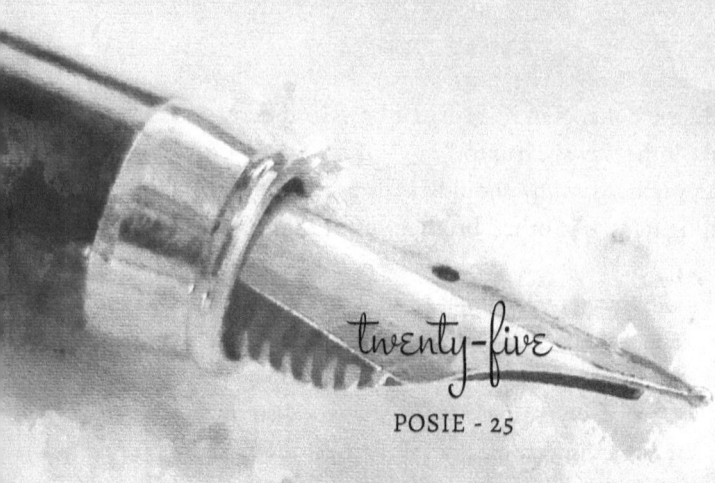

twenty-five

POSIE - 25

"Thanks again for seeing me home," I said. The man was gorgeous, I'd have to give Jen that much. She hadn't been trying to set me up with the bottom of the barrel dates. Nope. She'd gone for the top shelf potentials, I guessed, because she thought they had to be equal caliber to her boyfriend.

Mark was tall, though I didn't think he quite reached six feet. Still, pretty much anything over five, five was tall to me. He had a broad chest, sturdy shoulders, and toned arms that did more than hint at the fact that he liked to stay fit. His dark eyes were that type that made you feel warm, especially when he smiled, and they crinkled just the slightest bit around the corners. His smile was bright and wide, with straight teeth that spoke of serious orthodontia.

"I really hope you don't hold tonight, or Jen's involvement, against me. Despite everything else that happened, I was the one that asked about you. Whether Jen had other plans with her setup or not, I wasn't involved in that. I'll understand if you never want to see my face again, though."

I grinned and then hung my head sheepishly. When was the last time a man had truly been interested in me? There was the jerk that stole my virginity and bailed out like it was a prize he needed to win and then nothing else mattered. There was... Well, I wasn't going to mention him because it hadn't worked out, so there was no point.

Truthfully, I was tired of waiting to get my happily ever after with a man who had made his life too complicated to make it a reality. Seeing him looking all chummy with his son's mother, while she wore an engagement ring on her finger was the push I needed to really and truly let him go. I kept telling myself I did that when I stopped reading his letters, but there was still hope that one day, he'd come home and tell me that he couldn't live without me.

That was never going to happen, for so many reasons. "You know what?" I asked Mark. "I think maybe since you rescued me from that awful situation, I owe you a clean slate and a real date."

I could see the tension leave his shoulders as his smile widened. "You just made my night, sweetheart." Before I could even comprehend what he was up to, Mark leaned in and planted a sweet kiss on my cheek, just close enough to the corner of my mouth that I could almost taste the mint of his gum on the air between us.

"Do you think you'd be up to dinner tomorrow night?"

I hedged because I was supposed to have a family birthday tomorrow evening with Jack and his family, since none of the older Carters wanted to come out to the bar to celebrate with us tonight. "I was supposed to have plans, but I don't think they'd mind me canceling considering how badly tonight went."

"If not, we can do it another time," Mark offered.

"No, really. It's my birthday, and about time I started to put myself first anyway."

"Good, then you should know, I plan to put you first all night. If you hate something, it's your job to tell me, so I can make it right. Any foods you aren't fond of?"

"Nah, I will pretty much eat anything, except cake. Let's avoid that, and we're good."

He cocked a brow at me in question. "What does the birthday girl have against cake?"

I laughed. "My mom was a baker," I started to explain.

"Enough said. Too much time around the stuff, I get it."

I smiled and nodded my head as we both stood there staring at one another. It was only slightly awkward before he popped another beautiful smile and then took a quick step back.

"I'm gonna head out," he suggested as he tossed a thumb over his shoulder to indicate the direction he was headed. "If I don't leave now, I'll be tempted to stay and see you through the night. I'd rather have that clean slate we were talking about though, and I don't think that will happen if I'm here trying to make you feel better after the night you just had."

"I think you're right about that. I'll see you tomorrow." He turned and made it all the way to his car before I remembered my manners. "Thanks again for saving me back there."

"It was my pleasure, Posie."

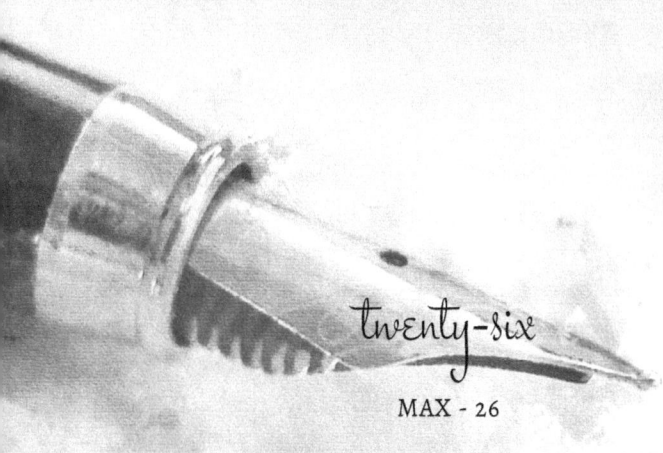

twenty-six

MAX - 26

"I brought pie," I announced. Posie told me once that she despised cake after being forced to make them and taste-test for her mom for years. I thought we could put the candles in the pie instead.

When I looked up, everyone was staring at me. "What?"

Mom had tears in her eyes, Dad looked angry and so did Pops. Evan's ears flamed red, and he wouldn't meet my eyes. "What the hell is going on?"

"Sorry," Pops finally called to me. "You can put the pie away, Max. Posie won't be around tonight after all."

"Why the hell not?" The whole reason I'd come home this weekend was to see her and celebrate her birthday. It was also the reason I hadn't brought my son. I didn't think she should have to meet him and have the baby steal all the attention away from her on her special day. Not that I thought she'd ever complain, but at the same time, I knew it would make her feel uncomfortable, even if she never bothered to show it in front of anyone.

"It's my fault," Evan said as he finally looked up.

"How is it your fault that Posie isn't here?"

He sighed and his shoulders slumped on the exhale. "I didn't

143

take her seriously when she complained about Jen before. Looking back, I know that I should have. Posie is never one to complain about anything, and the fact that she mentioned Jen making her uncomfortable should have raised blaringly loud alarms for me."

"Sometimes, we miss things," our mom offered her baby.

"Well, anyway, she said after last night, she wasn't up to doing the birthday thing anymore and asked that we respect her stance on that."

"Wait, so she's just not going to celebrate her birthday at all?" That wasn't happening on my watch. I'd screwed up far too many things to see her birthday completely ruined.

"Seems you could have brought my grandson around after all," Mom told me.

"I'm going to Posie's place to talk to her," I said.

"She ain't there."

I turned back to see Pops staring at his feet. He wouldn't say anything else though and when I glanced around at the faces of my family, I knew they were holding something back.

"Tell me." It was a demand and one that they wouldn't be able to deny because I was tired of these walls that kept going up to keep me from the woman I'd fallen in love with.

"She's on a date." Evan was the one who relented. "That's my fault too. I kept pushing her to move on because I didn't think you would ever be free and honestly, I thought if you really wanted her, you would have made it happen before now. You never bothered to come see her. Not once, did you ever try to come see her in person, even after you knew she tried to go to you. So, I told her to move on."

"We all told her to move on," My dad interjected, unwilling to leave his youngest out to dry.

"Then I guess Jen finally got a match right. Too late for her, because I dumped her ass last night, but her friend's brother..."

"The guy who took her home last night?" There was a sinking feeling in the pit of my stomach as he nodded his head. Fuck. She couldn't be on a date. Not now. I was so close to being able to come back home, to making things right. If she could handle the fact that I had a kid now...

I slumped down, unable to stand on my own two feet any longer. Last night had been a kick in the dick, and now, I realized Michael was right. I'd fucked it all up again when Jen told me that Posie had a boyfriend attending. I'd walked in with my son's mom on my arm while she wore that ridiculous fucking ring on her finger because she'd been a convenient shield for me. I didn't think about what it would feel like for Posie.

Instead of letting my jealousy fuck with my head, I should have just laid everything out for her like I meant to. Boyfriend, date, or not. I should have told her how I felt and how I was working on getting back home, so I could be with her.

I handed the pie off to one of my brothers. I'd even had the woman at the bakery write Happy Birthday, Posie on the top. "See she gets that," I told whoever grabbed it.

"Son," my dad called out, but I didn't stop. I left his house and made my way to my old truck. Then I drove to Pops' place and tucked my truck up beside the barn, so no one could see it from the road that headed back out of town. I felt a little like a stalker, but there were things I needed to see with my own eyes before I left town. If she was happy, she wouldn't get another letter from me. I'd give up my quest to get back home and try to make things work somewhere else.

One thing my entire family was right about was that I'd missed my window and fucked everything up for that girl. I didn't want to continue to be the undeserving man she put her life on hold for. It would kill me to see her move on with someone else, but no less than me having a baby with another woman hurt her.

IT WAS NEARLY MIDNIGHT WHEN HEADLIGHTS FINALLY lit up the road heading toward Pops' place. When his Dodge Charger pulled up, I wanted to roll my eyes because of course the asshole who was about to steal my girl drove a douchey muscle car. He helped her out of the car and it stung when I watched the way her eyes lit up as he tugged her just hard enough that she flipped right into his arms. It was a flawless gesture that made a huge impact. I knew that because her face transformed into that of an angel sent to Earth to bring all its inhabitants joy.

Yep, I was a dipshit for even thinking like that, but there was no other explanation for the way her happiness shone through. Then, the asshole's lips were on hers as she stood on tiptoes with her arms wrapped around his neck.

The picture my brother sent me of the memory Posie drew of the kiss between Cheyenne and me in the barn came to mind. I wondered if the sinking feeling in my stomach, the stench of defeat, and the immense pain of loss that felt like it might squeeze my heart right out of my chest were all the things she was feeling back then.

Maybe she had felt them to a lesser degree at the time, since I'd only been a crush she had on a stranger. When she drew that image, after finding out that I might be getting married, I imagine she felt a lot like I do now. That meant hearing about my son had to be torture, and somehow I could no longer blame her for not reading the emails I'd been sending.

Posie was going to move on, and I'd been the idiot who pushed her in that direction with my jealous bullshit behavior. What was worse, was that I couldn't just drive away and leave because the minute I started my truck, they would know I'd been sitting here watching them. As luck would have it, a set of headlights hit them as a car came down the road. Pops was back. I glanced at the clock and realized how late he was and wondered what the old coot had been up to.

It didn't matter, because I could have thanked him for showing up when he did. As he pulled into the driveway, Posie and her date broke apart and she said something to him that I couldn't make out. He smiled at her before leaning in and kissing her forehead, then he got into his car and took off.

"Jack?" I heard her call out to Pops as he got out of his car.

"Sorry, didn't mean to interrupt, sweetheart. Earlene decided she needed her beauty rest more than we needed to finish our game." He winked at Posie.

"You should really make an honest woman out of her one day," Posie teased.

"Nah, we have an understanding."

"Isn't that what all the kids are saying these days?"

Pops stared back off toward where douche nozzle's taillights still glowed in the distance. "Is that what you're saying? I had my time with the love of my life, Posie. Don't want anything less for you."

Posie took a few steps over and then threw her shoulders back and held her head high as she approached Pops. "I know what I'm worth," she told him. "You taught me. Now, let's get you inside and ready for bed. I want to see that you're taking *all* of your vitamins. You should have taken them all hours ago."

From the sounds of things, Pops wasn't too fond of some of his vitamins. I'd have to ask Dad about what the hell was going on with him.

"Ain't no damn vitamins, and you know it, girl."

She shrugged as they moved up the steps to his porch. "You're my dad and I don't want to lose you anytime soon. So, you're going to go in there and take your heart medicine, you're going to eat the nasty healthy shit I feed you, and you're going to smile when I pretend the medicine you have to take is vitamins because it makes me feel better."

"Aw, Petal." He cooed to her. "Ain't gonna leave you anytime soon, I promise."

Once they were behind Pops' closed door, I finally started my truck and took off to head back home. I'd seen enough to know that Posie wasn't mine to claim right now. The universe seemed to align against us every single time we got close, and I had to have faith that it meant that we would still get our chance, it just wouldn't be right now.

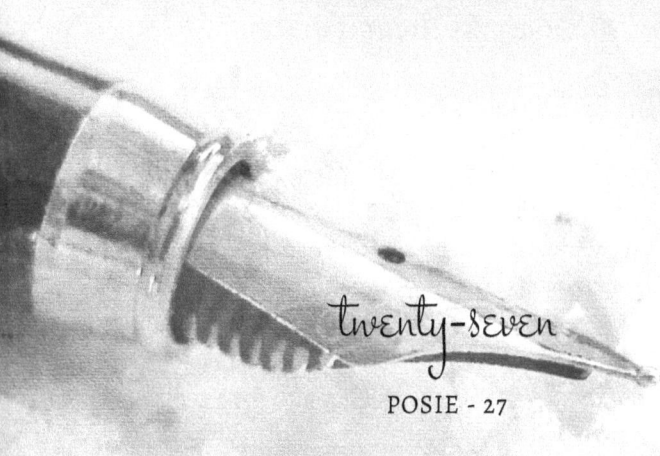

"Do you think he's going to pop the question for your birthday?"

I glared at Evan. How could I tell my best friend that I didn't think Mark was ever going to pop the question at all, let alone tonight, when we were all supposed to meet up for my birthday. I had refused to do anything special for my birthday last year, after the previous year's awful experience. You would think that I'd have been grateful for it, considering I got Mark out of the deal.

For a while, I was. For a while, everything seemed to be perfect between us. Not the kind of perfect where I had rose colored glasses on and thought the man shot rainbows out of his ass or anything. We had our share of disagreements, but we were genuinely happy.

"When are you going to let me in on what's going on?"

"What do you mean?" I asked.

"Something hasn't been right with you in months. You've been carrying around this weight on your shoulders, and it isn't healthy."

I sighed. "I've been spending more time here because Jack isn't doing well."

"Yeah, I know. We all appreciate that. I don't think Pops could have picked a better daughter if he tried." That made me smile.

"I couldn't have picked a better second-chance dad, either." A hot tear sprang free as I thought about him. "I'm worried," I admitted.

"We all are."

"He's too old. They won't even consider him for a transplant, and he won't agree to one anyway."

Evan nodded his head and kept it bowed. I was sure he had a few tears on deck as well. We all did these days when we talked about Jack. His health had been in a steady decline for the past couple of years and we were nearing the end of his fight.

I glanced at the clock on my screen and then back to Evan with another heavy sigh. "I guess I should head home and get ready."

"Thought we were working until four today?"

"Yeah, that was before you made me think of depressing things on my birthday. Now, I'm going home at one and maybe I can get a nap or something before I have to deal with whatever torturous birthday you guys have in store for me this year."

Evan gave me an odd look but shook it off. "Okay, well I guess we'll all see you later then." He turned back and grinned as he packed up his laptop. "I really think tonight is going to be the night for you guys."

If he had said that to me two months ago, I might have thought the same. Unfortunately, I knew that Mark had been distant when he was around and gone far too often of late to be chalked up to the work hours he claimed to be putting in.

I stared longing toward the loft, where I used to live before agreeing to move in with Mark a year ago. The barn was still my office, and I chose to come here every day to get some work done because Pops was still in his house, and I didn't want to be all the way across town, in case he needed me. It was one of the things

Mark and I had been fighting over for the past four months. He thought I spent too much time here.

What really blew everything up was that he made a point to tell me that the Carters weren't even my real family and that I didn't owe them the loyalty I showed. He had apologized, eventually, after I spent a full week not speaking to him. That's when things continued to sour in our relationship. He never meant the apology and I couldn't accept that he didn't understand that the Carters were more family to me than my mother had ever been, and I had no one else. Literally, every single member of my blood relations had died. I was the last.

Once I got all my things packed up and locked away, I grabbed my cross-body bag and left the barn. It now had an amazing security system on it. After word got out about where Evan and I worked, and a crazy fan tried to sneak inside to get a look at the next graphic novel in our series, we no longer had a choice. That had been almost a year ago, and Jack was quick with his shotgun. Thankfully, he scared the jerk away before he could gain access, steal anything, or heaven forbid ruin our work.

Jack had put his life on the line that night to protect mine and Evan's work. It was little things like that – well, major things to me – that made it impossible to understand why Mark didn't think I owed Jacks my complete loyalty.

When I got my bag placed in my car, I turned to see Jack rocking on his porch, his hand on the rocking chair next to his. It was weird, but the sicker he got, I swore I could almost feel his wife there beside him. Like she knew what was coming and was there to welcome him home to her arms.

"Dad?" I yelled to get his attention.

"Petal," He beamed over at me. "I can't believe you're 26 years old already. Been mine for a decade now, though I claimed you a lot earlier than that."

I moved to go to his side but refused to take the chair next to him. Instead, I stood, leaning against the porch rail in front of him with my feet kicked out. Jack was showing his age and then some these days. It hurt to see how frail he had become. His frame was too thin, skin even thinner, and his eyes had taken on a rheumy appearance over the past year. He was still a handsome devil, even in his decline.

"How are you feeling today, Dad?"

"Better now that the birthday girl is here. Do me a favor," he glanced toward his door. "I have a gift for you, but it's in the kitchen on the table. Can you go grab it for an old man. My bones are too tired today."

"Are you sure you don't need me to stay here tonight?"

"No, sweetheart. You need to go celebrate. That lovely daughter-in-law of mine is coming over to watch movies with me later. I won't be alone."

"Okay," I whispered before going in the house to get the little gift bag that was sitting on his table. I brought it back out and took up my position in front of him again. "Should I open it now?"

"Of course, Petal. I need to see your face."

"Okay, Dad." I said it in a teasing tone as I opened the bag to find an envelope inside. My eyes lifted to his and he could see the curiosity there.

"Answer to your question is right there. I'm not gonna ruin the surprise now." He chuckled as I rolled my eyes at him.

I set the gift bag down and opened the envelope. Inside was a land deed. I stared at the paperwork for a solid ten minutes before Jack leaned forward and put his hands on my shaking ones that were having a hard time hanging onto the paperwork.

"I know you have your daddy's farm over there. That barn is special to you, though. Wanted to make sure you knew that it would always be yours. No matter what, this is your home. From the driveway over ten acres and all the way back to the tree line. It's more than twenty acres and it's all yours. You have an easement for use of the driveway, but there's plenty of room if you wanted to put your own in. Hopefully, that won't ever be necessary, though."

"Dad," I whimpered. This was a beautiful gift, but I knew what it meant. More than a birthday present, it was my dad trying to take care of me because he knew that he wouldn't be here to do it much longer. I dropped to my knees and pushed forward to wrap him in a hug.

"I love you. I've never wanted a thing from you but your love in return but thank you for making sure my home and my office will always be mine. It's the best gift in the world after the one where I got you as my family."

"Aw Petal, you're making my old eyes mist up." He patted me on the back and then leaned in to kiss my cheek. "Best daughter I could ever ask for."

"I've been lucky, because I had two of the best dads in this life. He would be so proud of the job you did when he couldn't be here anymore," I told Jack.

"Your father was a fine man, sweetheart. You got his heart, my stubbornness, and your own shine. You're going to be just fine my girl."

"I love you," I said again because there was no way to get anything else out past the emotions clogging my throat.

"Go on now. I hear you have some shindig to get ready for. Don't let this sappy old man keep you."

"I'd rather be here with my sappy old dad than going out anywhere tonight." It was the truth.

"Nah, we'll have all day tomorrow, Petal. Go enjoy being young and have a drink for me."

"You're just trying to get rid of me so you can eat some of those doughnuts I saw on your kitchen counter," I teased.

"Caught me, almost red-handed." He grinned. We both knew that wasn't it. "Love you, birthday girl."

"Love you, Dad. Thank you," I told him again. When I got to my car, I put the deed in my bag so that I could run it by the bank on Monday and have it placed in the safe deposit box I had there.

I COULD HAVE SWORN THAT MARK'S DODGE CHARGER was parked at the end of the road when I passed by on the way to his house. That didn't seem right. Unless the damn thing broke down, we had a driveway and a garage that he normally parked it in. I shrugged it off, wondering if he was going to be inviting everyone over tonight, rather than us all going out somewhere. He thought I wouldn't be home until nearly five, so it was possible that I was about to ruin my surprise.

My heart hurt after accepting my dad's gift, so all I really wanted to do was go soak in a hot tub with a nice relaxing bath bomb and maybe a glass of wine. Nothing sounded better than drowning my troubles while giving myself a refreshing pick-me-up at the same time.

When I went to unlock the door, I realized it was already open. I pulled out the taser Evan had purchased me after the crazy fan was caught near the barn, and held it close to my side as I quietly eased the door further open. Once inside, I slid it shut again and then took a quick look around. There were two high heel shoes just off to the left of the door. One had been tipped over on its side and the other, while still standing, was facing in an odd direction as if someone had slipped them off so as not to ruin the carpet.

There was a woman's blouse hanging on the banister of the stairs and then a man's shirt dropped just a little further up. My stomach was in knots because there was no denying what I was about to walk in on, and it certainly wasn't a surprise birthday party for me, or the marriage proposal that everyone else seemed to think was coming.

Quietly as ever, I continued up the stairs, collecting the clothing that had been strewn the whole way up as I went. The clothing rested in my left hand while the taser still sat occupied in my right. I might have known what I was walking in on, but that didn't mean the taser wouldn't still come in handy. Technically, there was an intruder in my home, and messing with my life where they didn't belong.

When I got to my bedroom door, I had to fight the urge to be sick. My bedroom. Our bedroom. Mark had someone else in our bed. In the house he invited me to share with him as a committed couple. Now, considering his behavior over the past few months, I had to wonder how many times he'd done this before while I was at work or taking care of my sick dad.

I slipped the bedroom door further open and saw Mark behind a woman who was bent over the end of our bed. He was thrusting wildly into her as she grunted like a pig.

"Mark, let's get all the way on the bed this time. This position is getting old," she whined as he continued to thrust. His response to yank her head around by the grip he had on her hair. When he turned her head, she ended up facing me, but her eyes were for him only and she hadn't yet noticed that she had an audience.

"You know why I can't do that, Jen. It's too late in the day to launder the sheets and blankets. This is going to be bad enough. I'm surprised she hasn't noticed yet." He smacked her ass. "Now, shut up because you're ruining the mood."

"Why don't you just leave her?"

"Are you kidding? You know why."

"Marrying her won't give you free rein to develop her land," Jen snarked at him. He moved to thrust her head down into the bed, but before she turned all the way, her eyes locked onto mine. A harsh gasp erupted from her as she started smacking at Mark's thighs. "Stop, Mark!"

"No. You knew this was just sex when we started. Despite wanting her land, I also love Posie."

Well, wasn't that just sweet of him to declare his love to his side-whore. The asshole was fucking Jennifer, my business partner's ex-girlfriend. The woman who had hooked me up with Mark in the first place to keep me away from her man, was suddenly the woman coming between me and mine. Somehow, I didn't think that was coincidence.

"She's trying to tell you that you have an audience for this little show," I stated calmly as I threw their collection of clothes at them.

Mark turned with jaw slack at my announcement. "Posie? What are you doing here?"

"Last I checked, I lived here."

"I mean..."

"It's my birthday," I reminded him and watched as his face went even paler than it had upon noticing me standing there if that was even possible.

"Fuck!" He swore as his now limp cock fell out of Jen and the condom he'd been wearing – thankfully – dropped off his cock and onto the pile of clothing I'd just thrown at his feet.

"If you don't mind, I'll just pack my shit and be on the way, and then you two can carry on with your little affair." Then I turned my eyes to Jen, who looked like she was about to be sick. "Funny that it's you here fucking my boyfriend, when you introduced us because you were trying to make sure I never fucked yours. Not that I would have stooped so fucking low as to slum it with someone who was taken, but then again, you've never been a decent person, have you?"

"Oh my God! I'm so sorry, Posie. It just happened. Please, don't tell Evan."

And the light clicked on the minute she said that. "You've been trying to get Evan back while fucking my boyfriend? How did you think that was going to go for you?"

"You weren't supposed to know," she mumbled.

"Then why do it?" I asked, honestly curious.

"He was there when I needed someone."

"Yeah? When?"

"Don't!" That one word came out as a warning to Jen from Mark. He didn't want me to know just how long they'd been having an affair. Not that it mattered. One time was entirely too many in my opinion.

"Four months ago," she whispered, but I still caught it.

"Four..." I said in disbelief because that was before our problems even started. It made it clear that nothing I had been doing was the catalyst for him distancing himself. Maybe it had been guilt, fear of getting caught, or something that had built the walls between Mark and me, but it hadn't been the amount of time I spent working and taking care of my dad.

"You've been making up reasons to fight with me, blaming my family and the time I spent trying to help my sick father as the reasons, and all the while, it was because you were fucking a whore behind my back."

"Posie," Mark moved so quickly toward me that his dick flopped, making wet slapping noises against his thighs, which only worked to highlight how much he shouldn't be coming anywhere near me.

"Stop!" I yelled. He continued at me, and I had no doubt that he didn't mean me any physical harm, but when a naked man approaches you after being caught with his pants off and his dick in another woman, you can't be too careful. So, I raised the taser in my right hand and caught him right in the balls with it as he went to grab hold of me. He never made contact because the jolt of electricity that hit him sent him flying backward and too the floor.

"Oh my God! You killed him!"

"Nope, but he might not be able to have kids anymore," I suggested. "Now, get the fuck out of my house before I give you a shot to the fucking ovaries from the inside."

She reached down to grab her clothes and snapped her hand back as she came in contact with the gross, wet condom. I took a picture of the scene with my phone for evidence to show Evan, and then I moved closer to Jen.

"Get the fuck out. Now!" I kicked her clothes out of reach and lunged, like I was going to give her a jolt and she took off in all her

naked glory. I followed behind her and then called for an ambulance to come collect my cheating ex-boyfriend.

Then, I sent my best friend a text to come get me, along with
the picture, because I was probably going to need to be bailed out
of jail by the time the ambulance came to collect the asshole. While
I waited for someone to show up, I wondered if I'd just channeled
my mother's level of crazy or if any sane woman would have done
the same thing in my shoes.

I'd like to think that any woman walking into her house with a
taser in hand, after suspecting a break in, would react the same. I
wasn't sure how the cops and a judge would feel about that, so I
would have to get a good lawyer who could argue my case for me.
A sympathetic jury wouldn't hurt either.

When Evan showed up, it was to see the ambulance driving
away and a police officer attempting to question me. "I thought
someone broke in," I repeated again, as if I was in shock.

"Ma'am, a naked woman was reported running from this residence just before your 9-1-1 call came through."

Evan must have started to piece things together by the little bit
he'd heard, and he pulled me aside.

"This is my business partner's home. If a naked woman was
seen running from this place, then she wasn't meant to be here. We
get all kinds of crazy fans. You guys have it on record about the one
who was locked up after trying to break into our office. I bought
Posie a taser after that because she could have been hurt or worse if
she'd been there alone."

"Oh yeah," the officer slowly drawled as he attempted to
remember. "You two are the comic book people working out of
the barn on the Carter farm?"

"Evan Carter," my best friend proudly stated as he reached out
to shake the officer's hand. He didn't bother to correct the officer
or school him on the difference between comic books and graphic
novels. That might have kept us under his radar a bit longer.

"Are you sure you don't need medical attention?" He glanced

down again and noted the bruises on Posie's wrist that appeared to be finger marks wrapping around. The man took a picture of it with his cell phone.

"What is that for?"

"Evidence. You seem to be in shock, and I want to note it in my report that it appears you've been assaulted. Probably when you accidentally walked in on your boyfriend and another woman having an affair," he tacked on, telling me he understood more about what was going on than he'd originally led me to believe. "Seems to me, you were startled by what you thought were intruders and then one of them grabbed you and you used that Taser of yours in self-defense."

I nodded and that was when the tears started. To my complete surprise, the police officer pulled me in and wrapped his arms around me. "It will get better, sweetheart. Just hang in there." He released me into Evan's arms. "You have somewhere safe to take her?"

"I do. She's coming home to our family's place. Can we have someone come collect all of her things?"

"We got what we need. I suggest you get them here now, while the boyfriend is out of the house. Make sure you leave his things alone, no matter how tempted anyone might be to mess with them. I'd hate to have to come arrest any of you after what Miss Posie has been through."

twenty-eight

MAX - 28

Dear Posie,

It's been a while since I've written to you. I guess that's mostly because I didn't think you wanted to hear from me again after the incident with Beth on your birthday a couple years ago. I heard about what happened with your boyfriend. I want to tell you how sorry I am that your heart was broken, that your trust was betrayed, and your relationship destroyed. The fact that Evan's ex-girlfriend was in the mix probably added insult to injury too.

I want to tell you how much I wish you weren't hurting and that my arms are here, waiting to hold you, if you need that instead of these words. None of what I have to say means much to you these days though, and in an effort to keep your faith in me, this part will probably be hard to hear.

I'm not really sorry. I wish you didn't hurt, but I'm glad he's out of your life. Selfish, right?

I know it is, and I'm still saying it all anyway. Who knows, maybe I won't even bother sending this letter to you. I should keep it all to myself. I'm glad he's gone though, Posie. It killed me every fucking day to think of you even having a boyfriend, let alone living with a man. According to Evan, everyone was expecting him to propose. I haven't even been with anyone since your 25th birthday.

"You're not going to send that to her, are you?" Dev asked as he looked over my shoulder.

"Go to hell," I huffed before minimizing my screen. "What are you doing looking over my shoulder, anyway? I thought you were playing with J.J.?"

"I was until the little guy fell asleep in the middle of my epic build and knocked all the blocks down," Dev explained. "You really need to bring him back home sometime soon. I'm sure Pops would love the chance to get to hang out with his great grandson a little more before..."

"Before what?" I asked, not liking his tone.

"He doesn't have long, Max. I think that's part of why Posie isn't coping too well with everything that just happened. If you ask me, I don't think she was as 'in love' with the Wellington asshole as other family members were led to believe. She's taking it hard anyway, and I think a lot of that is because she knows she's about to lose her dad. Her second dad. That girl can't catch a fucking break."

An ache built inside my chest at the thought of Pops no longer being around. I didn't get home to see him in person as often as I liked, but we talked all the time. He was the one who updated me on all things Posie. Evan would only tell me so much and my other brothers didn't think I deserved to know, since I kept screwing things up with her. Pops, on the other hand, made it his mission to relay every juicy detail of that woman's life. He always followed it up with a reminder that it was never too late to change the course of history.

"Pops never did like her boyfriend," I tell Devon.

"What? That's not true."

"Yeah, it is. Not one day has gone by in the past two years where the old coot hasn't reminded me that it is never too late." I chuckled along with Dev.

"He really told you to go out and steal another man's girl?"

I shrugged my shoulders. "I think the way he sees it, she was always meant to be mine, so it's more like Wellington swooped in during a low point for Posie and me and took advantage of the situation and her heightened emotions."

"Yeah, I can see where he'd think that."

"Because it's true," I tacked on bitterly.

"Why didn't you stay and fight for her that night?"

"She looked happy when she got back from that first date with him and all I'd caused her was pain. Who was I to go busting up in there with all my baggage in tow? I didn't even live in town, I had a baby with another woman, and my baby's mother would never allow me to move back home with my son without her tagging along for the adventure. That night, all I could see was the way she laughed and smiled and kissed another man and that if it was me instead of him, there would be a baby screaming in the background for attention and another woman slinking around to cause trouble."

"Seems like she had another woman slinking around in her relationship anyway."

"Hindsight is a bitch like that." My brother didn't need to remind me that some of the baggage I'd been worried about her dealing with had been thrust upon her by Wellington. It wasn't fair that she had to endure part of what I meant to spare her, but then life rarely was. I stared off into space for just a moment more before Dev tapped me on the shoulder.

"Nothing has changed for you. Only now, you know that the things you're trying to save her from can happen anyway with someone else. When are you going to step up and take what you want out of life? I'm sick of seeing you go through these crappy relationships and failing all the time. There's only one reason they never work out."

"Yeah, because I'm bad at love," I joked. Though, if I was being honest with myself, it wasn't much of a joke.

"Nah, it's because you were meant for one woman, and you keep letting life get in the way of you having her."

"Dev, you have to know that she doesn't want me like that anymore, if she ever did."

"Oh, she did. Poor girl thought she hid it well, but we could all see through her bullshit, especially Pops. He's the only one who doesn't let her get away with lying to him or herself, though."

"What is everyone doing about Pops?" I asked. In part it was to get the heavy topic of Posie off my chest and because there had to be something that could be done for our grandfather.

"I wish I had better news. I think you should put in for some time off. I'm sure Pops would rather have time with you and his great grandson than have you there after he's gone for his funeral."

"That's why you came?" I asked. The answer stared me in the face without my brother having to say a single word. "Shit, okay, I'll get J.J. ready."

"Won't his mom have something to say about you taking him out of town without permission?"

"She can't really say much, since she left him with a babysitter while she took off with her friend to Vegas for a long weekend."

"She did what?"

Luckily, the babysitter was the daughter of one of the cops who worked with me. When Beth didn't come back for him that night, and instead called to ask if she could keep him all weekend, the girl told her she'd call back with her answer. Ferraro called me immediately and told me what was going on. I picked up my son and kept him all weekend. My lawyer also documented everything that happened, including the text exchange between the babysitter and Beth. "I'm one step closer to getting sole custody of my son," I told Devon after explaining the situation to him.

"In a way, I'm happy for you, but damn, Max. That's fucked up. What if she had used someone who didn't know you?"

"I don't even want to think about it. I have someone keeping tabs on her now. This is my weekend with J.J. She can't really say shit about me taking him home to see family, especially since Pops is so sick.

"You know you'll see Posie while you're there, right?"

"Obviously."

"Just try to remember that she's in the middle of a fresh breakup and that Evan's former girlfriend was the person that idiot cheated on her with."

I gave him a nod as I packed up my shit and called in to inform work that I might need to drop emergency leave, depending on how this weekend went with my grandfather. Having to tell someone, out loud, that my grandfather was basically on his deathbed made it all feel so real. We were going to lose him. I'd been away so long, trying to establish myself as someone separate from my sometimes-overbearing family, that I'd missed out on years with the old coot. My son had missed out on getting to know his great grandfather. It made me determined to fight to get back to my family before J.J. and I missed too much more time with any of them.

There was Posie to think about, too. I couldn't keep watching her slip through my fingers and nothing would ever change until I made my way back home.

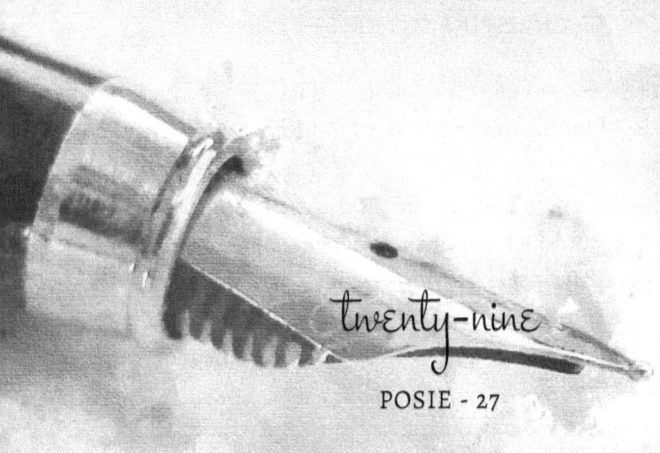

twenty-nine

POSIE - 27

"Petal?" Jack called to me as I got out of Evan's car. He tried to stand but I motioned for him to stay right where he was.

"I'm okay, Dad. Can't say the same for Mark, though."

He looked from me to Evan and back again. "Someone needs to explain," my father demanded.

"I left early today and went home to find Mark in our bed with Jennifer."

"Jennifer?" He asked.

"My ex," Evan enlightened him.

"That son of a bitch. I might be on my way out of this life, but he can sure as shit join me."

Evan laughed. "No need to worry about it, Pops. Your little Petal took care of his ass..." He glanced at me and grinned. "Or was it his balls?"

I shook my head and then looked up to see the question in my dad's eyes. "I may have zapped him in the balls with my taser. No need to worry, though. The police officer wrote it down as self-defense and took pictures of my wrist where Mark grabbed me to try to keep me from leaving."

Jack nodded his head and then he started laughing, which lead to wheezing, and him having to try to catch his breath in a horrifically painful way.

Evan and I looked at one another and then I moved closer to wrap my arms around Jack's frail shoulders. "Come on, old man, we need to get you inside. I think you've had about all the humidity you can stand for one day."

"Stop trying to take care of me when you're the one who needs to be cared for right now."

"You know what would make me happy?" I asked.

"What's that, Petal?" By his placating tone, I knew he was already aware of the answer.

"Taking care of my dad. It will get my mind off things while Evan goes back to help our family clear my things out of the house before Mark gets out of the hospital."

Jack nodded his head as we moved inside. "That's good. I'd like it if you would stay in the house for a while, instead of the barn. That is, if-"

I cut him off. "I was hoping you would offer, so I wouldn't have to ask. Honestly, I just want to be close to my dad right now." I couldn't help the sniffle that followed. It wasn't a lie.

"That's two birthdays of yours that bitch has ruined now. I hope you hit her with that taser of yours, too."

I giggled at his vengeful side. "Well, I didn't hit her with the taser, but I didn't allow her to get clothes on either. She ran from the house naked, and the neighbors saw her."

Jack laughed again, and wheezed, and then struggled to catch his breath. "Damn it..." Those two words were a struggle for him. "Proud of you," he finally managed.

"Have you eaten dinner?"

"No, Petal. I'm glad I waited. If you have any appetite left you could humor an old man and share a birthday dinner with me."

"I would love to."

"You knew, didn't you?" He asked as I worked on getting something ready to cook for us.

"I suspected, but come to find out, things had been going on for longer than I thought. There's also the fact that I overheard their conversation. He was planning on developing my family's farmland after we married." Dad looked like he was ready to hop in his truck and go murder Mark in the hospital. "He had the nerve to tell that bitch that he loved me, too. Marrying me wasn't just about the property. Can you believe that? He was having sex with another woman, in our bed, and had the nerve to talk about loving me."

"I'll never understand your generation," Dad admitted.

"No," I shook my head. "That's not my generation, that's just an asshole thing to do. He clearly doesn't know the first thing about love."

"Something tells me that maybe he knew he was climbing an uphill battle with you, Petal. Maybe he did love you, but knew that your heart was already claimed by someone else?"

I gasped. "Are you excusing his behavior?"

"Not at all. He took the cowards way out instead of having a real conversation with you about who held your heart. Far as I know, you never lied to him about your feelings." When I shook my head, Jack nodded. "Didn't think so. You've always been a straight shooter, Petal. He didn't have the talk with you because he already knew your heart would never belong to him. That's his problem. If he didn't think you could love him the way he hoped, then he should have said something and accepted you as you were or ended things. He also shouldn't have kept his intentions regarding your family's land to himself."

"No, he shouldn't have, and I can't believe it never crossed my mind. Dad, he's asked what my intentions were for the land so many times, but I just thought he was trying to get me to decide what to do with it – for me. Truthfully, I thought he was hinting that we should move there, considering the house is huge and family ready." I fought off the chill that winded its way through my body. I could never live there again knowing that my mother hung herself in that house for me to discover her body after reading the cold, uncaring note she left behind.

"Don't mean to be a downer, but I was hoping to talk to you about your family's land, too. I had a look at the books, in comparison to what I know has been going out over there. I hope you'll consider getting someone to do an audit. That bastard that's been running things has been skimming from you, and not by small amounts."

"I know."

"You... Wait... What? What do you mean, you know?"

I chuckled at Dad's startled response. "I already have Devon looking into things for me, and if need be I will press charges. I hope to not have to do that, but if my hand is forced, I will." When Jack continued to stare at me as if he'd never seen me before, I laughed. "Come on, Dad. I might be an artist instead of a farmer, but I'm far from stupid. I know the amounts that have been going out too. I might have been young when I lost my father, but all those times he took me out to work the fields with him, he explained how things worked, what everything cost, and how much he could expect to earn."

"He was preparing you to take over one day," Dad surmised while nodding his head. "Your father was a good man."

"Both of them," I corrected. "Both my fathers were damn good men and did a good job raising me."

His eyes closed but those thin lips of his tipped up at the corners in a contented smile.

"Always wanted a girl," he mumbled before his head dipped. Dad nodded off more often lately, and at random, concerning times. I swiped angrily at the tears that fell. It wasn't fair. This good man, this man who had taken me in and became my father when mine passed on, was about to lose his battle and there wasn't a thing I could do to help him.

While it stung that my boyfriend cheated on me while everyone else thought he was preparing to propose marriage, at least he did me an unknowing favor. I wouldn't have to feel guilty for spending what time my dad had left in this world with him. He was now my sole focus.

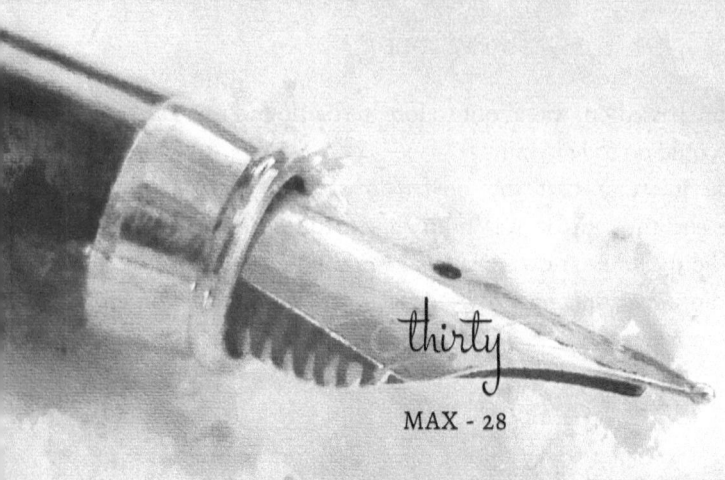

thirty

MAX - 28

We were too late.

"I'm so sorry, son." My dad pulled me into a crushing hug as my own son held on tightly to my hand.

"I didn't think we'd run out of time to get here," I admitted in his ear as my dad squeezed me hard. His hug, while meant to comfort me, was also a tool he used to try to pull himself back together. After a minute, he finally pulled away and then reached down to snatch my son up from where he stood by my side.

"Hey, little man, how about we give your dad some time here and we go hunt down some cookies?"

"Tookies," My boy repeated as his lip poked out in response to the tears in my eyes. "Daddy!"

"It's okay, J.J. Go get some cookies with your Pop. I'll be there in a minute. Save me one, okay?"

"Tay." He snuggled his head down into my dad's shoulder as they walked away. My heart lurched in my chest. My boy wasn't even 3 years old yet and he already experienced the neglect his mother put him through and then losing his great grandfather.

Even his innocence couldn't shelter him from everything

forever. As my dad marched down the hallway with his grandson in his arms, I turned back to the hospital room where the rest of my family had gathered. Despite the room being cramped with family, the only person who registered for me was her. Posie. She stood there looking like a wounded angel, pushing Pops' thin, silver hair back off his forehead.

I got the call late last night that he slipped into a coma and an ambulance was called to bring him to the hospital. "We've been waiting for you," she said without looking away from Pops.

"I thought…" The words were all but a whisper on my lips as I took in the steady beeping of the monitor the old man was hooked to.

Posie shook her head. "The machines are doing the work for him, only long enough for you to get here to say goodbye."

"But…" I was about to argue until my mother's hand came down on my shoulder. She shook her head, as if to tell me not to beg for hope. How could they all be so resigned.

"He has a DNR," Posie explained. "The only exception to the 'no machines' rule was to keep him here long enough to give everyone closure, time to say goodbye. You're the last one here, so once you say your goodbyes, he will be able to finally rest."

A tear travelled down her face and landed where her hand had joined with Pops' lifeless one. I moved a little closer to the bed.

"Come on, boys, let's give them a moment." Mom ordered as she began to usher my brothers out of the room. Each of them clapped a hand down on my shoulder before leaving the room. Evan stopped and looked me in the eyes, as if he wanted to give me some kind of warning.

'Don't hurt Posie.'

He didn't have to say verbalize it for me to get the message loud and clear. As Evan left and shut the door, I moved closer to the same side of the bed Posie stood on. "I thought we would have more time," she stated.

"I know. When Devon came to bring me home, I thought

there would be enough time to put in for the time off at work, pack up, and plan a week or two back home. If I'd realized..."

Posie shook her head and cut off that thought immediately. "We all knew it wouldn't be long, but I think denial is a bitch sometimes." She chuckled. "Sorry, Dad." She whispered to the man who could no longer hear her. It was weird hearing her call him "Dad". That was what he had become to her in my absence, though. Pops had been her father for the officially for eleven years and probably acted as one well before that too.

"I thought that it was perfect timing, having that idiot cheat on me, so that I could stay home with Dad and not have to feel like I was being ripped apart by someone demanding my attention away from him." She shook her head and sniffled back her emotions before watery eyes turned up to meet mine. "I thought I'd have more than a single day there at the farm with him."

I pulled her into a hug and held on tightly while she fell apart in my arms. My gaze slipped past her to Pops, and I could have sworn his lips tipped up in a smile.

"Don't worry, Pops, I've got her now," I promised. There was no telling if he heard me, or even if it registered to Posie what I'd just said. None of that mattered because I would hold true to my promise to the man I respected most in my life. It was time to figure out how to make my life work, so that my son and the woman I'd been in love with for years, could both be a part of it.

"I'm glad you were able to come," Posie whispered in my ear before backing up and swiping away her tears. "He was so proud of you."

I wanted to deny what she said. How could he be proud of me? The man wanted me to be with the girl he raised, and I'd let them both down. He'd been right all along, she was perfect for me, but I didn't think the opposite was true. By the time I realized that she was exactly who I needed, I'd already screwed everything up and made it damn near impossible.

"You don't have to believe me, but he talked about you often. Trust me when I say, he was extremely proud of you for following your heart, for taking on the thankless job of protecting people and finding them justice. The only thing that would have made it better, was if you'd been closer to home. That was the only complaint he ever made about you, that we didn't get to see you often enough."

"Fuck." The word dragged out in a hoarse whisper. That hurt. She was telling me something good, but at the same time, my heart sank. I should have been around more. My boy should have been able to get to know his great grandfather better before it was too late. It was something I would have rectified, if not for the poor choices I'd made. My son's mother was the point of contention with me coming back to town. She wanted me to pay for her to relocate here, otherwise she would fight me on the move and try to keep my son.

I wish I had fought her harder on everything. If I had, maybe all that time wouldn't have been lost. Not just with Pops, my boy, and me but with Posie, too.

"We should let them come in and take care of him," I finally said as I held Posie in my arms. She bobbed her head and allowed me to move her along out of the room. Just as we got to the door, her head swiveled, and she took one last look at the man who she had come to know as a second father.

"I hope he's sitting on a rocking chair somewhere with your grandma. He missed her so much all these years."

"I bet he is," I confirmed even though I didn't really know fuck all about what happened to people after they died. At least not what happened to their souls. I was the one to bring them justice, sometimes, if they died from a violent act but on the days when being honest with myself won out over the fantasy, I had to admit that there wasn't a single fiber of my being that believed the dead sought out justice for the wrongs committed against them. If there was a better place after all this, then they were enjoying it, not busy concerning themselves with what already happened and can't be changed.

"I'm not sure where you live these days," I admitted as we moved closer to the elevator. I pulled my phone out to text my parents, so that they would keep my son with them for a while. Posie needed me.

"The barn," she said. "But I think I want to stay at Dad's house tonight."

"Okay, we'll go there."

I knew she'd broken up with that tool who had swooped in when my son's mom played mind games with Posie on her birthday, but I didn't think she'd moved back into the barn. Last I saw it, the damn place looked exactly as the name entailed, a musty old barn filled with hay, horse tack, and all the crap projects that Pops thought he'd get to one day. Truthfully, I wondered why Posie had never taken over her own family farm and the house there. Despite what her mother had done, I didn't think Posie let that bother her these days.

"He really was my second dad," she whimpered. "He was everything."

"I know, sweet girl," I mumbled into her hair and then regretted my words as she stiffened in my arms. "What did I do?"

Posie shook her head. "That's what he always called me. That and Petal." She grinned up at me through her watery smile.

"Think maybe he was talking through me, then, because I've never called you that or thought of you as that."

The smile she wore grew wider. "That's good. Like a final goodbye from him." We took a few more steps before she spoke again. "Did you call me Sweet Posie before, though, in your letters."

"It seems so long ago that I wrote those," I admitted. "My brother caught me writing one to you yesterday when he came to tell me it was time to get my butt back here for Pops."

"You still write me?" She sounded surprised.

"I haven't written since you started dating that asshole."

"Oh." The one word came out more like a disappointed huff. I tipped my chin down to look at her.

"I didn't think you'd been reading anything before that anyway."

She shrugged her shoulders. "I may have skimmed them before adding everything to the box."

"The box?"

"I have a box filled with every letter you ever wrote me."

That brought a small smile to my face. "What a coincidence. I have a similar box, only it locks and no one else knows the code to get into it."

She giggled softly. "You keep my letters in a safe?"

"They're the most precious thing I own, so yes."

"Max," she muttered.

"I know. Now isn't the time to get into this. I won't lie to you though. Outside of my son, you are still the most important person in the world to me. The past few years, it has felt like I've been missing a limb by not having those little pieces of you anymore. I missed hearing about your day, how Pops was doing from your perspective, and how my brother would never remember what your characters looked like if you didn't draw him pictures of them."

Her soft chuckle warmed my heart a bit. "That sounds like something I'd say about your brother."

I squeezed her to my side a bit tighter before I realized that neither of us had paid a bit of attention to where we were headed. "I tossed Dad my keys since the car seat and all of J.J.'s things were in the truck. Where are you parked?"

"I'm just over there," Posie pointed, and I followed the direction until I saw an old seventies era Ford Bronco. It had a refreshed sky-blue paint job and somehow felt like the perfect fit for her. When we got closer, I glanced down and noted the license plate.

PtlPshr. Posie must have noticed, and she cracked a grin as I tried to puzzle out what it meant.

"Petal Pusher," she said and then cracked up. "Dad almost always called me Petal instead of Posie. It was a little thing he used to do to tease me when I was younger to get me to come out of my shell and cross the road to come talk to him. When I bought the Bronco, he shook his head at me and said, 'And everyone wonders why...'" Posie stopped mid-sentence and tried to shake it off.

"Please, finish."

She sighed as if resigned to do just that even though she didn't want to. "He said, 'Everyone wonders why I say you and my grandson would be perfect for one another if you both ever got your shit together.'"

Posie grimaced up at me and then back down at the license plate that started the conversation. "He said I was going to end up pushing the damn thing more than driving it because Ford vehicles were named with the acronym for Found on Road Dead for a reason." She giggled again. "That man was a trip. He dubbed my baby The Petal Pusher. So, I worked out how to get the gist of her title onto a license plate."

"I bet he loved that."

"He did. Every time he saw it, Dad smiled and winked at me." Her face crumpled as she said that, and I pulled her into my arms feeling the ache of missing my pops while she missed her dad.

"Come on, let's get you home for now." She handed me her keys without protest and went to climb into the passenger side. "Will people be headed to the farm?" I asked, not knowing if they'd already planned anything.

"I don't think so. That will most likely happen after..."

Posie couldn't bring herself to say it and neither could I. Instead, I gave her a quick nod and started her truck. The damn thing rumbled to life beneath my fingertips. Part of me was curious about how her idiot cheater ex hadn't heard her pull up to the house in this thing. He must have really been invested in whatever he was getting up to with my brother's ex.

"I can't wrap my head around the fact that he's gone," she whispered.

"I can't either. It fucking sucks. I kept thinking I had all the time in the world, and you'd think when I fucked up and didn't come after you that time that I'd have learned a lesson."

"What are you talking about?"

"Nothing. Never mind," I mumbled as we pulled into traffic.

"Can we not do that? I feel like most of our problems were self-inflicted because one or the other of us has always been afraid of saying the thing that needs to be said. I've learned lessons in life too. It's short. You never know how many years you get, and I'm tired of living with regrets, Max."

I glanced over at Posie's beautiful face that was pulled tight with grief and frustration. "Okay. I knew you came to my house that time and I let my brother talk me out of going after you because I didn't think I was ready for you yet. I still needed to put time in on the job and I figured you needed to stay back home to be able to work with Evan."

"You recognized me?" She asked.

I shook my head and kept my eyes on the road. "My neighbor had a Ring camera on his house that caught part of my front stoop as well. After Jake and I noticed you, and the way you pulled off, I had to make sure it wasn't someone watching my place because of a case I'd worked. I went and pulled the video."

"And you saw me looking like an insane creeper," she groused.

"I never once thought that about you. Myself, maybe, but not you."

"Yeah, okay. Since when has the great Maxwell Carter ever come off as a creeper?"

"The night after your 25th birthday when I sat there on the side of the barn, waiting for you to come back from your date with that asshole. I went there to convince you that I wanted you, but needed to figure out how to get closer to home without J.J's mom pitching a fit about it. I hoped you'd be willing to give us a shot." I shook my head as I remembered that night.

"You looked so happy when you got out of his car. I figured it wasn't fair of me to ask that you put your life on hold when you had the promise of something good. It wasn't fair to ask you to step in and put up with the drama Beth would sling your way, the fact that I had a kid with her, and that we still didn't live anywhere close to one another."

"Wow, we are so freakin' dysfunctional," Posie said before she started to laugh. "No wonder Jack kept trying to drag us together." Our awkward chuckles died down before she spoke again, and what she had to say completely blew my mind. "I would have moved there. I don't know why you thought anything was holding me back. Half the time Evan and I used video chats for meetings anyway because we could never link our schedules up with whatever else we had going on."

I didn't know what to say to that. If that was true, then that meant my brother was an asshole for not telling me it was a possibility. Then again, it wasn't really his place to work out the finer details of my relationship with his business partner. Hearing her say that was a kick in the fucking teeth though. It meant we could have been together this whole time that I had been a stubborn ass about my job and thinking she'd feel the same.

"Are you going to say anything?"

"I'm too busy mentally kicking my own ass for never talking to you about it. I thought I was doing both of us a favor by waiting until I was able to get my time in on the job and come back. If I had known you'd be willing to come stay with me and it wouldn't have fucked up your job... Jesus, Posie. Everything could have been so different. J.J. might have been yours. I know he wouldn't be the same, but we might have had our own."

"You can't say things like. You can never regret your son."

I shook my head. "I regret so much. In my mind, I'm not

giving him up to have been with you. He would have just been half you and half me instead of..."

"Half hers," Posie finished for me.

"Yeah. God knows he doesn't deserve a mother like her. He was nothing more than a pawn and a vehicle to control me when she couldn't find another way to make shit happen."

"I'm really sorry for what happened with her, but you two looked really cosey together on my 25th birthday, so forgive me if I don't understand the dynamic. It seemed like you were together again."

"No, Posie. No. We were never together. I don't even remember the one and only time we had sex. I didn't bring her to town for your birthday. Jenn invited her separately, and we just happened to meet in the parking lot. Jenn had told me that you were coming with your boyfriend, and..." I pulled into the driveway headed to Pops' house and detoured to go to the barn instead. As we pulled in, I explained exactly what I'd been thinking and how everything played out that night.

"I used to think it was fate that kept us apart, like we weren't meant for one another, but it feels more like," she paused to search for the right words. "Like," she tried again.

"We're bad at love."

"Yes, exactly that." I watched as a hint of red stained her cheeks when she realized what she just admitted to.

"Let's get inside." Posie hesitated and stared over at the farmhouse. "We can go there instead, if you want."

"No. I think I need to not be there tonight, or I may never leave that house again. Do you want to come in?" Posie glanced at the barn and then back to me and then her truck. "Oh, I guess you can just take my truck and get back to the family. Your son probably needs you."

"J.J. is fine with my parents. I'm sure they'd be more than happy to have you come over and stay with them, all things considered. You are a member of the Carter family, even without Pops here."

"I know. I just don't feel..." She sighed and pulled the door open to allow us both to enter. I followed in behind Posie as she did something with the alarm panel on the wall. Once the barn was secure again, we both moved inside to what had to be the studio where she and Evan worked.

It was the first time I'd seen inside the barn since it had been renovated and I was blown away. "The last time I was here, this place was full of hay, dust, and probably a few field mice."

"Hopefully, the field mice found a new home. I haven't seen any in years." I watched as she hung her keys on a hook along with the sweater she had worn in the hospital. It felt like a magnet pulled me in her wake as she moved through the open space. The floors were some sort of treated concrete now and they shined as though they'd recently been waxed and buffed. The walls were white with dark gray wood beams spaced about every eight or so feet. The truly remarkable thing was the six feet tall by four feet wide panels that were propped against the walls. Each one depicted another scene that I recognized from the graphic novels Posie and Evan created.

"These are amazing." I hadn't even realized that I'd walked over to the first one, closest to the door we'd come through.

"Those are original paintings, not prints," Posie informed as she stood next to me and watched me take in her work.

"I bet people would pay a mint to get just one of these."

I turned in time to see Posie shrug and walk away. "I think I have water, some locally crafted beer Evan brought to try, and orange juice. I haven't been staying over here much because of Dad." She stopped short and the minute her shoulders shook, my feet moved of their own accord.

"Posie, it's going to hurt for a bit, but he's with my grandma now."

"I know. He didn't think I heard him talking to her all the time these past few days." She turned in the circle of my arms, where I'd pulled her into my embrace to offer comfort. When Posie faced me, she offered a watery smile. "I swear, I could feel your grandma around the house. The powdery perfume she used to wear would be all over a room when I walked into it and Jack would be there talking to her as if she was seated right beside him."

"That must have been a little scary for you." It probably would have freaked me out.

"No," she insisted. "In a weird way, it was comforting to know he had her in the end. She was there to welcome him to whatever's next. I think we all wish for a beautiful transition like that when we leave this existence behind."

"I suppose we do."

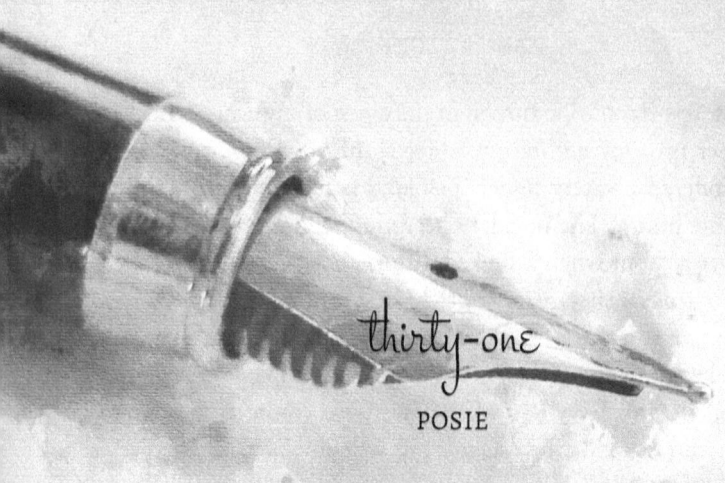

thirty-one

POSIE

The last time Max had been in the barn with me had been when I was 16. At 27, the experience was markedly different, though still tinged with sadness. My second-chance dad was gone, and even though I was prepared and knew it was coming, it still didn't feel real. My heart kept waiting for him to stroll over to the barn and give me hell for not coming to eat dinner with him.

"I don't know if I'm overstepping by being here," Max admitted as I pulled away from him.

"You're not. Sorry, I'm having a hard time convincing myself that Jack isn't going to barge in at any moment."

"How about you give me a quick tour and then we'll kick back and just relax for a bit. We can talk about Pops if you want, or something else if you're not ready."

"I have a letter for you," I blurted out. "Well, it's not from me this time. It was from Jack. He wanted me to mail it to you yesterday, but then everything happened, and the letter just got stuffed in my bag."

"We can get to that in a minute. I really want to see what you did with the rest of the place."

"It wasn't me. Most of this is what Jack had done. He wanted me to have my own place where I felt safe and comfortable. He knew I never wanted to step foot in my family's home again."

"Have you thought about selling it?"

I shook my head. "No. I want the land to remain in the family. Maybe, one day, I'll have the house torn down, so I don't even have to see it."

"You plan on staying here?" Max asked.

"I guess you didn't know. Jack gave me this barn and the ten acres from my side of the driveway all the way back to the trees and then west of the barn."

"I didn't realize." Max seemed surprised by that, but I wasn't sure why he should be since I was fairly certain Jack had left him a piece of land too. Evan had the ten acres on the other side of mine. Right now, it sat as a partially wooded, mostly empty lot.

"You seem surprised," I muttered.

"Not in a bad way. I'm trying to figure out why Pops wouldn't give you his house, too."

"I assumed it went to someone else."

"And you're okay with that?"

"I didn't even expect him to give me the barn or anything at all, Max. I have a huge property across the street. It wasn't that long ago that I went through the books and had the old farm manager fired. He was skimming off the profits for years. Michael has taken over now, and as a sign on bonus, he has a fifty percent stake in the farm. Eventually, I want him to buy me out because I can't bring myself to step foot over there. It's just across the street, in plain sight every day, yet it feels like there's this barrier that won't let me cross to the other side."

"Probably because you felt safe on this side with Pops."

"I still feel safe on this side, even with him gone."

"So, when you said you wanted to keep the property in the family..." Max left the thought hanging.

"I know you've been away all this time, so it's hard to grasp, but your family is my family, Max. We have all grown incredibly close over the years. Michael and I never had as strong a bond as Evan and me, but it's still there. I know he'll do that property proud, and my father, well actually both my dads, would be proud that the land passed to him."

Max swallowed and turned away as if to take in the rest of the barn around us. "The loft is your personal space?"

I grinned at him. "Yes."

"What if Evan is here working? It doesn't look like that gives you a lot of privacy," Max pointed out as he stared up at the loft that was open to the rest of the barn.

"Come on, I'll show you." I grabbed Max's hand without thinking and pulled to get him to follow me. When I went to release his hand, he held on tighter, and we walked up the stairs together.

"The stairs are a nice change from the old ladder."

"Yep, it was one of the first changes Jack made." I rolled my eyes remembering. "He was worried I'd fall one day, and no one would realize until it was too late."

"He loved you."

"I know it and I loved him back just as fiercely." When we reached the top, I turned to see Max's reaction to my space. Immediately, he moved over to stand in front of my bed as he stared down at the desks below where I worked in tandem with his brother sometimes.

"Still not seeing how you have any privacy here," Max grumbled. I moved over to my nightstand and pushed a button on the little remote control sitting there. A wall rolled down from the ceiling to settle into the track on the floor just inside the rails that kept people from falling off the edge.

"I didn't see that coming," he admitted as I giggled.

"That's not all." I tilted my head back over to the stairs we had come up and pushed another button. A separate wall came down, closing the space in completely, with exception of the windows behind where my bed sat. Another button, and those windows were also sealed up.

"Your personal space in the barn is a panic room?" Max asked as he turned back to me.

I nodded. "The retractable walls that block access to the stairs and window were features that Jack added for me after the incident where someone tried to break in. He wanted me safe when I stayed out here. It's not as secure as an actual panic room, because the walls can be busted down, but it gives me a little extra security at night to have a special door someone can't just bust a lock on or break down without a whole lot of effort."

"Wow. This place is remarkable."

"It really is. I was thinking about expanding the barn one day, if I had a family. Evan and I talked about making a new office space right on the edge of our two properties since they adjoin, that way the whole barn could be converted into a house and the downstairs area could be split into living space and walled off for a couple bedrooms and a bathroom. I didn't like the idea of taking away all that open space, though, so I thought adding the bedrooms and bathroom would be a better option."

I couldn't read Max's face as he had pushed the button to roll the wall back up and faced away from me to look out at the open space below. "I agree with the open concept down there. It probably helps when you're creating those masterpieces."

A warm blush suffused my skin at his compliment. "It does, thank you."

Max turned back to me and seemed as though he was about to say something, but shook off whatever it was. "Maybe I should read Pops' letter now."

I reached into the bag that still dangled over my shoulder and pulled the letter out to hand to him. Max pulled me over to the corner – the same one where I'd once sat curled up in a ball drawing when he'd brought his girlfriend to make out in the barn.

Instead of bales of hay and dust, a comfy, overstuffed chair sat there. It was still a favorite spot of mine to sit and sketch.

Max took a seat and pulled me into his lap before opening the envelope and pulling out the folded pages. Once he unfolded them, his arms wrapped around my middle and situated the pages so we could both see what Jack wrote to him.

Maxwell,

I wished you had come back home sooner, so this letter wouldn't be necessary. I wanted to make you an offer that I didn't think you could refuse. Let's start with that.

My house and the ten acres surrounding it from the driveway over to Shady Creek and from the road to the forest are yours. The deed with the property lines drawn up is in my safe at the house. Either your dad or Posie can get you into the safe to get the official paperwork. I wanted you and your boy to have a safe place to land after everything the two of you have been through.

I understand that the timing may not be right for you to come home, but if you keep waiting on the time to be right, you're going to miss out on the life you and that boy are supposed to have.

She won't admit it, but my girl is still hope-lessly in love with you. Sure, she moved on, but everyone with a set of eyeballs could see she was just phoning in that relationship with the pond scum she hooked up with. I have reason to believe that the bastard is just in it to get his mitts on the land she owns. The bastard likes her well enough too, but I don't trust him, Max.

When he betrays her, she's going to need someone she can rely on. Her heart won't be broken by him because my Petal never gave it away - not to that idiot anyway. You need to stop being stubborn and get home so you can put her pieces back together and fit them into the life you're building with your son. J.J. couldn't ask for a better woman to influence his life than my Posie. She's one of the good ones, my boy. She has the same heart her daddy carried in him before he was taken from this world.

I know you've fought it for years because you thought you had something to prove outside of our family. Too much like your dad. Probably too much like your Pops, if we're being honest. I need you to know that we are all proud of you and everything you've accomplished on your own, but it's time to come home.

In my safe, you will find some information that might make that possible sooner rather than later. I had a man looking into that woman who birthed your boy. She's a snake in the grass, but she's not as slick as she thought. Take what's there, use it as leverage if you need to, and get you and your boy free and clear from her. Then get your butts back here. I have it on good authority that the local police are looking for a good detective.

I'm sorry that we weren't able to spend some time together before...

I'm old and not much longer for this world, Max. I need you to take care of my house, but more importantly, you need to look after Posie for me. She's seen far too much loss in her life. That girl needs a steady dose of sweet and I've always known it was you who would give it to her. Even if she's still with that prick when you read this, you should step in and see to it that she chooses you instead. Be a homewrecker I can be proud of. Ha! Your grandmother would have boxed my ears for saying something like that, but in this case, I think she'd agree with me.

Get the girl. Love your family hard and never again let go of the best thing that ever came into your life. We only get so many chances before they're all gone. Make them count.

No matter what, know that I love you and that boy of yours with all my heart. Your grandma and I will be looking out to make sure you don't screw things up again. Lord knows, you're too stubborn for your own good sometimes. Since I know I won't be around to give you a stern talking to in person, you get this letter. If you're smart, you read it with my girl. If not, you should let her accidentally find it, so she can see my true last wishes, too. She's just as stubborn as you are. It's why you'll be great together, once you both figure out that you fit.

Love her hard, Max. Never let go.

Love,

Pops

PS - If for some reason things don't work out between you two, know that I wish for the best for all of you anyway. All that matters is that you're all happy. If it does work out though, I want you to think back to the times I told you that you should get to know that girl and remember I told you so! Ha!

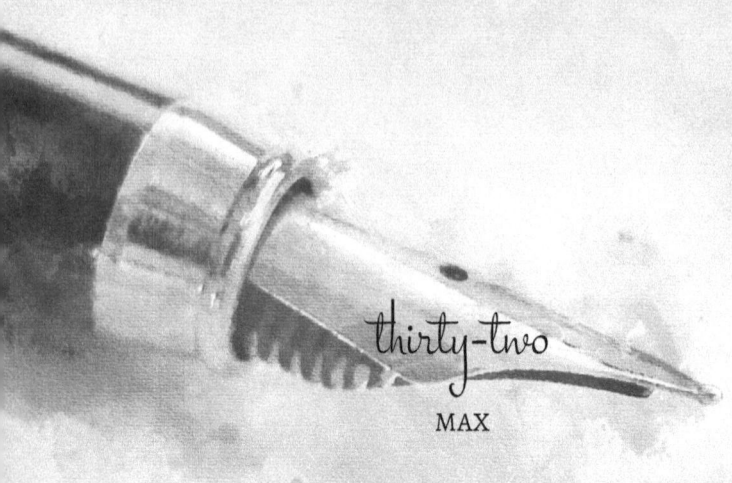

thirty-two

MAX

The letter sat there in my lap, well Posie's lap, as we both quietly processed everything Pops had to say to me. My fingers slid up and down Posie's back as she sniffled back her emotions.

"He always said you would be perfect for me one day when you grew up and got your shit together," she said.

I turned her, so that her legs were draped over the side of my own and she was sitting sideways instead of with her back to me. Those beautiful, red-rimmed eyes of hers had a steady stream of tears overflowing down her cheeks and it took every bit of willpower I had not to kiss them all away and finally make her my woman in all the ways that would bond us physically.

"When did he tell you that?"

She giggled and shrugged her shoulders, but looked away as if the answer embarrassed her and she couldn't face telling me when we were eye-to-eye. "When I was 15."

"Fifteen?" I questioned. Posie nodded in response and turned to finally lock eyes with me again. "That was before..."

"About a year before you ever even noticed me at all."

"Why didn't he tell me?"

"Probably because you were too busy trying to date every girl in our school except me."

"That's not true," I stated. When she gave me that looked that had her eyebrows arching and a smirk firmly engaged, I dug my finger into her side. She squirmed away and giggled, which helped to dry up the tears I couldn't stand to see slipping down her beautiful face.

"It was definitely true. Cheyenne wasn't the first girl I saw you kissing."

"She wasn't?"

"Nope," Posie stated as she shook her head and grinned at me. "It was the first time it hurt to see it happen, because by then Pops had been convincing me for almost a year that his grandson and I would be a perfect match if only the boy would open his eyes."

"Maybe he should have written me a letter back then," I suggested.

Posie shook her head. "No. I think Jack handled things the way he was meant to. You needed to grow up and do your thing. If we had come together sooner, Evan and I might never have grown close enough to realize we needed to work together toward our same career goals. And even though the circumstances that brought him into your world hurt us both, you were meant to be J.J.'s dad and that couldn't have happened if we were together."

That was a hard pill to swallow, but I knew that Posie was just as right as my Pops. The fingers of my right hand continued to run up and down her back as my left rested on her thigh.

"I wonder what Pops would think if he could see us now."

Posie laughed as her shinning eyes met. "He would probably say, 'About damn time' and then give us some privacy so we could seal the deal."

"Maybe the first part. I can't see him willingly giving his precious daughter privacy to be with any man, even the grandson he wanted for her." She hummed a noise in the back of her throat before changing the subject.

"I missed him even before he was gone. There were pieces of him I've had to watch fade away as he lost his battle. Promise me that you won't ever replace those rocking chairs on that porch. If you do, then I want them here at the barn. It won't be the same, but-"

I cut Posie off. "There's no way I'd ever replace them anyway, but sweetheart, if I'm living in that house, then you'll be there with me."

"I have the barn here."

"You said yourself that you wanted to expand the barn. Until you do, the farmhouse will be your home just as much as it will be mine and J.J.'s."

"Wait, does that mean you're going to move here?"

I sighed heavily. "I already had a position with the local department here. There were a few loose ends I had to tie up before J.J. and I could move. It was supposed to be a surprise, since I thought there was still time." Fuck. It hurt to know that I had to waste so much time dealing with Beth that I'd missed out on my son and me getting to spend time with Pops before he was gone.

"You were... Wait, what about," Posie swallowed and seemed to have a hard time getting the rest out.

"Beth?" I questioned. She gave a slight tip of her head to indicate that was who she meant. "She's being dealt with, but I want to go check on the information Pops said he had. Maybe it will help put a few more nails in her coffin. My lawyer is delivering papers for her to sign this week to relinquish custody of J.J. willingly."

"You think she'll do that?"

"At this point, she'd be stupid not to. I already had to get an emergency injunction against her because she basically abandoned him with a babysitter to go on a vacation. Luckily, the girl was the daughter of an officer on the force, and they called me when Beth never showed back up. She sent the girl – who was only 17 – a text telling her that she needed to watch J.J. for the rest of the week because she was out of town."

"I don't understand how someone could do something like that."

"That makes two of us. My private investigator was able to track her down and get footage of her supposed emergency. She was a on a beach in Florida with her friends. He got some good pictures of her doing coke in the bathroom and a few other things we're going to use in court if she refuses to sign."

"How did he get bathroom coke-snorting pictures?"

I chuckled then. "One of her friends needed a few hundred dollars more for her vacation and had no problem selling her out."

"Some friend."

"When you treat people – even friends – the way Beth does, it's not surprising when they turn."

"I wouldn't know."

"Of course you wouldn't. You're one of the most genuine people I know, Posie."

She snuggled into my side and put her head on my shoulder. The gesture caused her silky hair to drape over my arm as her warmth seeped into my chest and left me feeling content even in a moment when I should have felt anything but. My grandfather just died. We were discussing my son's good-for-nothing mother. I was still in limbo waiting to move closer, though at least it finally seemed to be moving forward instead of backward. Still, I felt the most contented I'd ever felt in my life just sitting in an overstuffed chair in Posie's surprisingly homey barn as she sat snuggled up in my lap.

"It would be great if we never had to move."

"Did you mean to say that out loud?" She asked, and I could hear the humor in her voice as she did.

"No, but it's not something I'd hide from you either. Having you in my arms feels like a dream, too many years in the making."

"It really does." Her agreement had a tinge of sadness mixed in. "He would have been so happy to see this."

"I'd bet anything he knows."

"You're probably right."

I closed my eyes and allowed the warmth of her body to seep deep down into my very soul. She claimed my heart years ago. It had been done in pieces; another little section was given over to her with each new letter. Every time I held my breath, as I checked the mail and hoped to hear from the one person who had been such a puzzle to me in the beginning, made me yearn for her even more.

The only thing that disturbed us was the insistent buzzing of the cell phone I had stuffed in my pocket. "You better get that," Posie explained as she slowly removed herself from my lap. She stood there and waited while I retrieved my phone, but as soon as I had it in hand, I pulled her back down onto my lap. There wasn't a single cell in my body ready to give her up just yet.

"Hey, is everything okay?" I answered immediately after dialing my mom's number back.

"Everything is fine. We wanted to check to make sure you were both okay and see if you needed someone to come pick you up."

I tucked Posie closer to me and she burrowed her head into the crook of my shoulder where I could feel each of her breaths flutter across my neck. The sensation caused goosebumps to sprout all over my arms and neck.

"We're both fine. Posie gave me a letter from Pops and we just got done reading it. Did you guys know he left his house to me?"

"Did he?" My mother asked, though I could tell by her falsely high voice that she already knew the old coot had been up to something.

"Why didn't someone tell me? I've been looking for a house to buy."

"We all thought you would come to do some in person house hunting and your pops wanted to give you the deed then, but then your visit got pushed back because of that woman."

Mom refused to say Beth's name. She hated her. In fact, on more than one occasion, I'd heard her compare Beth to Posie's mom. She probably wasn't far off, but her need to keep making that comparison needed to end. I wasn't sure if it would hurt Posie to hear that, and it wasn't something I was willing to take a chance on.

"Well, that will be dealt with soon. Is J.J. okay there with you guys? If not I can come pick him up."

"He's absolutely perfect and being spoiled by his Uncle Evan as we speak." Posie must have heard because she patted my chest and smiled into my shoulder. "There is an official reading of your grandfather's will at the end of the week. Do you think you can stick around for that?"

"I'll be here for that, if not a little longer."

"Does that mean you're still going back?"

Posie stiffened at Mom's question, but I squeezed her tighter to my body in reassurance. "I have to go back and get things packed up, but I'm thinking of taking some help with me."

"Oh! Do you need your brothers?"

"Not at all." I laughed because, once again, Mom wasn't fooling anyone with her inane questions. "I'm hoping Posie will go back with me to help get everything set for my move back home."

Mom shrieked and it sounded like she may have dropped the phone in her excitement, but none of that mattered as Posie sat up and locked eyes with me.

"You want me to go help you pack up?"

"I'm already mostly packed, but I thought it would be nice if you came and helped out and got to know J.J. a little bit before we move in officially." Posie's wide eyes turned almost panicked as she glanced around the barn. "Next door," I tacked on before also adding, "for now." She nodded her head in agreement just as my mom picked the phone back up.

"Don't worry about J.J. We have him for the night. If he needs anything, I will call you."

I pulled the phone from my ear to double check what I was hearing. "She hung up on me."

"She sounded excited to have her grandson spend the night."

"I think she sounded more excited that we were about to have a sleep over."

Posie giggled and then tipped her head back down onto my shoulder. "Is it weird to feel all of this and be happy about finally being in the same place? I feel like I'm betraying Dad's memory somehow."

"Pops wanted us together. He tried to get us on the same page for years. I don't think he'd agree that it was weird. I bet anything that he would think it was perfect. We have each other to lean on in his absence now and that's really all he wanted from the very beginning."

"I wonder why he thought you needed me to lean on?" It was a mumbled question, more like a thought slipped out than Posie was looking for an answer. Still, I couldn't stop myself from going there.

"I know exactly why. You're everything I should have been looking for all along. We enjoy enough of the same things to give us a solid building block for a relationship, but we're different enough to keep things interesting. Plus, Pops loved you. The real question would be why he thought I was the right Carter brother for you, especially since Evan is closer to you in age."

Posie's beautiful laugh filled my heart with hope. "Evan and I are too much alike. We would have either been at one another's throats or gotten bored too quickly."

"Yikes, I guess I can keep your secret for how you really feel about him," I teased.

"He knows."

Anger swirled deep in the pit of my stomach. "How would he know?"

"We talked about this very thing before." She shrugged as if it wasn't a big deal. I knew better. Evan had pretty much told me that he was interested in her at one point, but she was too hung up on me. Posie must have caught on to how I was feeling because she lifted a hand and traced it across my jaw. "He knows how I feel.

He's just as much a brother to me as Michael and Devon are. Ev thought he had a crush on me for about five minutes before he realized the same thing I've always known. We're too much alike and not compatible at all."

"That doesn't really make me feel better when I have to wonder if my brother's hugs mean something completely different than everyone assumes."

Posie giggled again and then leaned in to kiss my cheek. "Are you always this possessive?"

"I've never been possessive a day in my life."

"Really? I find that hard to believe."

"The only reason you find it hard to believe is that you are the one person who I get possessive over. I know we have a lot to figure out and it will take time to see where this thing between us is going, now that we'll be near one another, but I can tell you now that I won't be able to handle other men pawing all over you."

"Ditto," she insisted.

"Great, it's settled. Other men aren't allowed to paw all over either of us." She smacked my chest playfully and laughed.

"Other women better not be doing it either," she tacked on as I squeezed her body reassuringly.

"Come on, we need to get some food and then get some rest. I have a feeling tomorrow is going to be a long day with the family."

Posie sighed. "I suppose we can't stay in this little bubble forever, huh?"

"How about we promise to revisit the bubble as often as possible?" When she stared blankly up at me, I rephrased. "I like sitting here, with you in my lap, having random conversations about life, family, and even the future. I think this is something we should make time for every day, if possible. Even if it's just an hour out of our day, to catch up in the quiet hours when we're together."

"I'd like that a lot, Max."

"Good, it's a date then."

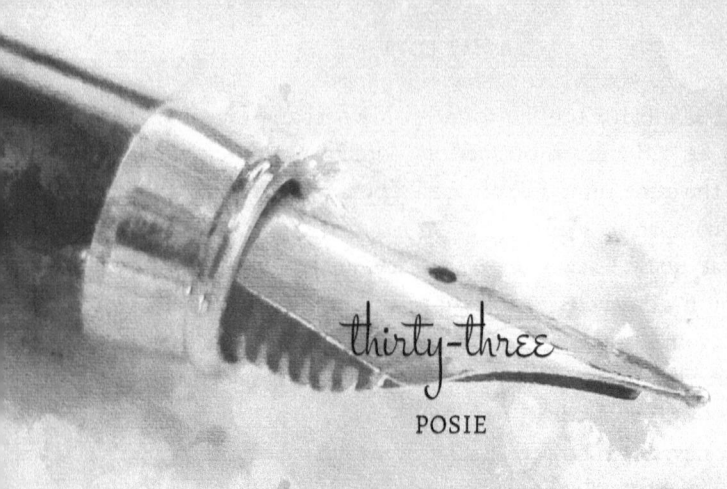

thirty-three

POSIE

Maxwell Carter stayed the night. In. My. Bed.

My brain must have short-circuited after Jack passed away because the universe wasn't this good to me. There was no way the man I'd been pining for since I was 16 years old was lying in bed next to me. His five o-clock shadow from the night before had grown in thicker and darker overnight. My fingers itched to trace across his cheeks to see if the texture of his impending beard felt the way I imagined it might.

Maybe I was a coward, but I couldn't bring myself to do it. Part of me worried that this was all a dream. Truthfully, it had only been a few days since the big breakup with my live-in boyfriend. Shouldn't I feel guilty for having a new man in bed with me so soon – even though we didn't do anything but sleep? I didn't remember getting into bed with Max. The last thing I remembered was sitting on Max's lap in my comfy chair and talking about little, every day mundane parts of our lives.

"I hope you don't mind," his gruff voice said, startling me from my thoughts. "The chair is comfortable, but sleeping in it all night would have killed my neck and back."

"I don't mind, just trying to figure out how I got here because that memory doesn't exist."

Max chuckled. "You were drooling on my chest, and I carried you to the bed."

"You honestly could have left that part out."

"Pretty sure we promised to be open and honest with one another at some point."

"Yeah, well, when it comes to seeing me do gross shit, I think we can dull the details down." We both laughed and moved a little closer to one another. Just as Max's head tipped down, and appeared to be coming in for a kiss, someone pounded on my door.

"Who the hell is knocking on your door like the police serving a warrant?"

"No clue." I pulled my phone up to log into my security camera feed. Max moved even closer, so he could see too. The minute I pulled the video feed up, we also heard him yelling at my door.

"Open up, Posie. We need to talk about this. We aren't over."

"That motherfucker had the nerve to come here the day after you lost your dad and demand you don't break up with him?"

"He might not know that Jack died. We haven't exactly announced it yet."

"He shouldn't be here at all. He was cheating on you and you caught him with his pants down."

"I did more than catch him with his pants down."

"Posie!" Mark yelled again. "Come open this door up before I break it down!"

Max jumped out of bed before I could, and it was the first time I noticed that he hadn't been wearing a shirt or pants. The man was on full display in just his boxers and there wasn't a force on Earth that could get me to look away.

"I want to see your eyes on me like that again, but right now, we need to deal with your ex."

Max was down the steps to the main floor before I could even blink, but the minute he shot out of sight, I finally came to my senses and tore off after him. The last thing any of us needed was Max getting locked up for killing Mark.

"What the fuck are you doing here banging Posie's door down?" Max growled the words at Mark as he opened my door. Both men forgot I had a security system and the alarm started to go off.

I ran over and punched in the code as Mark stood there with his jaw hanging halfway to the floor. It didn't take him long to pull himself together after noticing that I was only wearing a t-shirt that barely covered my assets. I must have been really out of it for Max to get me out of my jeans the night before without me having noticed.

"I came to apologize, but here you are being a hypocritical, cheating slut," Mark snapped.

"Watch your fucking mouth," Max warned.

"What the hell is he even doing here, Posie?" Mark asked.

"The real question is what the hell are you doing here? Max was invited, you weren't."

"Max? As in Max Carter?" Mark asked with a smug set to his jaw. "So not only are you cheating, but it's all incestuous and shit, too."

I rolled my eyes. "First, it can't be cheating, because in case you missed the memo – when I tased you in the balls after catching you fucking Jenn – we broke up. I am single. I can fuck whomever I want, where and when I choose to do it. Second, Max is not my blood relation, nor was he around for all the years that Jack Carter claimed me as his daughter, so you can fuck off with that bullshit." I took a breath and then narrowed my eyes on my ex-boyfriend. "As a matter of fact, you can simply fuck all the way off anyway."

"I'd ask what Jack thinks of you whoring around, but since its with his precious grandson he always wanted you with, I guess he doesn't care."

"He can't care seeing as how he is dead, but yeah, he very much would have chosen Max for me over a cheater who just wanted me so he could sell my land and make a tidy profit he thought would go into his pockets."

"Jack's dead?" Mark asked, obviously stunned by the news.

"Yeah, he passed away while you were too preoccupied with your sidepiece to try to make up with the girlfriend you were cheating on."

"Fiancé," he corrected.

"You never asked me to marry you."

Mark pulled a ring out of his pocket and held it up. "I had the ring already."

"Then I suggest you go give it to your fuck buddy because I sure as hell don't want it. Now, a man I considered a second father to me just passed away and the last thing that I want to do is stand here arguing with the rotten bastard who cheated on me for months. Not just the one time I caught him, but MONTHS. Fuck you, Mark. Do not ever come here again or I will make sure to turn the voltage up on my taser so that it can do more than singe your ball hair. Come to my home again, and I'll be sure you leave without working testicles."

When Mark stood there, balled his fists up as if he might hit me, and gave me a death glare, Max stepped between us. "You heard Posie. Get the fuck off our property."

"Your property?" Mark asked in a stupor.

"You heard me. Mine and Posie's. Pops was a very generous man, and as you already pointed out, he wanted us together. We own all this property and everything across the street too." Max smirked at him, and I wasn't about to call him on the bullshit that we owned all of it together. If it got Mark to leave, then he could tell him purple pigs were flying out in the pasture for all I cared.

Mark backed up a step. "This is not over," he insisted.

"Oh, it's really fuckin' over. You come near Posie again and we're going to have a big fuckin' problem."

"What do you think you can do about it? It's not like you even live here. You might be a fancy detective in that town of yours, but here, you ain't shit."

Max grinned at Mark. "I'm the new detective here in *this* town. I suggest you get right with that fact and take heed of my warning."

Mark spun around and stomped to his car, but not without looking back as he pointed his beefy finger my way. "We're not done, Posie. You know it was a mistake."

"You're right about that. Dating you was always a mistake," I countered before Max shut the door and locked it.

"Reset that alarm." He pointed out as he moved out of the way. "Are there cameras at Pops' place, too?"

"There are."

"Good. I want to know if that asshole comes back and tries to harass you. Same goes for phone calls and texts." I nodded my head at his authoritative demands and grinned at him. "What?"

"Bossy looks good on you." Before Max could reply, I turned and made my way back to the stairs. "Family might start showing up over at Jack's place, well, I guess your place, soon. We should get dressed and head over there."

"Why would they show up?"

I shrugged my shoulders. "Isn't that what people are supposed to do when someone dies?"

"What happened after your mom...?" His voice trailed off and I could almost taste the regret in the air after he thought better of what he asked me.

"No one came to offer condolences about my mom because they never really liked her. Jack Carter was a beloved and respected man of this community, though. I'm shocked no one has shown up yet."

"I suppose you're right. We'll probably be knee deep in weird casseroles by the end of the day." I snickered at the way Max shuddered.

"This might sound strange, but I always wondered if it would be awkward between us in person," I admitted.

"What do you mean?"

"I guess since you never really knew me before you left town, I thought if we were ever really together in person, it would be awkward and not at all the easy banter we have in our letters and emails. I guess, maybe that it would be too good to be true if we were as at ease in person as..." I didn't get to finish my thought because Max reached over and grabbed my hips to pull me to him.

"I never had a doubt that you'd be as amazing in person as in your letters."

"No?"

"Nope. In fact, I kicked my own ass a lot over the years for not taking the time to get to know you when I was home. The only saving grace in me not doing that is I got to leave and make a fresh start for myself. I think if I'd gotten to know you and stuck around for you, there may have been some resentment due to unfulfilled dreams, especially when I was younger."

"Jack always said things work out when they're meant to, not when we want them to."

Max rolled his eyes. "Funny coming from a man who tried so hard to put us in each other's orbits."

"He also said sometimes things needed a little shove in the right direction." We both laughed because if Jack were here with us, we'd be teasing him while he told us how absolutely right he had been all along. "I hope to one day be as wise, kind, and loving as that man. He was my hero."

"He was mine, too, sweetheart."

Max moved us so that he held me in a tight hug instead of simply holding onto my hips the way he had done when he first stopped me from moving upstairs.

"Let's go get dressed and over to Pops' place."

"Your place now," I corrected.

Max shook his head. "That will forever be Pops' house. I could live in it for a million years and my earliest memories would still be of sitting on that porch with my grandparents as they sneaked cookies or candy to my brothers and me while our parents huffed and puffed about having to deal with us."

"The only reason I'm not completely crippled by the loss of him is because I know without a single doubt that he is with your grandma right now. They've missed one another."

"That'll be us one day, Posie. If I go first, I'll be waiting until you're back in my arms. If you do..." He swallowed thickly. "I'll be just like my Pops sitting on the rocking chair beside yours, talking to your spirit until you guide me home to your arms on the other side."

"Max," I whispered. "You can't know that. We haven't even... We aren't even dating."

"The way I see it, we did something far greater than dating."

"How do you figure?"

"We got to know one another over years of letters, with no physical temptation to get in the way."

I raised an eyebrow at that and gave him a wide-eyed stare. "There was plenty of physical temptation, Max. Have you seen yourself in a mirror?"

He laughed at me. "I meant that we weren't in proximity to take what we had to a physical place, so we nurtured the heart of us first. We have years of learning the ins and outs of one another to fall back on where most couples don't. I promise you, there isn't a bit of doubt in my heart when I tell you that we are going to spend the rest of our lives together."

"I really like the sound of that."

"Good because that means Pops is truly at rest, since his job here on Earth is well and truly done."

"Dammit..." I sniffled. He was right. Pops wouldn't have anything left to worry about if he knew that his final breath brought us together after everything.

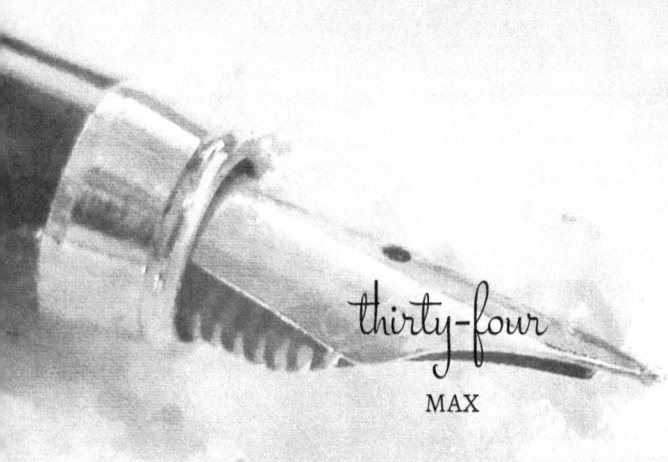

thirty-four

MAX

Ever since the night before when I'd laid there beside Posie staring at her beautiful features as she slept peacefully, I'd wanted desperately to know what it was like to have her beneath me. To taste her. To make the woman of my dreams come from everything I always dreamed of doing to her.

I knew it wasn't the right time then. She was worn out after caring for my Pops, dealing with her very recent breakup with the cock weasel ex of hers, and then the death of Pops that still felt unreal. Even I expected to see him at his house whenever we made our way there. There was too much going on to add intimacy to our relationship even though I desperately wanted to. When Posie grabbed a shirt to throw on and started to lift the one she'd been wearing last night over her head, I had to look away. It was either that or pounce on her then and there.

Instead, I reached over and caught hold of the pants I'd taken off the night before and stepped back into them. My clothes were still packed away in my truck and my family had driven it, along with my son, back to my parents' house the day before.

By the time I got my day-old clothes back on, Posie was also dressed in a simple t-shirt, jeans, and slip-on shoes. We locked up the barn and walked over to the house my grandparents had lived in my entire life. When we got to the porch steps, it became harder and harder to put one foot in front of the other. Posie seemed to hesitate as well with her eyes glued to the rocking chairs.

"He should be sitting there," she said so quietly that I had to focus to hear her. While the man had been my grandfather all my life, there was no way to deny that the bond between Posie and Jack Carter was stronger than even the one he had with his grandsons. She had truly become his daughter after all the years he spent looking out for her.

"Come on," I said as I grabbed her hand and tugged her onto the porch and down to the chairs. You take that one." I pointed at the one my grandmother used to occupy every time we came over. Then, I sat down in the chair my Pops always sat in. Once we were both seated, I reached over and took Posie's hand in my own and we sat there staring out across the street at the home she lived in the last time these two chairs were occupied with a couple who loved one another fiercely.

"The day in the barn all those years ago, I went home and told my dad about you."

"Did you tell him what a weirdo loser I was?" She asked with a hint of amusement in her voice.

I shook my head. "I was so confused that day. There was a part of me that needed to protect my Pops from someone I thought might be taking advantage of him, but then there was the other side who was curious about the sad girl hiding out in his barn."

"Well, that sounds loads better." Sarcasm dripped from her lips right alongside the words as she continued to avoid my gaze by staring off into the distance.

"I wasn't ready to know you back then. My dumbass was too selfish, too ready to get the hell out of here and leave this little ass town in the dust."

"What if you decide you hate it here again?"

"Nah. I've come to appreciate this town, what it represents, and who lives here more than any other place on the planet."

"Still, you might change your mind."

"Posie, the thing I stupidly left here to find was my own identity outside of my family's influence. I found that years ago. You even helped me do that through our letters. Staying gone longer than necessary was all about bad timing and being trapped in a situation I wasn't able to get out of quickly. I wanted to come back years ago. This town, these people, my family, you... I want J.J. to be raised here where I know good people will always be looking out for him. I want the peace of mind of knowing that the people I love the most are close, so if anything ever happens, there is someone that we can count on. My family needs to know that they can count on me to be there for them too."

"It's a powerful feeling, having your family surround you. You Carters are good at making someone feel like they have an Army at their back." Posie grinned over at me as she said that and it hit me, maybe for the first time, that this girl who I had fallen in love with through many years-worth of letters was already a part of my family. A very loved and cherished part.

"I never want to force you to live without them at your back either. I need you to understand that the decision to come back here was an easy one for me because it was past time to bring my ass home."

"Okay."

"Okay," I mimicked with a wink as we both turned to see my mom's car pull in followed by the rest of my family and my truck that was being driven by my dad.

"Looks like the calvary have arrived." Her assessment made me grin as my parents each got out of the vehicles they were driving and approached the porch first.

"Nice to see those chairs getting some use," Dad called out. From the corner of my eye, I noticed Posie run her hand over the arm of the chair she gently rocked in. As soon as my parents hit the porch, my woman stood to greet them. My son, who had been helped out of the truck by Evan came barreling up to me with his arms wide open.

"Dad, Uncle Evan had so much fun wiff me."

"He did?" I questioned and glanced over to my brother who laughed at his nephew's assessment of how the night went.

"Yup. We pwayed cars and then we drew pictures." While my son leaned in, to make it harder for his poor uncle to hear him, he forgot to lower his voice for the quiet part. "He's not good at making people wike me."

"That's impossible, buddy. We won't tell Uncle Evan that he can't even draw a stick figure right. That might hurt his feelings," I admitted rather loudly while trying to hold back my laughter.

"It's so good to have you both here, even if..." Mom started to say as Posie hugged her tighter.

"Let's go on in the house. It's starting to get muggy as hell already. Too early for air this thick." Dad complained. He moved to open the door before stopping. "Sorry, the house is yours now, Son. Have you been inside yet?"

It was like I was being called out by my own dad for having a sleep over with Posie. "Where did Daddy sweep last night?" My own son asked. I rolled my eyes at my dad as Posie giggled by my side. The noise caught J.J.'s attention making his head snap around. "Dad!" He yelled and pointed at her. "It's Posie! She's here!"

"She is, buddy." Posie seemed shell-shocked to be called out by my son, who I didn't think she'd ever officially met. He was too young to pick up on the fact that he startled her though, and instead, ran over and threw his arms around her legs to squeeze her tight. "Posie! Daddy wuvs you."

Mom sniffled as Posie leaned in and fluffed my boy's hair. Once she had him untangled from her legs, she bent so that they were eye-to-eye as he stood there, and she kneeled before him. "I could use a helper to get breakfast started for everyone. Do you think you can be my helper today?"

"In the kitchen?" He asked with comically wide eyes.

Posie nodded emphatically. "Yep, we have to crack some eggs," she started, but before she could get any further my son yelled, "YES!" Then he took off for the door after he made a fuss of yanking Posie to her feet. She followed in dramatic fashion as Dad held the door open for them.

"Well, that was a sight to see." Mom sniffed back her emotion and dabbed at her eyes as we all followed them into the house. Despite not having changed a bit since the last time I visited, the house felt empty. It was missing its soul with Pops' departure. He should have been there to see his great-grandson enamored with his favorite girl.

Before I made it inside the house, my dad reached out to grab my arm and hold me back. After Mom and my brothers made their way inside, Dad leaned in close and spoke quietly.

"It's not lost on me how much you've been wanting to be close to her over the years, but I needed to remind you that Posie has been through a lot in a relatively short amount of time, Son. She just lost the second man she considered her dad and that was on the heels of breaking up with her live-in boyfriend who she caught in the act of cheating on her with the woman who previously sabotaged her 25th birthday and purposely set out to mess things up between the two of you."

"I am aware of everything that has happened. All we did was talk and reconnect last night. Don't worry, your pseudo-sister's virtue was safe from me." I tried to make light because it was weird to have my own dad throw a caution flag up on the situation.

He shook his head. "Posie probably doesn't see it this way, because she considered your Pops to be her dad, but she's like a daughter to your mom and me, too."

I couldn't help but chuckle. "Things are going to feel really weird when we send out the invitations and you're listed as her father-brother and my father."

Dad smacked me on the side of the head but turned his face because he couldn't hide his own laughter. "Dad would be laughing his ass off over that."

"Pops did set this whole thing into motion," I reminded him.

"He would have been ecstatic to walk out and see the two of you sitting in those rocking chairs this morning."

"For a minute there, before you guys pulled up, it felt like he was there."

"Probably so, Son." He threw his arm around my shoulder and tugged me closer to the door. "Now, remember, that girl means a lot to me – to the whole family, really – so you treat her well."

"Is she going to get the same lecture about dating your son?" I teased.

Dad shook his head. "Nah, because she doesn't need it. That girl has been infatuated with you before you ever even noticed her."

"That part kills me."

Again, my dad shook his head as he held the door for me to pass first. "It shouldn't. You weren't ready for her yet, Max. If you had really taken an interest back in high school, and then left, things probably wouldn't have ended up being long-term and it could have caused issues with her being so comfortable around the rest of us. Everything happens for a reason."

"Yeah, so I keep being reminded." We walked in just in time to see J.J. splatter an egg across the kitchen as he slammed it down on the counter.

"I think we can scratch chef off future career paths for destructo-boy," Evan called out.

"I can dwal stick people," My son taunted his uncle back.

"Fair enough," Evan laughed as the tips of his ears turned red. "I have Posie to draw pretty pictures for me, though."

"No!" J.J. yelled at him. "Posie is ours, right Daddy?"

I had to clamp my lips down between my teeth to keep from revealing the shit eating grin that wanted to sprout. Instead, I nodded my head and watched as my son did the same. "You can dwawl with me later, Posie."

"I would love to, J.J. How about we get that sticky egg cleaned off your hands?" She took him to the sink and held him lifted up between her body and the counter while Mom tackled cleanup on the egg splattered across the kitchen island and part of the floor.

I HAD BEEN RIGHT ABOUT THE NUMBER OF WEIRD casseroles that were delivered at Pops' house that day. As soon as word started to spread, townsfolk who had known my grandfather started popping in to offer their condolences. According to my parents, most everyone knew that Pops' health had been on the decline, so there weren't a whole lot of people shocked by his loss.

By the time the last person who didn't belong in our immediate family left, everyone was wiped out and emotionally drained. J.J. had fallen asleep on the couch an hour earlier, despite the noise of everyone who left saying their goodbyes in that room.

"I'll go make a bed up for him," Posie managed to garble out through a yawn.

"We can take him back with us again for the night," Mom offered.

"Thanks, but I think it will be better if he wakes up in the same house he's been in all day." Posie climbed the stairs and was out of sight before Mom could respond.

"I thought maybe the two of you needed time to grieve."

"So do you and Dad," I reminded her. "We'll be fine. If we're not, we'll call. I promise."

Despite how exhausted she looked; Mom managed a small

smile. "I really like the fact that you're throwing out "we" so naturally."

"It's been a long time coming. We're not really there yet, but I have hope that it will all work out now."

"Me too. Our girl will be good for you and J.J. Love you, Max. See you tomorrow."

"Careful going home."

After my parents left, Evan was the last man standing. "You headed out too?" I asked him.

He shook his head. "If you don't mind, I'd like to stay the night. I'm too tired to go anywhere and I can run interference with the little man if he gets up early, so you two can sleep in without questions being asked."

"Not that it's any of your business, but I think we're all too tired for..."

"Not my business and don't want to hear anything you might have been about to say about you and my sister hooking up." Evan mock gagged. "It fucking sucks that Pops' death was the catalyst to get you back here, but I'm really happy you are. She deserves to get exactly what she wants in life and that's always been you, Max."

"You once told me you had a thing for her," I reminded my younger brother.

"Nah." He sighed and ran his fingers through his hair to push it back out of his face. "Posie is special. I loved her – still do. It's not in that way, though. Never was. I was always jealous of the time that you being with her would take from me. I love working with that girl. Love hanging out and doing movie nights or going on silly little mini adventures to get inspiration for our graphic novels. There was a time when I was selfish enough to make you believe I would step in and make her mine." He choked out a laugh. "If Posie knew that she'd kick my ass from here to the end of the Earth and back."

"Don't worry, your secret is safe with me." I glanced around. "I'm guessing you have a room picked out for the night?"

"I'll take the one next to your boy and leave my door open. You can go join Posie in her room."

I offered a quick nod to my brother as he moved to lock up. "I'll check to make sure everything's secure. You head on up."

I grabbed my son off the couch and carried him upstairs to find Posie coming out of one of the bedrooms. "The bed is all made up for him," she whispered and watched as I went to lay my son down and quickly removed his shoes before tucking him in.

When I moved back into the hallway, Posie had secured a baby gate across the hall, so that J.J. wouldn't be able to tumble down the steps if he woke up sleepy.

"Thanks for that," I whispered as Evan came upstairs and stepped over the gate.

"Night, Sis." He leaned in and kissed the top of Posie's head before tipping his chin up at me. "Night, Max."

I offered a return tip of my chin and wrapped my arms around Posie. She looked like she could crumble at any moment.

"Night Evan. If you or J.J. need me-"

"I know where to find you," he insisted after cutting me off.

I followed Posie into the bedroom she still had at Pops' place. It no longer looked like a girly bedroom. Instead, there were tons of pictures hanging on the walls of her with my family over the years. There was a giant teddy bear sitting on a chair in the corner. I assumed it was the graduation gift she had been given by my parents because he wore a graduation cap.

Posie's gaze followed my own and she smiled warmly at the bear. "I bet J.J. would love cuddling up in his arms to watch his shows in the morning."

"Nah, that bear is special to you."

She waved off my concern. "He is special and that's why I want to share him with J.J. I don't believe in having things simply sit around and collect dust. The bear deserves to be well-loved, and I have a feeling your son is just the person to do that."

"You are so fucking perfect," I whispered into her hair as I helped her out of the shirt she'd put on that morning. "Why does it feel like a week has gone by since we got dressed this morning?"

"Grief, plus too many energy vampires draining our reserves today." Her list was short, but highlighted the biggest reasons we were both bushed.

Posie moved to her dresser and yanked out a tank top and a girly set of boxer shorts to put on. When I groaned, she chuckled softly. "I'm not sleeping naked with your son just down the hall for the first time."

"I know. I'm going to go see if Evan has something here I can borrow. My bags are still out in the truck, and he's already locked up."

Truthfully, I would have slept in boxers again, but I didn't think I could handle watching her get changed. After removing her shirt, my dick was already semi-hard. It had been a long day, as much as I wanted to sink inside of her and never come back out, we both needed some rest first.

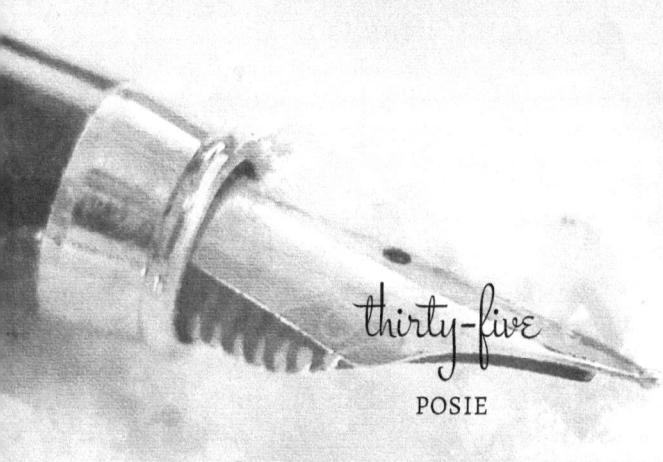

thirty-five

POSIE

Max never did come back to the bedroom after leaving to go find some clothes. I waited for him to do just that, until I heard an excited little boy voice harassing his uncle. After it became apparent that J.J. was wide awake, there were no more reasons to wait in my bedroom. Instead, I grabbed my human-sized graduation bear off the chair in the corner of my room and tucked him up under my arm. Then, I thought better of it and held him in such a way that it appeared the bear was walking beside me.

As I descended the steps to the main floor, I heard a squeal and the pitter-patter of little boy feet chasing after me. His father and uncle joined him in watching me walk downstairs with the bear while having a one-way conversation with him.

"Of course we're going to get breakfast. People two states away heard your tummy grumbling this morning." Little boy giggles followed behind. "What? No! My tummy grumbles were not louder than yours!"

"Daddy," I heard J.J. whisper-yell. "What do giant teddy bears eat?"

"You really want pancakes again?" I asked the bear. "Fine, I'll make us some."

"Can I hab some too?" J.J. asked.

"I'm making enough pancakes to feed all the people in this house plus the stinky, giant bear." J.J.'s giggles were a balm to my wounded soul. It was day two without Jack in my life. It felt as though he'd be waiting downstairs for me. Instead, the house felt lonely, as if it was missing its heart.

The bear grew heavier in my arm at the thought of Jack not being downstairs to see its arrival along with the peals of laughter coming from the little boy following us down.

At the bottom of the stairs, I tripped over a tennis shoe and nearly went tumbling along with the bear. "Dammit, Evan. How many times..." I cut myself off because that was Jack's rant for him. As soon as I realized my dad's words were about to fall from my mouth I stopped short and then laughed. He was here in spirit.

"I swear, I didn't leave them there." Evan came over and helped me by taking the bear off my hands. "I'll help the big guy to the table while you pull yourself together, crackpot."

My laughter continued to flow out of me until the tears of joy turned to ones of sadness for missing the man who had been my rock for more than a decade.

"Go with your uncle, J.J."

"No. Posie is sad." Little boy arms wrapped around my body where I had slid to the floor in an effort to stop myself from falling hard after tripping over the shoe. "Don't be sad. Big hugs makes it better."

I wrapped my arms around the little boy and felt his father engulf us in his embrace too. Their warmth filled me up again and made it possible to keep moving forward. "Sorry, I just missed my dad, especially after nearly chewing Evan out with the same words I heard Jack lob at him year-after-year whenever we stayed at the house with him."

"It's okay, Posie, we know."

"My daddy is gonna marry you some day."

J.J.'s admission shocked all of us. Evan had come back from depositing the bear in the kitchen and stopped short before he got to our pile on the floor. I glanced up to see him grinning from ear to ear.

"Well, I guess there aren't any secrets in this family," Evan teased.

"That was supposed to be a surprise, Jay," his father admonished playfully.

"Posie gonna marry me too?"

I ruffled his hair and leaned in to give him a kiss on the cheek. "Sure thing, kiddo. Maybe we should go eat first, though."

He jumped up and pumped his fist before sticking his tongue out at his dad and running off to the kitchen. "Looks like little man just stole your woman right out from underneath you." Evan laughed as he taunted his brother.

Jack didn't want a funeral or to be buried anywhere. He wanted his ashes scattered at a special place on the property where he had done the same with his own wife years earlier. The piece of land, near a little natural spring-fed pond in a clearing surrounded by a copse of trees, was deeded to a family trust so that no one person owned it, and it could not be sold off out from under another family member.

When we all found out about it, everyone agreed that they wanted the same done with their remains if they should die before everyone else. While morbid, it was also a beautiful moment to know that we all wanted the same thing, to be together again in the end.

Two days after we scattered Jack's ashes together, Max came to me and asked to talk. My nerves were on high alert because over the past couple days, there had been so much going on that we didn't have any time to really spend together. Not in the ways I wish we could have anyway.

"What's going on?" I asked when we both found a seat out on the porch in those old rockers.

"J.J. and I need to go back to finish packing up our stuff and get things settled with Beth. I have a court date next Thursday."

My eyes widened at that. "I didn't realize you were going to court or that you had to wait around that long."

"She refused to sign the papers when she realized I haven't been in town."

I sighed. Max had been hopeful that Beth would be out of their lives soon, but something in my gut told me that snake of a woman wouldn't disappear as quietly as he seemed to think she would.

"Okay, what do you need from me?"

"I need you to come back with us."

"Seriously?"

"We talked about it before and you agreed, but since then, we've been kind of swamped and I wasn't sure if..."

I reached over and put my hand on his thigh to reassure him.

"I am not backing out on going with you. Of course, I will be there if you want me to be. I didn't know if my being there would cause more problems for you two. Beth sounds..." I hesitated to say it, but as Max remained patient and quiet by my side I shrugged my shoulders and dove into my feelings. "Well, frankly, she sounds a lot like my own mother was. I worry for J.J.'s safety. Knowing what my mom did to the woman my dad was in love with, I also worry that Beth will go nuts if I'm around."

"Can I tell you a secret?"

"I hate secrets," I admitted.

"The reason Beth started going off the rails before is because I was trying to get J.J. used to the idea that you were going to be in our lives soon. He started going back to her telling her all about the lady his dad was going to marry, and Beth started to spiral."

I gasped. "Did you do that on purpose?"

"Nope. As a matter of fact, I tried not to make a huge deal about it and included talk of you in with the rest of the family, so it felt normal. I think my boy was looking for a mother figure who actually cared about him, and he ran with the fantasy of someone who was going to come into his life and be better than his mom was."

"That's so sad, Max."

"It really fucking is. If there was one thing I could change in my life, it would be to change who my boy's mother is. He didn't deserve for it to be that crazy bitch."

I squeezed his thigh and leaned over to place a kiss on his cheek. Since Jack died, we had moved the chairs closer and took the little table between them out of the way. It sat on the other side of the chair I always sat in, and we got a matching one for the other side of Max's chair.

"I will be there by your side."

"Thank fuck."

WE LEFT THE FOLLOWING MORNING AND GOT IN BY MID-afternoon on Saturday. When we got inside Max's house, it was in shambles. There were half full moving boxes everywhere.

"Shit," he hummed the word as we all glanced around at the chaos my two boys left in their wake in their packing attempt. "I guess I forgot how bad everything looked here."

I chuckled and held J.J. close to me. "I'm hungwy," he complained.

"How about you order us some food, since I doubt you have anything we can make quickly. Then, after we get the little monster fed, so he stops growling at us, I can help you organize this."

"There's a reason I'm going to marry you one day."

I grinned at Max. "Well, let's hope I live up to your organizational expectations then."

After we got J.J. situated with some crayons and a bunch of left over boxes to decorate, we started in on labeling the boxes Max already had full, as we sealed them up. After the food arrived, his son went down for a nap and his best friend Jake came over to help out.

"It's good to see you two finally together and not running the hell away from one another," Jake teased when Max wrapped his arms around me after grabbing us all a beer from the pack Jake brought with him.

"It's a long time coming."

"Too bad you didn't stick around that last time you were here. I feel like I owe you both an apology for that day."

I waved Jake off. "Nope, you really don't. Me showing up was a total surprise, so you couldn't have known."

"I did though," Jake admitted. "Obviously, I didn't know you were coming that day, but I thought it was unhealthy that Max was always pining away after a girl he couldn't be with. I knew the girl I was seeing back then was bringing a friend along."

"So, you lied to me?" Max asked him while he rolled his eyes. It was clear he knew it had been a setup all along.

"Well, if I had known she was a clinging weirdo, I never would have tried to set you up with what basically amounted to a Beth Junior, but yeah, I thought you needed to get out and start dating women who were accessible to you. It feels like I fucked things up between you guys."

"Nah. We weren't ready for one another then. Don't sweat it," I told Jake and Max must have agreed or liked the fact that I let his buddy off the hook because he squeezed me tight and then kissed the top of my head. Just as he was about to lean in and kiss my mouth, someone knocked loudly on the door.

"It's after ten," Jake growled.

"If they wake up J.J., we're going to have a problem. I don't care who that is," Max added as he let me go to answer the door.

"I heard you were back in town, baby," a woman's voice cooed to Max. I didn't hesitate to go see who in the hell thought she could show up at Max's door at night and call him 'baby'. I wasn't surprised to see Beth standing there in nothing but an open coat and skimpy lingerie.

It was my turn to roll my eyes as Jake walked up beside me.

"What is going on?" Beth snapped as she snatched her coat closed. It barely covered her bottom half, but at least her boobs were hidden from sight.

"What the hell are you doing here, Beth?"

"I came to welcome you back home and give you another chance to realize what you're missing out on," she snapped at him.

"I'm not missing out on anything," Max informed her as he pulled me into his side. Jake stood slightly out of the way, and I wasn't sure if Beth could see him there, but I noticed his cell phone was up and made sure Max slid closer to me, so Jake had a clear view to film whatever happened.

"What in the hell is that whore doing here? Hasn't she caused enough problems for us?"

"There was never an "us", Beth. You took advantage of me when I was not able to consent and got yourself pregnant the one time we had sex. I'll remind you again, I don't even remember that happening. I refused to date you time and again when you badgered me to do so until I had to threaten legal action against you."

"That's not true," she huffed.

"Oh, it's entirely true and on record, so don't try to lie to cause problems because Posie is here."

"Such a stupid name," Beth bit out. I rolled my eyes again. The woman was ridiculous.

"What in the hell are you doing at my house after ten at night, banging down my door, and showing up in lingerie?"

"I told you that I came to make things good between us again."

"There was never an 'us', Beth. I won't tell you that again. You have repeatedly been told that you are not welcome at my residence. When you were allowed to pick up our son, we always did that at a neutral location, never at my house because you are not welcome here."

"I thought you would change your mind," she suggested as she ran her fingers down the seam of the coat she allowed to spread open again.

"I do not, under any circumstance, want you in my life, my son's life, anywhere near where we live, work, or go to school. I do not want further contact with you and our son won't have any either. If he changes his mind about that when he turns 18, then that's his decision. We are a long way off from him reaching that age, considering he's only 3 right now."

"Max, stop this. You're embarrassing me."

"No, you're embarrassing yourself. You shouldn't be here."

"He's my son and you are my man!" Beth screamed at the top of her lungs just as a man walked up with his cell phone held high, obviously recording the event as well.

"Everything alright here, Max?"

"I just instructed Beth that she needed to leave and should have never shown up at my house."

"She's been slinking around the house a few times since you've been out of town. I guess she didn't know when you'd be back and kept trying her luck. Have it on my cameras and saved the files for you," Max's neighbor informed him.

"Appreciate that, man. Beth, you need to go."

"NO! My boy is in there! You are mine! You were always supposed to be mine, not hers!" She screamed and then lunged as if to attack me. Both Jake and the neighbor continued to film the scene, for use as evidence later, while Max stepped between Beth and me and took the brunt of her attack as he pushed me deeper into the house away from her.

"Daddy!" J.J. called out, having been woken by the noise. I went to him, and he ran willingly into my arms. "No!" He screamed as he saw his mom standing there attacking his father. "No mommy. Don't want to. No. Pwease, no mommy."

My heart broke in that moment as I wondered what this poor boy had endured when he had been required to stay with his mother. Max took a solid hit to his jaw as he snapped around to see the way his son reacted to his mother.

Beth took the opportunity to charge at me, once again, even though I was holding her son in my arms. "He's not yours. You can't have them! I will kill you, bitch!" The woman screamed as Max tackled her to the ground. "I will kill you too and then I'll kill that little brat. He was supposed to make you stay with me and he failed. Max is mine!" She screamed as her wild, crazy eyes locked on mine. "He is MINE. Mine. You can keep the little brat, I'll find a way to take you both out. Max is mine."

"You're insane!" Max yelled as he took something from Jake and slapped it down on Beth. It took a minute for me to realize he was cuffing her hands behind her back. "Stop this, Beth! J.J. doesn't need to see or hear this shit."

"I will kill him and her too," she screamed at the top of her lungs.

That finally pulled me out of my shocked state and I moved quickly to take J.J. back down the hall and into his room at the back of the house. When we got there, I started to hum to him to block out the sound of his mother's screaming. It didn't do much good, considering we could still hear her, but J.J. sank into me and his poor little muscles relaxed a bit.

"No mommy," he chanted over and over again into my shoulder as my heart broke for the little boy.

"No mommy, I promise." I cooed the words into his ear as I ran my hands reassuringly over his back and kissed his head repeatedly. "You're safe, baby. I won't let anyone hurt you, okay?"

"Otay. Posie, be my mommy?" He asked after a series of hiccups racked his poor little body.

"I will always be here for you, baby. I won't let anyone hurt you."

"Otay."

"Okay. I love you sweet boy," I offered the only comfort I could, my truth where he was concerned.

"Wuv you too." His voice was a hoarse whisper as he settled his head on my shoulder and calmed a little more.

I sat there rocking his body against mine in a gentle back and forth sway as I heard sirens approach and then listened as statements were taken and Beth was carted away. An officer came in to speak to me, and thankfully, she did so whisper quiet as J.J. had fallen asleep on me. I refused to relinquish my hold on him and spoke in quiet tones about what I'd witnessed. I didn't think it was necessary, considering there were two men filming the whole scene from different angles, but if it helped keep her away from my Carter boys, then that was what I would do.

Once we finally got J.J. down in his bed, Jake volunteered to sleep in the room with him in case he woke up with nightmares. Max guided me across the hall to where he only had a mattress left on the floor with a sheet and blanket draped over it. The frame had been disassembled and was off to the side ready to be packed up with the rest of his belongings.

"I'm so sorry you had to deal with that," Max apologized.

"No honey, I'm sorry you and J.J. had to deal with her. There's no telling what she has done to traumatize that boy so much. He did not want to go with her. His little body was shaking in my arms before she ever even threatened to kill anyone."

Max scrubbed his hands down his face, and for the first time that night, I saw as tears trailed down his face. "I worried about what she was doing to him. He started wetting the bed again a few months before the incident where she left him with the babysitter, but I had no proof of anything. There were no marks on him. I couldn't put hidden cameras inside her apartment. I felt so fucking helpless. A parent should never have to feel elated that their kid was abandoned, but I did. I was never scared for him because he was in good hands, but when his babysitter called to tell me his mom never came to pick him up... My instant reaction was pure fucking joy because I finally had something that could be used against her."

"I understand. You have a hell of a lot more now, and don't even need to use what Jack had gathered about her."

"Yeah, I do. I just wish you and J.J. didn't have to be here for that."

"Max, I'm here for both of you. I'm glad I was here to help him through that while you dealt with her. It enabled Jake to keep filming everything while you took care of the problem. I'm so glad that I was here to take care of him through that. I wish the shock of the situation hadn't kept me frozen so long, but hearing the things she said was unavoidable at any rate."

"Let's forget about the crazy bitch for the rest of the night. I need to hold you in my arms, sweetheart."

"We can do that," I said as we undressed and climbed onto the mattress together. The minute his arms wrapped around me, I was lost to the comfort he provided and needed more all at once. "Max, I need you."

"Need you too, sweetheart."

Before he could say another word, I moved down his body after throwing the sheet off of us and placed kisses all along his chest and abdomen as I went. "Posie, that's not what I meant."

"It's exactly what I meant," I told him. Going down on a man wasn't something I had a lot of experience with. I hadn't liked to do it with Mark because he was too aggressive with the way he used me. With Max, I wanted to please him, to ease some of the tension I still felt rolling off him in waves.

He blamed himself for what his son and I witnessed earlier, instead of blaming the crazy bitch for being a psycho nutcase. When I got down to his cock, I took it in hand and licked from the base to tip and back down again before going lower where I sucked on his balls.

"Holy fucking shit, Posie," he growled. "Feels so good, sweetheart."

The little anxiety I felt at giving him oral drained away in that moment to be replaced with a sense of power. Not in the sense that I had power *over* him, but that I had the power to make him feel good and forget his troubles, even if briefly. After sucking his balls into my mouth and massaging them with my tongue a few times, I relinquished them and licked all the way back up to his tip before sucking him into my mouth and down to the back of my throat until my lips wrapped around the base of his dick.

"Fucking hell, woman. You're about to make me shoot off faster than I ever have in my life."

I released his cock and smiled up at him. "Don't hold back on my account. I'll bring him back to life again when we're done here," I promised with a teasing tone.

I could have sworn I heard him say something about, "So many regrets." It wasn't something to take personally though because I knew exactly what he meant. Like me, he wished we had been doing this a lot sooner.

I continued to bob my mouth up and down his cock while massaging his balls with my hand. Every time I gave a little tug on them, his cock jerked in my mouth and spurted a little more precum. He was so close to tipping over the edge that I swallowed him back down to the base and sucked hard once there.

I didn't have a gag reflex that ruined the moment, so I stayed there sucking until the need to breathe again won out. Three more rounds of that and Max groaned as his release slid right down my throat while his hands grasped at my hair. It was almost as if he was at war with himself as one tried to hold me down while the other pulled tightly on the hair clasped in his grip, as if to pull me off his cock.

That was just the beginning of our night together, making one another forget that there were evil bitches who ruined things for people in the world. Max made me feel, forget, and find heaven itself in return and both of us ended up a little worse for the wear when his son woke us in the morning.

We got the moving truck packed up and Jake offered to drive it to our hometown for us, since we still had to stick around for court in a few days.

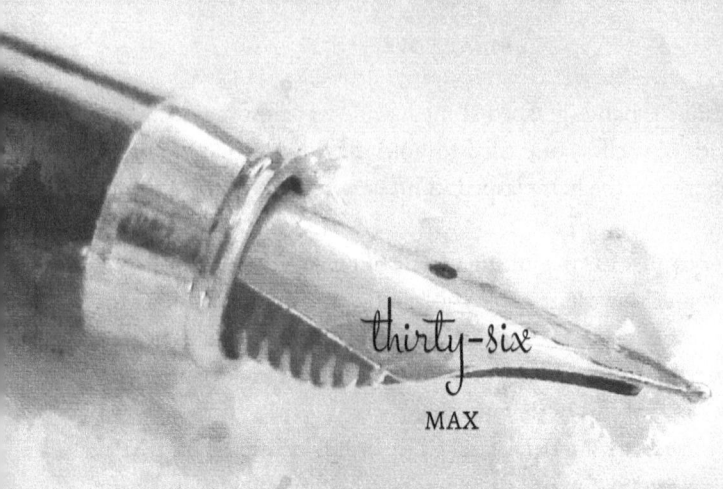

thirty-six

MAX

Not only did Beth have parental rights to my son terminated, but she also racked up a slew of criminal charges. Thanks to my previous court order stating that she wasn't to come to my home, and my neighbor's video evidence that she had done so many times, including trying to find a way into my home when she realized I wasn't there, stalking charges were added to the others she faced. She had already been charged with communicating threats, assault, child endangerment, trespassing, unlawful entry of an occupied dwelling, and possession of a schedule II-controlled substance that Beth did not have a prescription for.

She was remanded to jail until her criminal trial since there was no one available to bail her ass out. Having her locked up made for a less stressful move. There was no doubt that Beth would be able to find us easily once she was released, but with the combination of stalking, violence, and controlled substance charges, we hoped that she would be in prison for a good long while after her trial. I was also issued a restraining order against Beth for my son, Posie, and myself just in case justice wasn't served the way we hoped.

After moving all of our stuff into Pops' house, and storing

some of it, I was crushed when Posie tried to go home to the barn on our first night back.

My family were all gathered in the living room as we recounted everything that happened with Beth when Posie yawned for the fifth time. J.J. had been down for the count two hours earlier. "Why don't you go on up to bed?" I asked her.

She stood and nodded but didn't head for the stairs. "Yeah, I'm wiped out." When she headed in the direction of the front door I ran after her.

"Where are you going?"

"To my place," she insisted.

"No."

"Yes."

"Posie, why?"

She huffed her way through another yawn. "Max, your son has been through enough."

"Exactly why you should be here if he wakes up. He loves you."

"I love him too, but he just went through a whole ordeal with his mother, moved his belongings to a new place, and it hasn't really settled in yet that he's not going back to the only home he's ever really known besides Beth's apartment. He needs time to adjust before we throw me into the mix in a permanent way. I adore him, but I'm still a new person in his life. I'm also a new relationship for you, whether we've written letters to one another for years or not."

"I'm his dad, and don't see a problem."

"That's because in your mind we've sort of been together all along, even though that isn't true."

"It is true, though."

"Your son doesn't know our whole history. Let's wait until he's more adjusted."

"You're overthinking things," I argued.

"Son," my dad called to me, and I turned to see my parents and

Evan standing there watching us. "I don't want to step on anyone's toes, but we think Posie is right about this. J.J. has had a hell of a couple weeks. It won't hurt to give him an adjustment period. He can still spend time with Posie, so they can get to know one another, but moving in together should probably wait."

"You never know what will happen with that evil mother of his either. It's best to have all your ducks in a row for legal reasons," My mom added.

"I have full custody of him now," I argued again, though it was weak as their arguments started to penetrate my own selfish desires. While it was true that my son knew all about Posie, she was still a new person in his life, and it probably wasn't fair to drop her in as a new member of our household all of a sudden.

"You have to check in at the station tomorrow," Posie said which drew my attention back to her. "You can bring him to the barn, and I can show him around and hang out while you do your thing there. It will give J.J. and me a little one-on-one time to get to know one another better."

I nodded and then moved in to give her a kiss goodnight. "See you in the morning, sweetheart."

"Don't be mad at me," she begged before backing out of our hug.

"Sweetheart, you're looking out for my son's best interest over ours. I could never be angry about that."

Posie's smile lit up the entire room the minute I reassured her.

"See you guys in the morning. You have the key and code, so help yourself inside whenever you guys are ready in the morning."

After getting to spend a few nights with Posie in my arms, it sucked that she wouldn't be there again for a while, but I understood what everyone had been trying to say to me. My son came first, even if I thought Posie fit into our lives like a puzzle piece that had been missing, J.J. had never had that puzzle piece in his pile to start with to know that she needed to be plugged in with us.

OVER THE NEXT FEW MONTHS, POSIE AND I DATED LIKE A normal couple. Like a normal couple who knew one another a lot better than most, at any rate. She watched my son some days while my mother took him other days. When J.J. finally started asking questions about why we don't live with Posie, we knew it was time to start addressing that situation.

"You ready to move in?" I asked her one day when she brought lunch to me at the station.

She shook her head. "Not yet. I have someone coming by to discuss the barn expansion."

My brows went up in shock. We had discussed expanding the barn to a full house and studio before shortly after Pops passed away, but when it was never brought up again, I assumed she would eventually move in with me and J.J. in Pops' old house. "I didn't realize you were still thinking about that."

Posie smiled at me and nodded her head enthusiastically. "If you don't want to, we can discuss other options, but here's what I was thinking..." She took a deep breath and then dived into her plan to give us all a fresh new space for our new start together. My woman wanted to have a barndominum built on the other side of her barn with a roof over that attached the current structure to the older one, to leave an outdoor area in between them where J.J. could play or we could entertain outdoors even in bad weather.

"I'll still be able to keep my studio for work in the old barn and have it separate from where we live, while giving us all a new beginning in a house we work on building together."

"What about Pops' place?"

"Well, I have an idea about that, too."

"Do tell, sweetheart."

"Jake still wants to move here, right?"

"Yeah, once he's finished with the assignment he's working

on." My best friend was undercover in an operation that could take as long as a year to finish. Posie knew about it, but we didn't normally bring it up in public spaces.

"Right, and that could take a while and Angela won't want to move here until he can come with her, so it gives us time to get our house built and then we can rent Pops' house out to them."

Angela was the woman Jake had been dating seriously for the past two years. I wasn't certain that she had staying power with him undercover, but that didn't mean Jake wasn't ready to move anyway. The undercover work was wearing on him. It was rare that I received updates, but his handler kept me in the loop as much as he was able. I worried for my friend, considering he was only three months in on the assignment and already voicing his discontent.

"You would be okay with Jake living in your dad's house? I asked after putting my worry for my best friend aside for later.

Posie rolled her eyes at me. "Jack has been gone a while. You've complained more about wanting to update the place, while Jake loves the old, homey feel. It would mean that your best friend lived next door, which is a huge plus in my book. We can design our own home to be a good mix of modern and homey. You love my barn and have talked about incorporating updates that I have into the old house where it will be costly to do so." She offered up a shrug of her shoulders as if to say, 'Seems like a no-brainer to me'.

"Okay," I agreed.

"Seriously?" She hopped up and down in her seat, which worked to get my dick hard.

"Fuck my life, Posie. I have to hide under my desk for the next few minutes now. Keep your luscious tits from bouncing in my line of site and I'll let you have veto power for everything on our new house."

My woman giggled and stood up to lean over and give me a sizzling kiss that did nothing to cure the problem I had in my pants.

After Posie left, my Chief came to my desk and grinned down at me. "You are one lucky son of a bitch," he stated.

"I fuckin' know it. Took me long enough to get here with her, so I appreciate every fuckin' minute."

He knocked on my desk twice. "Glad to hear it. Her father was a friend of mine a long time ago. He'd be happier than a pig in shit to see his little girl glowing the way she does around you."

I didn't realize that my Chief had known Posie's dad. It should have clicked, since he was a couple years older than my own father, that he was probably around when all that shit went down with their first child. Still, it made me feel good to know someone else – who I wasn't related to – thought her father would have approved.

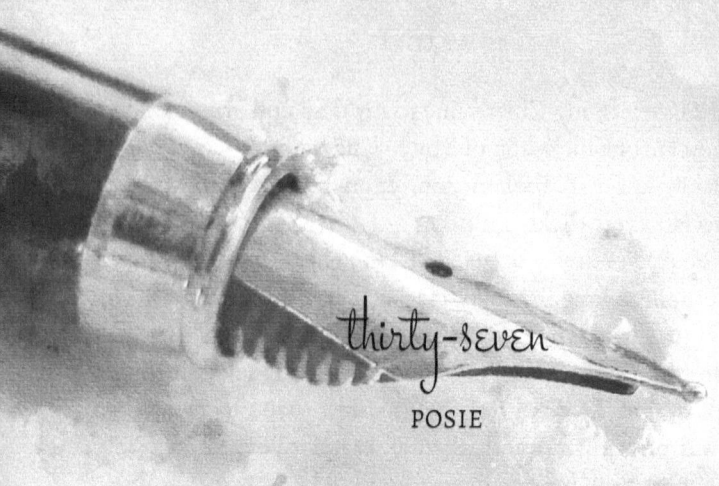

thirty-seven

POSIE

After I left Max at the station to figure out the problem in his pants and turn over my idea of letting Jake rent the house while we built a new one, I drove over to his parents' house to pick up J.J.

"Jackson Jacob Carter," I heard Sharon yell as soon as the front door was opened.

"My name is J.J." He corrected in a snotty tone.

"What did you just say?" I asked after walking through the door. J.J. came up short when he realized I was there and heard him talking back to his Nana.

"She said my name wrong," he whined.

"Jackson Jacob Carter is your name. J.J. is your nickname." The little devil huffed at me and crossed his arms in defiance. I glanced over at the amused face of his grandmother. "I take it today has been a challenge?"

Sharon full-out belly laughed at me.

"Oh, sweet girl, you have your hands full today. He refused to take a nap and his Pappa has loaded him up with the candy they've been sneaking all day."

We both rolled our eyes at that.

"Greg!" I yelled when I heard him snickering behind the door to the den.

"Mind your business, girl."

"I'm gonna mind *your* business if you keep doing this. I'll mind your business all the way to his next dentist appointment, you giant brat!"

"Hey!" J.J. stomped his little foot down and poked his bottom lip out. "Don't call my Papa a brat."

I teasingly jabbed my finger into his puffed-out belly and stuck my tongue out at him. "Or what?"

"Or I'll tell my daddy." He insisted.

"Maybe we should tell your daddy about all that candy you've been eating," I suggested.

His eyes rounded out and he turned to glance back at his Nana who refused to save him. "I'm sowwy Nana." I rolled my eyes as Sharon tried to hide her laughter and failed. The smug grin that spread across J.J.'s little face spoke volumes for the trouble he knew he could wiggle out of by being cute.

"Come on, Mister Troublemaker, we have some paintings to work on at the studio until your dad gets off work."

"We gets to paint!" He yelled before he ran to grab his shoes.

"Sorry, we weren't ready," Sharon muttered as I followed her further into the house and leaned into Greg a hug as we passed his hiding place.

"You're rotten," I told him.

"You love me anyway," he teased back.

I rolled my eyes and patted his arm as it came around me to pull me into a side hug. "I ran the idea about Jake and the new house by your son today," I explained.

"How did he take it?"

"He pouted at first until I brought Jake into it and reminded him of all the updates he wanted to do to the house anyway."

"I knew the best of both worlds approach would be the ticket." Greg preened since it had been his idea. It was Sharon who rolled her eyes that time in the wake of her husband's not-so humble attitude.

MAX MADE IT HOME JUST BEFORE DINNER WHEN J.J. AND I were still hard at work on our projects. I had to touch up a few spots on my own painting where he became overzealous at times and tried to help me instead of working on his own.

"You drew an outline for him to paint in?" Max asked as he took in his son's work of art. Truth be told, J.J. showed a lot of promise for an almost four-year-old.

"It helps to keep him focused on his own canvas rather than mine," I explained.

Max laughed. "Sorry about that. If you need more time to work on your stuff, I don't think my parents would mind keeping him longer."

"Tell that to your mom who had to put up with the sugar fairy supplying your son all day."

"Dad was always the softy of the family," Max offered in explanation as he chuckled and walked away to go get all of our dinner dishes put away. After not having a nap at his grandparents' house, J.J. crashed immediately after eating most of his dinner.

"You mind if we spend the night, since he's already crashed out?" I rolled my eyes at my boyfriend for being so damn transparent.

"Of course, you're both welcome to stay." I had already walled off a portion of the downstairs to create a little bedroom for J.J. He enjoyed being there even more than his room at the house because he didn't like the brown walls there. His room still had old fashioned wood paneling in it. In the barn, everything was new and light to make the best environment for me to work.

"Perfect. I think we should just stay here now that we decided to build our dream house. Might as well get J.J. used to the move early before it happens," Max pressed.

"If I roll my eyes any harder at you or your dad today, I might just permanently injure them," I teased.

"You better get upstairs so I can make sure you roll them the opposite way for a while, to even things out." I giggled at his innuendo but didn't waste a moment in running upstairs to be with my man. Long day be damned. I was ready for the comfort being with my man provided.

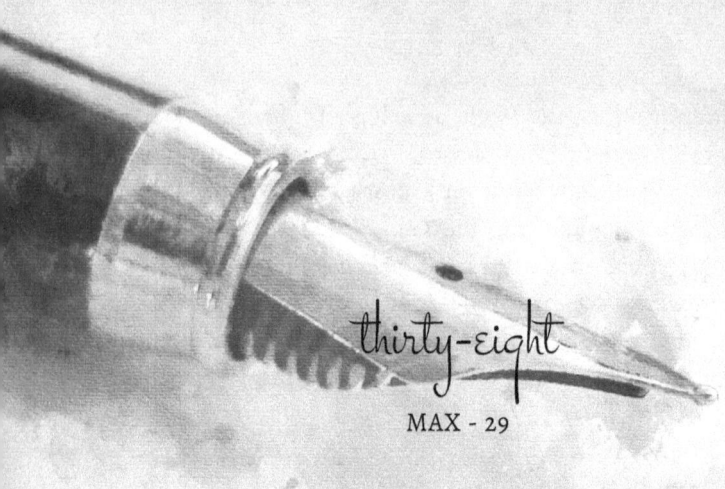

thirty-eight

MAX - 29

Our house was almost complete. There was something I needed to do before we moved into it and the longer my eyes tracked the way Posie led my son through how to paint his trees, the more I was determined to do it today.

Patience had worn completely thin over the past six months. My patience over the delays in getting our home finished, my family's patience in me for not proposing to my woman yet, and the fact that my best friend was still on assignment was another nail in the coffin that ate away at my resolve.

I had wanted to wait until he could be a part of our celebration, but every time we thought Jake would wrap up the undercover operation he was on, something would come up to postpone the bust. If I was frustrated with the situation, I knew he was, especially since Angela was rumored to have been seeing someone else. She didn't even give my friend the courtesy of a Dear John letter. Instead, she sent word through the department to let him know they were over. Then the department had to put eyes on her, to make sure she didn't spill the beans about what he was up to.

We still had Pops' house cleaned up and cleared out for him to take over whenever he finally got clear of that situation.

I glanced back down to watch as Posie cleaned my boy up and then took him to his room. It was past his bedtime already, but he was bound and determined to get those trees right.

I smiled with pride as I saw that he had done just that before they finally gave in. Pops would have been so proud to see his daughter pass on the skills she had to his great-grandson. It still felt weird to acknowledge that my girlfriend was my grandfather's daughter. It wasn't something any of us brought up in public. Even though there was no blood relation, some people didn't understand the dynamic and passed judgment that we didn't care to address. We also never talked about J.J.'s mother who was serving out a twelve-year sentence for the nightmare she put us all through.

While my girlfriend painted with my son, I made myself busy with writing her a letter. It was something I missed doing and decided this was the prime moment to start it up again. I glanced down at what I had written and smiled as I tucked it into an envelope and slid it onto my dresser. She would get it after I was certain my son was asleep and wouldn't interrupt us.

Posie faced me after crawling in bed. I could see that she was exhausted and while I wanted to give her a reprieve and allow her to drift off to sleep peacefully, there was a question I needed an answer to that was burning a hole in my proverbial pocket.

"What's on your mind?"

"I wrote you a letter."

"You did?" There was no way to hide the curiosity or excitement in her voice as she questioned me.

My smile grew as I reached behind me and offered it up to her. She took the envelope and stared at it for a few minutes before turning her eyes back up to meet mine. There was a shimmer of wetness in them when our eyes locked.

"I know this might seem weird, since we see one another every day, but I miss our letters."

"Me too. That's why I wrote you today while you painted with J.J."

Her smile grew as she slid the envelope open and discarded it on the bed between us as she pulled out the pages. I didn't expect her to read my words out loud, but that's what she did.

> My beautiful, sweet Posie,
> I missed giving and receiving these letters. It's been a long while since we used to do that. Seeing as it was my fault that we stopped, I wanted to remedy the situation.

Posie glanced up at me and offered a sad smile. We both knew why our letter writing stopped – hers long before mine – because while we were wonderful at putting our day-to-day lives on paper, our communication about feelings was where we lacked.

> There were things I should have said in letters long before you came to surprise me that one time. Things like: 'I've fallen in love with you, you mean everything to me, please don't let anyone else take your firsts – I want to claim them for myself'. There were other moments I wish I had written what was really on my mind. Moments that might have brought us together sooner without all the drama.
> Still, as Pops reminded us both frequently, every-

thing happens the way it does for a reason. We weren't ready then.

I am ready for the next step now, though.

I hope you're on the same page with me, sweetheart.

When I looked down into your studio today and watched you spend hours with my son patiently teaching him how to do something that is nearly effortless for you, I was in awe. Your beauty knows no bounds. You love with all your heart and do it openly for anyone to see.

Thank you for loving my son as if he was your own.

It made the love I already felt for you grow beyond anything I ever thought possible.

I need you to know something, Posie, and a letter was the only way I could tell you.

I want you in our lives forever.

I want you to be my wife.

I want you to be J.J.'s mother.

I need you to be the mother to more of our children that we will get to raise together. One day, I want you to be the Nana while I'm the Papa to our future grandchildren and I want to start that journey today.

I love you with everything I have to give, sweetheart. Please, tell me you will always be mine as I ask you the most important question of our lives...

Posie swiped away moisture from her eyes before it could fall and then she locked her eyes on mine. "I've always been yours, Max. That's never going to change."

I grabbed her hand and slid the ring I'd been hiding for months onto her finger.

"Then say 'Yes' and promise you'll become my wife, and we'll never stop writing letters and loving one another."

"Yes, Max. My answer is always going to be yes."

She leaned over at the same time I did, and our lips met in the middle over the discarded envelope that once contained my heart in word form.

"I love you, Posie," I whispered against her lips.

"I love you, too, Max. Now, show me how perfect we are together."

We were already both naked, except for the ring I'd just put on Posie's finger, so I slid over further and pulled her closer until she was lying there with me draped across the top of the lefthand side of her body. I brushed my hand down her cheek to her neck and traced it feather-light across her collar bones and the sides of her breast before moving back to the middle and trailing my fingers down the center of her abdomen.

"You're so fucking beautiful, sweetheart."

"You're a handsome specimen, too, Max."

I grinned at her. "Calling me a 'specimen' isn't exactly romantic, Posie."

She grinned back. "We can't take ourselves too seriously. Now, why don't you finish showing me how much you appreciate being the only man to have access to my body for the rest of our lives."

I leaned in further and kissed Posie until she gasped for more. After I gave it to her, I trailed kisses down her jaw, neck, and followed the same path my fingers traced earlier until I came to her slick center. My tongue shot out to swipe up the whole of her pussy from her entrance back to her clit with the flat of my tongue. I took my time to lick, suck, and nibble every single inch of her delectable cunt until she squirmed beneath me with one hand fisted in the sheets as the other gripped the hell out of my hair in an attempt to get her to climax faster.

I chuckled as she attempted to move me where she wanted, and the sensation sent her into a mini orgasm before I could pull back. "Cheater," I accused.

She giggled as she shot back, "Tease."

"Just for that," I said while crawling up her body, "you're going to have to come big around my cock now instead of on my mouth."

"That's not exactly a punishment, my love."

I grinned at her endearment. "I can't even remember why I would need to punish you after hearing 'my love' spoken from those sweet lips."

"Okay, my romantic, cheeseball fiancé, how about you get up here and fuck me until we're both half-blind puddles of bliss, so we can celebrate our impending marriage?"

"When you put it like that, how could I deny you?"

"You can't." Posie reached between us and took hold of my cock with her hand. She gave it a quick wank or two before lining me up with her entrance and lifting her hips to help drive me inside. I would have helped her but was mesmerized by watching her take charge.

When I didn't move to help out, Posie rolled her beautiful eyes at me, grabbed my hips, and pulled me forward until I was lodged completely inside her. Only then did I break and grin at her.

"You're a pain in my ass."

"Not yet, but I could be," I teased before pulling out halfway and slamming home again.

"Don't threaten me with a good time," Posie huffed.

I pulled out, flipped her over, and sank my dick back inside her hot, wet pussy as she laughed. Her laughter made her body pull tight against my cock and I groaned in appreciation.

When her laughter stopped and she wiggled her hips at me, I slapped a hand down on her ass. The sudden sting of the impact made her pussy clench around me again. "Yeah, baby. Just like that," I grunted.

"I can't even complain because..." She moaned as I pulled out, slammed back in and gave her other ass cheek a dose of the same medicine. A full body shudder and pussy squeeze later had me losing my damn mind. I grabbed her hips and held on tight as I pulled her body to meet each and every forward thrust I made. Our thighs slapped together as my balls battered her clit and Posie's back arched giving me just the right angle to hit that magic spot inside her that made her squirt all over me the minute she came.

After I emptied myself inside her and rolled us so that I was lying behind my fiancé, I kissed the back of her neck and tucked the sheet up around us. "Fuckin' love you sweetheart."

She mumbled something like, "Love you, too" but it was difficult to understand in her fuck-drunk state.

I decided to push my luck and let her know what I was thinking. I reached around and splayed my hand over her tight stomach and whispered in her ear, "The minute I wife you up, you're going off the birth control, and I'm going to fill you up until you're carrying our next child in here, sweetheart."

"Shut up before you have to fuck me again. It's been a long day and we're going to have to announce our engagement to family tomorrow."

"I think we should go for round two then. They're going to keep us busy, and we don't want to be too tired to celebrate again tomorrow." Posie giggled but didn't hesitate to turn over and climb on top of me.

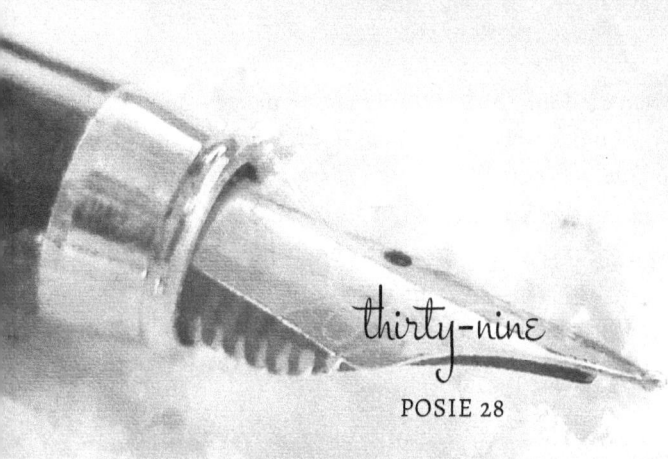

thirty-nine

POSIE 28

I would have married Max the same night he asked me to. Truthfully, I probably would have married him at 16, if I'd been able to. He didn't want to get married without his best men by his side, though. Jake had been instrumental in helping Max keep his sanity during everything that happened with Beth, the birth of his son, and the eventual silence from me, so I understood.

Eleven agonizing months later, Jake was finally free of the assignment that kept him undercover far longer than he ever intended to be. His assignment cost him the woman he had when he took it, not that I thought that was a big loss. It also cost him the woman he had fallen in love with while undercover.

When that woman found out that nearly everything she thought she knew about her boyfriend was made up, she told him to kick bricks and disappeared almost overnight without a trace.

Jake was probably too heartbroken to be the best man throughout a wedding where his best friend was deliriously happy and in love, but he chose to be there for Max anyway.

The whole time I got ready, Sharon threw me a knowing grin. I'd purposely chosen to wear my cowgirl boots instead of high heels. There wasn't a doubt in my mind that my fiancé – soon-to-be-husband – would be wearing his and for some ridiculous reason, I wanted us to match.

I wasn't wearing the old pair. My 28th birthday had been two weeks ago, and Greg and Sharon had gifted me with a new pair of boots that I cherished, especially since my feet had grown since Jack gifted my last pair to me when I was 16. I still had them in my closet, unable to part with the memories attached to the worn-down leather.

Max would be 30 in a few months and J.J. would be 5. I couldn't believe how quickly time had flown by for us.

"Are you sure about this?" My Man of Honor asked as his mother let him into my dressing room. I turned to see Evan standing there looking charming as ever in his tuxedo and cowboy boots.

"I've never been surer of anything in my life."

He and my soon-to-be mother-in-law both grinned at me. "Well, then let's get you out there, so Dad can walk you down the aisle."

A tinge of sadness overwhelmed me to know that I wouldn't have either of my fathers to do that, but Greg had stepped in and offered, and I had gladly accepted.

Sharon went to take her place in the front pew of the church as everyone else took their places. My Man of honor and Max's best man were going to walk down the aisle side-by-side with J.J. leading the way. He was our ring bearer, so we wanted him to get up front where his uncle Jake could keep an eye on those rings before something happened to them.

"You look absolutely stunning," Greg complimented as I walked up and put my arm in his. "I know that considering your relationship with Jack, you probably think of me as more of a brother," he said. I kept my mouth shut and listened. "The thing is, I never saw you as a sister. I've always seen you as the daughter that Sharon and I were never blessed with. Jack had your heart and gave you that title when you needed it, but I hope, considering your about to marry my son, you won't mind us Carter men passing that torch down one more time, Petal." He winked at me as he tacked on Jack's nickname for me.

"I love you so much," I whispered, unable to speak louder because my emotions clogged my throat and it felt as though anything above a whisper would trigger tears to fall before I was able to walk down the aisle.

"Too much?"

I shook my head. "Just right, Dad." The wedding march started, and I thanked my lucky stars that Sharon convinced me to hire a videographer for the wedding because I'd completely missed the guys walking down the aisle in the wake of Greg telling me he hoped I'd consider him to be my third dad.

"I'm a lucky girl," I admitted as we took our first step.

"Nah, we're a lucky family."

My wedding was a blur. Between my excitement and emotions, it was a miracle I made it through while still on my feet. It wasn't until halfway through the reception that I truly checked back in and realized what was happening outside of the tiny little bubble that consisted of my new husband and me.

"Shock finally wore off?" Max asked as he leaned in to tease me.

"Hush. Today has been so emotional."

"I know it, sweetheart. Dream come true for both of us."

That made me smile because he wasn't wrong. There was only one – well two – things that could have made the day better. That would have been to have Jack and my biological father – Eric – there with us today. Even knowing it wasn't possible, I felt like they were still there with us in spirit.

"I have a confession to make," Max stated as we watched J.J. dance with Sharon. I turned to see my husband's eyes turned down.

"What is it?"

"My bachelor party..."

I sighed, knowing there weren't any strippers or anything, so not sure what my husband would have to confess to me.

"Well?" I prompted when he didn't finish.

"My brothers bet me I couldn't get through that mud pit out on the back field where Michael just tilled up the ground before all the rains." I sighed, knowing exactly where he was going with his story. "And... Well..." He paused before bringing his eyes back to meet mine. "The truck got a little muddy."

I laughed. "What is it with you and muddin' the night before formal occasions?" I questioned.

"Boys will be boys?" He muttered his semi-question with a sheepish shrug of his shoulders. I pulled my husband's face to mine as I rolled my eyes at him. Then, I kissed the shit out of him.

As I pulled away, I whispered against his lips, "Be glad I love you."

"I am. Every single day of my life."

WE HAD TO GO BACK HOME TO THE NEW BARN HOUSE after the reception because our flight to Montana, where we were going on our honeymoon, didn't leave until early afternoon the next day. As we left the party amidst all the cheers, I couldn't help but anticipate our first night in our home as man and wife.

That was until I saw the true state of Max's truck. As soon as it came into view, I almost busted out of my wedding dress when I doubled over in laughter. Someone, probably Evan, had written

"Just Married" in the mud on the back window of Max's truck that was almost unrecognizable thanks to the sheer volume of dried on dirt covering the front, sides, and rear almost to the top of the truck.

"You are out of control, Maxwell Carter."

He grinned at me and then glanced back at his truck with pride. "Devon had to be pulled out of the mud and I made it through on my own, so it all worked out."

I would have rolled my eyes again, but my husband took the opportunity to pick me up bridal style and carry me over to his truck while his best man raced to get there to open the filth-covered door for him.

Max worked hard to get me into the truck without my dress touching the mess, but I didn't care. I like the messy parts of our lives just as much as I loved the serene moments. My only require-ment was that as many of them as possible were spent with one another.

When we got back to the barn, we were both in for a bit of a surprise. Our bedroom had been transformed into a romantic honeymoon suite complete with rose pedals adorning the bed. The only thing that felt out of place were the two envelops that sat atop each of our pillows. As soon as I got closer, I noticed one was addressed to Petal and the other to Maxwell.

I picked them up and handed Max his. The handwriting was familiar to me and as I traced it, I could almost feel Jack swallowing me up in a giant hug.

> *My Dearest Petal,*
> *I couldn't be there today, so I asked my son to step into my shoes and make sure you got this letter as you set out on a new adventure. Hope-fully, you married my grandson, otherwise this letter might be a little embarrassing for both of us.*

I giggled as I read that part.

I always knew that you two were meant to be.

That's not true, but do you know who did? My wife. She used to tell me all the time that one day, when the two of you grew up and found yourselves and one another, that you and Max would make a perfect pair.

At first, I couldn't believe my wife. Max was always a bit of a lady's man with an ego when he was younger and that didn't seem to fit with my far-too-serious Petal. Still, she proved me right. As you both grew older, I could see it too. I could also see that you both needed time before it could happen.

I'm so proud of you and all you've accomplished my pretty Petal. I'm excited to welcome you into the Carter family in one more way. The fact that you've held so many titles amongst us shows just how loved and cherished you really are. If you remember nothing else, always carry that knowledge in your heart.

Love my grandson with everything you have in you. I have no doubt you will be an amazing wife, mother to J.J., and to the rest of the kids I foresee the two of you having together. Thank you for shining your brilliant light on my family, my sweet daughter.

I'll see you again one day, but until then, live the best life you can with no regrets. We'll swap stories when we meet again.

Love Always,
Your Dad, Jack.

I glanced over and saw Max's eyes were just as misty as my own. We swapped letters and I read his too.

Max - my boy,
There was a day a long time ago when I told you that one day you would realize there was a woman who would appreciate you and your quirks. Because you were stubborn about it, you've had some misses over the years. You weren't bad at love, Max. I know you said that to me a few times, but I begged to differ. You were bad with those other women simply because they weren't the right one.

I'd be willing to bet the farm that those idiot brothers of yours talked you into muddin' just before your wedding. She didn't mind one stinkin' bit about the dirt on your truck or the cowboy boots you wore through the nuptials, did she?

I couldn't help the smile stuck on my face as I realized Jack really did know us better than we thought.

She's going to make you one happy man, Max. All you have to do is give her that happiness back and never forget that she's the one who would smile through the mud and chaos that life slings your way. She'll do it with her own pair of shit kickers on while raising your babies to grow to be the best kind of people. Never lose sight of what you have, Max. I never did and I want that kind of love for you. More importantly, I want it for my Petal. Give her a giant hug for me, I bet she misses them.

All my Love,
Pops

what to read next

HIS BITTERSWEET REGRET

By: *Christine Michelle*

Opal Morgan was always meant to be mine.
And she was, right up until I let everyone else inside my head and threw her away.
Six months after our last goodbye, I was on another lackluster date, regretting my life choices, when I finally saw her again.
She took my breath away for more than just one reason, the biggest being the well-rounded baby bump she couldn't hide behind her bulky sweatshirt.

Marshall Kennedy was my one true love.
There had never once been a doubt in my mind, even as everyone around us tried to tell me that a love like ours could never last.
Then, one day out of the blue, he told me it was over and just like that, he walked out of my life.

I had to tell him my news via text and all I got back was that it didn't make a difference. Goodbye meant goodbye.

So, why was he surprised when he finally saw me again?

Maybe it was just wishful thinking on my part, or bittersweet regret on his, either way, he was back and now I was the one second guessing everything.

Chapter One

Opal

"When are you guys going to grow up and try new people on for size?"

"Excuse me?" I turned to see the smirks on Marsh's brothers' faces as Cassy Andros asked the awful question. I pretended not to know what she meant, but it was stupid to do so. Marsh and Opal, together since they were fifteen years old, had always been the running joke amongst most of our friends and family. We had been one another's firsts. Well, not first kisses, but everything else. It had been me and Marshall Kennedy against the world since we started dating in our sophomore year of high school, and nothing had changed since. We were now both going on twenty-three years old and still together. Even though we were still happy together, everyone around us still tried to tear us apart. I often wondered if it was just jealousy because we had found our other halves so soon without having to go through all the crap everyone else seemed to. Who knew?

"Oh, come on, isn't it time you two took a break and explored new people?" I didn't miss the way Cassy's eyes wandered hungrily over Marsh's body. He kept himself in good shape, even though he would never be mistaken for a gym rat. Sure, he ran and worked out, just not to excess. His hair was trimmed short, with the top portion of his light brown locks hanging down his forehead while the rest was tapered down from a buzz cut to a close shave by the time you got to his nape. The hair he lacked on top of his head was made up for by the full, well-maintained beard and mustache, a few shades darker than what grew on his head.

I loved his beard. I remembered when he couldn't grow one at all and just had sparse little sprigs of hair everywhere as he tried. It always brought a grin to my face when I thought of it, and that was one of the things that made us special. We had history together. We grew together as the people we were now, and that meant we had a closer bond than most of the couples we knew.

"Why in the world would he need to do that? Just so you can have a turn on the only Kennedy brother you haven't managed to sink onto?" Granted, it was a bitchy thing to say, but it was the absolute truth. Cassy had been with Bastion, Brixton, and Jimmy. I doubted she had been with Ryker, since he was still only seventeen, but I honestly wouldn't put it past her. That meant the only brother who wasn't disturbingly close to the age of consent was Marshall.

Cassy laughed at me. "Oh honey! If I wanted your little boytoy, I would take him from you. You guys think you have this crazy bond, but..." She pointed her finger to the left, where Marsh was laughing at something a cute little blond was saying. She looked like a pixie, but one that had her law degree and fought crime for a living. Cassy tittered as my eyes lingered on the scene she pointed out.

"Good for him," I heard Brixton mutter. I turned to face him, more because I didn't want Cassy to see the moisture building in my eyes, than anything else.

"What have I ever done to you?" I asked. At least the flush on his cheeks showed that he was a little embarrassed, but that didn't stop him from speaking his mind again.

"Listen, Opal, it's nothing against you. I just don't want to see my brother plodding along miserably five years from now, with two toddlers underfoot, wondering why he never bothered to live his life to the fullest while he was able to."

"I don't understand why you guys hate me so much," I whispered. There was no mistaking the fact that the Kennedy boys didn't want me with their brother. The twins had tried, numerous times, to break us up while we were in college. That started because instead of going to their father's Alma Mater as the rest of the boys had, Marsh had gone to a local state university with me. The whole family had been disappointed in his decision.

I don't know why they were. The rest of the boys – except Ryker who was still in high school – all carried six figure student loan debt. Marsh didn't owe a dime thanks to scholarships, cheaper tuition, and being able to live at home, and then our apartment, rather than dorms.

I watched Marsh, who was still chatting with the pixie girl, until he finally glanced over and remembered that I was there. He immediately left her side and came to mine.

"What's wrong?"

"Nothing. I'm not feeling well. I'm going to head home, but you should stay."

"I'm not staying if you're leaving."

"Marsh, please, stay. Your brothers already hate me. They think I trapped you into a life with me somehow and that you're not living it up to the fullest."

"This again?" Marsh asked with a roll of his eyes. When I said nothing, he glanced back down to see the hot tears that threatened to fall. "Opal."

My name was a whisper on his lips as he leaned in and kissed the top of my head. I was dainty compared to Marsh. In fact, the blonde pixie was probably an inch taller than me. While other people might have described me in the same light that I had done for her, I never saw it when I looked in the mirror. I was girl-next-door pretty with my black hair, short, tanned legs, and slender body. My boobs were a B-cup on a good day and my eyes were just as dark as my hair. There was nothing spectacular about me.

The crazy thing was, knowing all that, I knew there didn't have to be anything spectacular because Marsh loved me for the whole package – inside and out. It gave me the confidence to know I never had a thing to worry about. At least, I never had before tonight. I recognized that look in his eyes when he'd been talking to the pixie. It was interest. Cassy – though I'd never admit it to her – had been right.

"You know I don't mind coming back home with you."

"I know, but honestly, you should stay and have a good time. I'm feeling a little queasy and don't want to ruin anything for you."

"If you're feeling queasy, I should be there to help you."

"Yeah?" I asked with a little tease in my tone. "How are you going to help me to not be queasy?"

His brows pulled together as he thought, then he grinned down at me. "I'll be your snuggle pillow. That always makes you feel better." I couldn't hide the smile that his answer elicited from me. He wasn't wrong about that. I patted his chest with my hand in appreciation.

"Stay, please. It'll give me a chance to get a little rest before you get home." I glanced over toward Brix, who was scowling at me. "Besides, Brixton was looking forward to you being here tonight. Please, don't let your brothers down on my account."

"Fine, but I won't stay long, just long enough to appease them." I sincerely hoped that wasn't true, because I was beginning to think the only thing that would appease Brixton Kennedy was if I fell off the face of the earth and his brother nailed at least three of the single women at the party before going home.

Chapter Two

Marsh

"Where did your ball and chain go?" Brix asked me when I made my way back over to him after walking Opal out.

"What the hell is your problem with my girlfriend?"

"Aww, come on little brother, you know we don't have a problem with Opal."

"Really? Could have fooled me. She left here feeling unwell."

"What's her tummy ache got to do with me?"

"Maybe nothing, but the tears in her eyes definitely seemed to be a problem that maybe you caused."

Brix threw his hand up as if to wave away my words. "I can't help that your little high school crush is sensitive. It wasn't even me that made her that way."

"Yeah? Then who?"

Brixton laughed as our brother – his twin – Bastion stood there watching us banter back and forth. "Well, little brother, she was being schooled by Miss Cassy Andros about that longing look you were throwing to Tandra."

"Who the hell is Tandra?" I asked, seriously not having a clue. "And why would Opal ever be ruffled by anything Cassy had to say? She knows what her agenda is and that it will never happen in this lifetime."

"Tandra was the cute, blonde fairy-like girl you were just hanging out with while your soon-to-be-wife stood over here with Cassy in her ear, pointing out that longing look on your face."

I got ready to deny it, but Bastion stopped me. "Don't bother denying it. We all saw how interested you were, man. Opal included." He tacked on the last bit as I glanced back toward the door. My stomach clenched as I thought about Opal leaving after thinking that I might be interested in someone else.

Why had she done that? As much as I wanted to deny it, what

they were saying was true. I might not have known the girl's name, but she had been fascinating in a way other women hadn't been for me in a long time. I rubbed my hand across the center of my chest, trying to ease the discomfort there.

Did she think I wanted to stay for the other woman – for Tandra? I hoped not.

"Hey man! Been looking for you." My best friend, Cramer – who I'd called Crayfish since we were in grade school – called out while slapping my back.

"Been standing right here for a while."

"Yeah, I know. I was going to talk to you earlier, but saw that you were finally interested in someone other than Opal and wanted to leave you to it." That aching pang hit my chest again – dead center. Did everyone in the whole party notice? "Don't get your nuts all bunched, man. Don't think anyone else realized."

"Wrong!" Bastion called out before he walked away to go grab another drink. Brixton sniggered and followed in his twin's wake.

"Damn, the twins caught you too, huh?"

"Worse," I admitted while allowing my head to hang heavily on my shoulders. "Apparently, Cassy had to go run her mouth to Opal again and she managed to point it out."

"Damn, what did your woman have to say?"

"Not much. She said she wasn't feeling well and left. That was before I knew that Cassy pointed out that I was talking to Tandra and ran her mouth about it."

Cramer laughed, and not for the first time, I kind of wanted to punch the asshole in the face. "Seriously? She didn't even want to force you home or stick around to make sure you didn't follow through?"

That question might have been what was gnawing at my chest. She simply left and didn't seem worried about leaving me behind either.

"What if she's the one getting sick of you, and this is her way of setting you up to take the fall?" Cramer surmised. "Oh shit!

Seriously! Imagine if she was the one to leave your ass in the dust after all these years. Maybe she finally saw the writing on the wall and figured it was time."

I punched the bastard that time. "What the fuck man? I asked you before to stop talking about Opal like that. Why is everyone so against the two of us being happy together?"

"We're not, dude. We've all told you before, we think you just need to take a break from her to go fishing for a while. There are tons of other women in this vast sea. The fact that you noticed one tonight speaks volumes. You two settled down early, it's not natural."

"My parents met in high school. They're still together."

"Remember that time we overheard them yelling out in the garage about your dad's secretary?" Cramer asked, eyebrow cocked up in a questioning gesture. My heart sank. We had overheard that argument a few years ago. My parents were still together, but their marriage had been on rocky ground for a while there, and if I were being honest, it still wasn't back to normal.

"I just want what's best for you. I know it would kill you if you ever stepped out on Opal while you were together. Look at your dad, man. He's been miserable ever since we heard them fighting, maybe even before that. He's had to scrape and claw to keep your mom and I don't think he even stuck his dick in the secretary, it was more like a sexless relationship where he carried his marital problems to her and she thanked him for it with hugs and the comfort he wasn't getting at home."

Unfortunately, I heard more than just that one argument between my parents over the past couple years, and Cramer wasn't wrong. Just because it happened with my parents, after nearly thirty years of marriage, didn't mean shit, right? That didn't mean it would happen with Opal and me.

"I was planning on going to get her a ring this weekend."

"What? No! No fucking way. Brix, Bas! Get over here, quick!" Cramer shouted. I wanted to fucking punch him again.

"What's up?" Bastion asked as they both sauntered over.

"This idiot wants to get a ring for Opal this weekend and make it official and shit."

"Aw, man, and here I thought we were finally getting through to you!" Brixton lamented before sipping on his beer again.

"Dude, you don't even know if you're having good sex," Bas taunted.

"I get off just fine, thank you."

"My point exactly. You think that just because you get off, that the sex with Opal is good. You two fumble-fucked your way through losing your virginities to one another and it's probably just been trial and error – if that – ever since. You know what variety is, brother? It's the spice of life. There are things other people teach us that we didn't even know we needed to learn, and that can't happen if the only woman you're ever with is Opal."

Oddly enough, that was the one point my brothers had made that I couldn't argue with. There were times when the sex was just a way to scratch an itch. There wasn't really anything exciting about it. It wasn't always like that, but it had been a lot lately.

There was also the issue of the intense buzzing energy I felt when I'd talked to Tandra earlier in the evening. I hadn't felt that kind of energy since I first asked Opal out and we started dating at fifteen. It was a crazy mix of excitement and anticipation. I stared at my best friend and brothers, wondering if maybe I should have stopped being hard-headed when I was in college and listened to them.

I knew I'd missed a few experiences by living at home and going to a local state college as opposed to what they had all lived through. Granted, I was also more financially stable already because I wasn't bogged down by major student loans the way they all were. Truthfully, I think the tradeoff was better on my end in that respect, but it didn't stop me from wondering what I'd missed out on. Who I had missed out on. What would those experiences have been like had I not been hooked on Opal all this time?

I loved her. There was no denying that. Still, there was a part of me, especially recently, that wondered if maybe there was something more out there. That voice in the back of my mind always nagged that I was missing out, like everyone kept telling me I was. Even my father had given a few subtle hints that maybe I needed to truly be on my own for a bit to see what life was like without Opal before settling down with her. He told me he didn't honestly see me with anyone else, but that he also didn't want to see me struggle with regrets and what ifs the way he had from time-to-time through the years.

"Looks like he's finally giving things some serious thought, fellas." Brixton was a dick, but he also wasn't wrong.

"Think about all that sex you could be having. Right now, Tandra could be sucking you off in the bathroom, or you could be fucking her on the counter. If not her, maybe you could make Cass's dreams come true and let her have the final Kennedy brother."

"What about Ryker? Wouldn't he be the final one?"

"He would have been if he hadn't fucked her last weekend when his girl broke up with him," Bastion informed me.

"Jesus, are you serious? He's not even eighteen yet."

"So what? Our baby brother was plenty willing."

The scowl I sent my brother's way only made him laugh. "Come on, Marsh, let's go find that little blond you were so hot for. You've never been with anyone else. Maybe, it's time for a real change of scenery to realize that you've been missing out on quite a bit of life while playing happy couples with the first girl you dated."

My stomach tossed and turned with nerves as I allowed my brothers to guide me back over to the girl who I had been so infatuated with earlier. Guilt tickled somewhere in the back of my mind, but I quickly doused it in another beer. I wasn't doing anything wrong. I was talking to another girl, but that was it. For some reason, the argument that my parents had, played out in my memory, and reminded me that my father hadn't physically done anything wrong with another woman either. My mom had still felt completely betrayed by the actions he took.

The minute Tandra smiled up at me, I forgot all about the troubles my parents had and how they related to what I was doing. I forgot all about my girlfriend, and the fact she had gone home not feeling well. I definitely forgot that I told her I wouldn't be much longer before I joined her at home. Instead, I let myself go and enjoyed talking to a woman who intrigued me and offered a heightened level of excitement I hadn't felt in a really long time.

also by christine michelle

The Broken Beginning – Part One

The Broken Beginning – Part Two

Aces High MC – Tallahassee

Crushed

Aces High MC – Cedar Falls

Redemption Weather

Smoke and the Flame

Proven

Redemption Duology Box Set

S.H.E. MC

Angel Girl

JoJo

Keys

Dark Leopards MC (paranormal)

Ridden by Darkness

The B Team

T.I.E. Series

The Infinite Something

The Infinite Beat

Valhalla Rising

Revived

Robeson Family Novels

The Forgotten Wife

When the Last Petal Falls

Mirage Island Mates

Into the Grasslands

Beyond the Grasslands

about the author

Christine Michelle also write's under the name Anne Storm.
Anne Storm's books:
Dark romance/subjects with major triggers
Christine Michelle's books:
(mild) MC Romance, Rock Star Romance, and other
Contemporary Romance
Paranormal Fantasy & Romance

If you want to learn more about Christine, her books, or her crazy adventures into the wilderness, you can find out more through the following links:
Website:
christineandanne.com
Newsletter Signup:
https://christineandanne.myflodesk.com/newsletter
Signing up for the newsletter also gets you first option at future Beta reading and ARC (advanced reader copy) giveaway opportunities!
Universal links to everything
(social media, book links, and more)
https://linktr.ee/christinemichelle

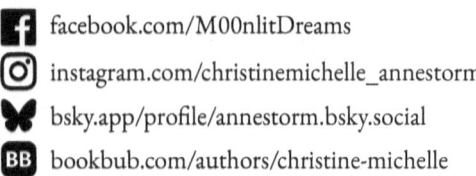

facebook.com/M00nlitDreams

instagram.com/christinemichelle_annestorm

bsky.app/profile/annestorm.bsky.social

bookbub.com/authors/christine-michelle

www.ingramcontent.com/pod-product-compliance
Lightning Source LLC
Chambersburg PA
CBHW021003260626
47169CB00006B/1921